"I AM GLAD WE ARE ALL TOGETHER HERE, BECAUSE I HAVE WHAT I CONSIDER TO BE SOME VERY DISQUIETING NEWS..."

J.R. brought an envelope out of his pocket. "What's in here affects us all, the entire Ewing family, I do believe."

"It's me," Lucy heard herself saying. "It's me you're after. What a hateful human being you are, J.R."

"I have only the good of the family in mind," J.R. said. He withdrew half a dozen photographs from the envelope. "You know who these people are, Daddy? The girl is our own Lucy. Without any clothes on..."

"You filthy bastard..." Lucy said.

"There they are," J.R. said harshly. "Undeniable in what they present. You and Beam in a disgusting display. You've been seeing him on the sly... All these nights you claimed to be studying at your friend's house, you were with Beam, in his apartment. Doing... *this*..." He cast the photos onto the coffee table as if they had scorched his fingers. "You make me ashamed, Lucy. You have shamed us all."

The Ewings of Dallas

A Novel by
BURT HIRSCHFELD

Based on the series created by
David Jacobs and on the teleplays
written by Rena Down, D. C. Fontana,
Richard Fontana, David Michael Jacobs,
Leonard Katzman, Arthur Bernard Lewis,
Barbara Searles, Worley Thorne
and Jeff Young.

BANTAM BOOKS · TORONTO · NEW YORK · LONDON

THE EWINGS OF DALLAS
A Bantam Book / October 1980

ISBN 0–553–14439–1

Published simultaneously in the United States and Canada

───

Bantam Books are published by Bantam Books, Inc. Its trade-mark, consisting of the words "Bantam Books" and the por-trayal of a bantam, is Registered in U.S. Patent and Trademark Office and in other countries. Marca Registrada. Bantam Books, Inc., 666 Fifth Avenue, New York, New York 10103.

───

PRINTED IN THE UNITED STATES OF AMERICA

0 9 8 7 6 5 4 3 2 1

"If I owned Texas and all hell,
I would rent out Texas and live in hell."
—GEN. PHILIP H. SHERIDAN

"This is a very special corner
of God's real estate."
—PRESIDENT LYNDON B. JOHNSON

They've plowed and fenced my cattle range,
And the people there are all so strange.
—OLD BALLAD

The Ewings of Dallas

The sun dropped out of the western Texas sky and nighttime settled over Dallas. The early evening cocktail parties along Main Street ended in a raucous yell or two and occasionally a drunken whimper as the working folks headed out to their air-cooled suburban tract houses. Late supper for some. Lonely night in front of the television for others, picking at a frozen dinner. The streets of Dallas were as empty as a pumped-out oil well. And atop Reunion Tower the restaurant revolved slowly, flashing its computer-triggered light patterns, visible for miles around.

For J.R. Ewing, this was natural, a part of that sleek urban landscape that Dallas had become, and therefore not to be remarked on. As if by reflex, he guided his Mercedes up to the sidewalk and parked in front of the Ewing Building. At this hour, the building was mostly dark, the offices emptied out. Only the night lights in the fire stairwells and in the main corridors on each floor were lit now, sufficient to the needs of the security force.

J.R. marched across the open plaza and hurried into the building. His building, he thought with some pride. That is, it would be some day. All his: the building, every bit of the Ewing interests and investments, Ewing Oil, South-fork . . . A smug, hard smile curled the corners of his mouth. J.R. Ewing was a big man, he told himself, in so many ways, and growing bigger and more powerful every day. There you had it, a fact of life, although there were still some holdouts who refused to learn their lessons. They would. Oh, yes, indeed, they would.

He strode through the marble and glass lobby, noticing, at the nighttime check-in desk, the absence of the uniformed guard. Stealing a smoke somewhere, or putting in naptime in some empty office. J.R. made a mental note to report the man, have him fired. All employees of Ewing Enterprises were expected to perform at a high level of efficiency all of the time: duty, commitment, loyalty. J.R. demanded these qualities in everyone who worked for him.

He rode the elevator upstairs. The reception room was still and empty. No clatter of typewriters to intrude, no chattering female voices. There was a strange and ominous attraction to the silence, as if almost anything could and would happen. J.R. experienced a dull craving in his middle, a subtle crotch-shift of desire, a sudden longing for a warm smile and a kind word.

Foolish weaknesses. All men were susceptible. But J.R. Ewing was equipped to suspend, dismiss, and keep such feelings at bay.

Inside his private office, he tossed his white sombrero on a chair, placed his attaché case on his desk, and carefully extracted from it the papers he wanted. Seated, he began to read. After a while he frowned and shook his head in disbelief. J.R. was not a man to tolerate mistakes for long. He would not condone disloyalty for even an instant. He re-read the last paragraph; somebody, he said to himself, was going to have to be taught a lesson.

He stood up. A tall, broad man with a face precisely assembled yet strangely bland, without emotion or vulnerability. A stranger might view J.R. as soft and accessible; he was neither. A spine of polished steel was at the core of the man; rigid and unbending, except when his own interests were at stake. There were many people in Dallas who would have insisted J.R. had no interests, other than personal profit and pleasure. Few cared to disagree.

J.R. went to the bar and poured himself some Scotch over ice. Being alone in his office at night was not unusual for him, yet an unsettling irritability stirred his middle, as if he were missing something. Committing some monumental blunder. He glanced again at the papers on his desk. That was a matter to be taken care of in the morning. No big deal. A phone call, a brief conversation and—problem solved.

The uneasiness returned. And the thick sensuous longing. He paused momentarily and reached for the telephone and dialed a number. It rang a dozen times. Go to damn hell! Where was the woman? He checked his watch. Out catting around, making herself available to every sweet-talking young hustler on the make. Well hell's bells, that was all right with J.R. Long as he got his, what was bought and paid for, what was coming to him. He slammed the phone down and threw back the rest of the Scotch.

He took a key out of his pocket and unlocked the bottom drawer on the right side of his desk; brought out a packet of letters and began to read them, comparing the contents with the reports on his desk. After a few minutes, the peevishly content smile reappeared on his mouth. He went after another drink and tried the number again. Still no answer.

He checked his address book and dialed another number. A woman's voice answered.

"J.R. Ewing here . . ."

"Oh, hello, J.R."

"I'm at the office. Why don't you put your sweet little behind in your car and trot over here for some drinkin' and good Texas lovin'. . . ."

She hesitated. "I'm afraid I can't make it tonight, J.R. I've got other plans."

"I see," he said coldly. "Anybody I know."

"We all have our private lives, J.R. That was part of our deal."

He forced a note of lightness into his voice. "That's right, sugar. Talk to you later." He hung up and went after a refill, this time bringing the bottle back to the desk.

The phone rang and he snatched it up. "J.R. Ewing . . ."

There was a silent second and the line went dead.

"Damn!" he said aloud. "Nobody's polite anymore. Just hang the hell up. Can't even say 'wrong number,' way things are these days."

His irritability rose in direct ratio to the amount of Scotch he swallowed. He splashed more of the amber liquid into his glass and drank. He tried the number again; still no answer. He sat back in his chair staring up at the ceiling. Damned people! Never occurred to any of them that J.R. Ewing was *human*, that he was a man and had *feelings*. Desire, need, loneliness. Yes, dammit, loneliness. He admitted it. But where were *they* when he needed company? When he yearned for companionship, affection, somebody to stroke his fears and his insecurities?

He almost laughed aloud. What in hell did he have to be afraid of? What could possibly make him insecure? A soft suggestion of sound in the outer office brought him up in his chair.

"Hey, there! Somebody out there?"

When no response came, he slumped back. Goll-eee. A man did as much for folks as he had, you'd think they'd be on call when he was off by himself. You'd think they'd be downright anxious to keep him happy and contented. Not so, not a bit of it. Well, so be it! J.R. Ewing knew how to flow with events. How to deal with shifting tides of favor. No different than herding cows. Concentrate on what you're doing. What has to be done. Remember those cows are wild animals and scared, and not stupid, either. They know for sure you're not out there to do them one bit of good. Keep your mind on your business and you'll be okay. Let it wander just one time and they are gone, mister.

That sound again. Must be one of the security people making his rounds or his imagination.

"J.R. Ewing here!" he said, raising his voice. "Anything I can do for you?"

When no one answered, he reached for his glass. It was empty. He was about to pour another drink when a distinct sound came from the outer office. Damnit, somebody was out there. Striding across the plush carpet, he pushed open the door. In the halflight he saw a figure. "What are you doing here?" he asked angrily. The only answer was the sound of two gunshots reverberating in the empty offices.

J.R. felt as if a runaway train had steamed into his middle, doubling him over, spinning him off to one side in searing agony and terror. He fell to the floor, the world sucking him down into an infinite cushioned maw from which no escape was possible.

Until there was only endless silence and eternal night.

PART I

The Ewings

TODAY

1

*L*ess than a month before, with the sun in descent over the western reaches of Southfork, Jock and Ellie Ewing sat on the patio of their ranch enjoying a soft breeze. Jock, a big man with a mane of white hair capping his weathered face, was working oil into a favored pair of boots. His strong hands kneaded the worn leather expertly, without thought, fingers performing a remembered process.

His wife, sitting next to him and engrossing in a book, was a pretty woman in her middle years with a bemused expression in her bright eyes. There was a universal look to Miss Ellie, as Jock had long called her, a woman at home in the 57th Street art galleries of New York City or at the San Francisco opera or as mistress of one of the State of Texas' finest ranches. But a closer examination of Miss Ellie's evenly spaced features would have revealed that here was a strong woman, smart in the way that hard experience makes one smart, a woman determined, courageous, and able to deal with anything life might throw up at her.

She looked up from her book. "Anything I can get you, Jock?"

He kept working on the boots. "I'm just fine, Miss Ellie."

She smiled. "You always have been, my dear. Which doesn't mean I can't still do something for you."

He looked into her face, those far-seeing plainsman's eyes narrowed but soft. "I love you too, Miss Ellie."

She smiled and he went back to the boots.

A few minutes later, J.R.'s Mercedes came cruising to a stop near the garage and he headed up to the patio, a bounce in his stride, a pleased smile across his face. Someone had once said of J.R. that only his mouth smiled, never his eyes; even in the presence of his parents, in the secure precincts of Southfork, those eyes jerked around as if to reassure himself no enemy was closing in.

"Evening, folks." he greeted them.

In answer Jock frowned. "Evening, J.R. Anything to report? Anything you're willing to tell me, that is."

"Now, Daddy, when are you going to relax and start trusting me?"

"Just as soon as you give me reason."

J.R.'s eyes clouded over. He started to speak but caught a slight warning flicker on his mother's face. He produced that mechanical smile of his and put his attaché case on the patio table, snapped open the locks and brought out a sheaf of business papers.

"Maybe this will help, Daddy."

Jock accepted the papers, looked them over. "What's all this?"

"The bank loans for the Asian leases were paid off today, one hundred percent to the dollar. Southfork is free and clear."

Jock's reaction was restrained. He went through the papers again.

J.R. was disappointed. "Aren't you pleased, Daddy?" More than anything else, J.R. craved and required a repeated and strong show of approval from his father. Jock, a hard man who seldom displayed his feelings in words or in gestures, expected a man's best work every day, was quick to criticize anyone delivering less than that, and slow to issue compliments. "Southfork is in no danger anymore."

Jock grunted softly. "Bobby go with you to the bank?"

"Yes, sir, he did." J.R. wanted to shout imprecations at his father, claim some of the interest and affection that went to his younger brother, Bobby, for his own. Instead he went on in a normal voice. "Everything was done out in the open, sir. Above board." Then, impulsively, as if unable to contain his emotions, he let the words come gushing out. "Dammit, Daddy, aren't you the least bit proud of me? Those Asian leases have made Ewing Oil one of the richest independent operators in the United States."

"No need to swear in front of your mother," Jock said.

"Now, Jock . . ." Miss Ellie put in.

Jock kept his eyes fixed on J.R. "I can't forget it was you almost lost Southfork in all this wheeling and dealing, son."

"That's all behind me, Daddy. I learned my lesson the hard way. I'll never do anything to put Ewing Oil or Southfork in jeopardy. I swear . . ."

"Well, son, you keep tight to the line like you are right now and I'll be happy with you."

A pleased, proud laugh broke out of J.R. "Folks, I do not mind telling you, I am enjoying this. Watching all that money come pouring in. Hearing those cartel boys pleading every hour on the hour for a piece of the action."

"Are you being fair to them, J.R.?" Miss Ellie said without emphasis.

"Fair! Let me tell you, Momma. If they hadn't been too chicken to come up with the money for those leases in the first place when I asked them to, I would never have had to mortgage Southfork a-tall. You ought to see them, Daddy, sitting up like a pack of hungry hounds begging for a handout."

A businessman's grin spread across Jock's mouth. "Don't blame you a bit for the way you feel. Nothing like a good deal going your way, 'specially when other folks can't abide the idea of your success." He stood up, slightly stooped but still tall and strong, still possessed of an outdoorsman's physique. "Come on inside, son, I'll buy you a drink. . . ."

After dinner that evening, the family assembled in the living room. Pam Ewing, a strikingly beautiful young woman with faintly exotic features and copper-colored hair, stood off by herself, lost in thought. Seeing her daughter-in-law alone, Miss Ellie spoke matter-of-factly.

"Oh, Pam, I forgot to mention, Harrison Page phoned you today."

"Thank you, Miss Ellie."

"What did he want?" Bobby said. A few years younger than his brother J.R., Bobby was compactly constructed with dark hair and a strong level gaze. The kind of man who looked as if nature had designed him to fit into any surroundings, comfortable and competent, his confidence running deep and strong. Bobby had never been entirely convinced of the wisdom of his young wife going back to work, and a phone call from her employer during the day only reinforced his doubts. But his feelings for Pam ran true and deep. He had supported her whenever possible in the past, and would continue doing so in the future. Still, the doubts remained.

Pam shrugged, a little too casually, he thought. "He was returning my earlier call. I didn't go into work again today and I wanted to explain . . ."

"Where did you go?" Bobby said, unable to conceal his annoyance.

"To the cemetery."

Bobby's lips tightened. The death of Pam's father, Digger Barnes, had made more of an impact on her than he had anticipated. Now, after all this time, he was beginning to worry.

Standing nearby at the bar in the living room was Sue Ellen, J.R.'s wife, a glass in hand. An angelic smile had transformed her pretty face into a mask. She stood in place, as if waiting for an unwelcome visitor. The visitor arrived in the person of J.R., who snatched up a brandy bottle and held it aloft.

"Didn't see you eat much dinner, Sue Ellen."

"I wasn't hungry, J.R."

"Guess you get all the nourishment you need out of one of these, darlin'."

She offered him her glass. "Straight club soda, in case you want to make sure I'm not lying."

"That's not necessary," Miss Ellie put in.

J.R. grimaced. "What I'd like to know is what you were drinking out of other glasses, at other times, darlin'?"

Bobby said, "Let it go, J.R."

J.R. felt the old antagonisms rising to the surface. For reasons he couldn't fathom, he was unable or unwilling to control his temper.

"What?"

"I said, let it go. You're not accomplishing anything."

J.R. spoke through his teeth, a cutting edge to his voice. "Why, Bobby, don't you know the first step in curing drunks is to get them to admit what they are. I am just trying to help my ever-lovin' wife here by getting her to say what she is—a damned alcoholic!'"

Eighteen-year-old Lucy, petite and blonde, with a feisty quality and a bold sensuous glint in her eye, challenged J.R. "Why should Sue Ellen admit anything? Are you willing to admit what you are?"

J.R. stared long and coldly at his niece, child of his second brother Gary, long absent from Southfork. "Lucy," he said deliberately. "This is between Sue Ellen and me."

"Not when you attack her in front of the whole family," Bobby said. "That makes it our business, too."

J.R. shifted his attention to his brother. "I'd say you have problems enough right now handling your own wife. Leave Sue Ellen to me."

"Don't start, J.R. . . ."

J.R. went on, ignoring the warning note in Bobby's voice, heedless of his mother's protestations, of his father's rough admonition to stop.

"Your wife is crackin' up, Bobby, slowly but surely. Anyone can see that except you. Not that anyone would blame her, things being what they are. That trash Digger Barnes, that dear ole daddy of hers. Hell, that useless piece of human meat was no relation to her at all. Everybody knows her *real* daddy was a saddle tramp named Hutch McKinney, a thief. And her momma was a whore—"

Pam gasped and ran from the room. Bobby, oblivious of everything except the deliberate pain J.R. had inflicted on his wife, heaved his glass at his brother. It missed, shattering against the mantle. Without hesitation, he hurled himself forward, swinging a swift right hand that caught J.R. on the cheek and sent him reeling backwards. Bobby went after him again, flailing away. It was Jock who separated them finally, his imposing presence a concrete announcement that the fight was ended.

"Hold it right there, both of you. This is where your mother and I live, our home, not a saloon. Next time any punches have to be thrown, I'm not too old to do the throwing. Now, Bobby, you back off, hear? And J.R., keep that mouth of yours shut. That clear enough for you?"

"Yes, sir," J.R. said, holding his bruised cheek.

Sue Ellen swayed his way, looking up into his face. "Looks to me, J.R., as if you're the one needs a drink right this very second. . . ."

With a muffled oath, he stormed out of the room and out of the house.

Bobby found Pam in their bedroom, seated on the bed and staring dry-eyed into space. He gathered her into his arms and she pressed close, as if to absorb his strength, that surging life-force that coursed through him.

"Oh, Bobby, is J.R. right? Am I cracking up?"

"Don't you believe it."

"I feel so lonely, so confused."

"Your father died, that is a great loss. You're shocked. Anyone would be."

"But Digger was not my daddy. Hutch McKinney. A few days ago the name meant nothing to me. Now I'm supposed to believe he was my father. A skeleton with a bullet hole in his skull, a man I never heard of, never knew . . ."

"Digger was your father. He raised you and your brother, Cliff. That's what makes a man a father. . . ."

"They say my momma died . . . but I don't remember. There was a watch in Daddy's belongings, with an old photograph in it. A woman, faded like my memory of her. I want to find out what happened to her, Bobby."

"What difference does it make now?"

"I feel as if the bottom has fallen out of my world. How can I know who I am if I don't know who my father was, or my mother? The way it is, I don't belong to anyone. I don't belong anywhere."

"You belong here, with me, Pam. You're my wife and I love you."

If she heard the words, she gave no sign. "I have to know," she said, as if to herself, "I have to . . ."

2

$\mathcal{K}$ristin Shepard's apartment was owned by Ewing Oil and so she was able to live in comparative luxury and splendor, courtesy of J.R.'s always controlled generosity. The irony of her situation was not lost to Kristin who, though still a very young woman, was neither stupid nor slow. Kristin and Sue Ellen; J.R. had married one sister, made the other his mistress. Yet it was not a situation that displeased Kristin. As one of J.R.'s secretaries, she did interesting work, was well-paid, and met fascinating, successful people. Even more important, she possessed a reflected prestige—a Ewing by marriage if not in fact, a working member of Ewing Oil with access to the way decisions were made at the top, privy to information few other people her age would ever have.

She knew she was beautiful. That men were drawn to her in large numbers, that they wanted her. She also understood that her desirability was enhanced by her proximity to J.R., Ewing Oil and Southfork. Her momma had taught Kristin well: get everything you can out of life, in any way you can, use all the attributes you have, all the wiles you can summon up. All that counted, momma had stressed over and over again, was the bottom line. Winning was everything.

But even Kristin had her limits. And they began with a man like Vaughn Leland. The banker was necessary to J.R. and his varied business interests, he was wealthy and to some degree powerful; and he turned Kristin's stomach. Especially when he put those big, soft hands of his on her.

He kept doing that before J.R. arrived. Stroking her arms, the small of her back, touching the swell of her breast. Kristin was not above using her body to get what she wanted; but not with Leland.

Now J.R. was ushering the banker out, saying a last few words. In the bedroom, having withdrawn so the men could talk privately, Kristin had listened to every word said. There were times when J.R. asked for her help. Besides, Kristin believed a girl could never have too much information and information was ultimately the key to success. And power.

She heard J.R. thank Leland for coming. "Now you drop a word here and there, Vaughn, discreetly, hear. Test the ground, see what response you get."

"I'll carry your message, J.R. Tell the boys just the way you told it to me. They'll be straining at the leash, I tell you. Plain greedy, those people . . ." He left laughing as if he knew something nobody else knew.

"I don't like him," Kristin said, returning to the living room.

J.R. shrugged off his carefully tailored Western jacket, let it fall to the floor. He took off his tie, going past her into the bedroom. "Can't say as I blame you. If he'd've done his job the way he's supposed to I would never have had to use Southfork as collateral in the Asian deal."

She trailed after him. "Before you got here he was all over me. A damned snake oil salesman is what he is, always touching, feeling me."

J.R. sprawled out on the bed and raised one foot. Kristin tugged one boot off, then the other. He stood up and removed his pants.

"Wait a minute, J.R.," she protested. "I want to talk."

"Go right ahead, darlin'."

"If you hadn't walked in when you did, I would have had to fight for my virtue."

He laughed, mean and thin. "Your virtue?"

"I mean it. Dammit, J.R. You just leave the rest of your clothes right where they are."

He took off his T-shirt. "Now why would I do a thing like that?"

"Come on! You can't just walk in here and expect me to go to bed with you. . . ."

"That's exactly what I do expect."

"Look here, J.R., I am not here for your convenience. I

am a person with rights. We made a deal, you remember that? I am not going to sleep with you again until you divorce Sue Ellen and marry me. I mean, she's a hopeless alcoholic. Everybody knows that. You are going to have to commit her. You need a wife who knows you the way I do, J.R., a wife who shares more than your bed."

He reached for her and she stepped back. "What would your momma think about having you involved in a scandal?"

"Scandal?"

"Well, of course. You named as correspondent in your sister's divorce action."

"That doesn't have to happen . . ."

"Be hard to stop, if Sue Ellen knows about us."

"Does she know?"

"Always possible, isn't it?" He stepped out of his undershorts. "Now get your body over here, Kristin."

She shook her head. "Even that piggish Leland treats me better than this . . ."

"Well, then, maybe you ought to try him out."

"What are you saying to me, J.R.? Doesn't it bother you when one of your so-called friends comes on to me like that."

"Take it as a compliment, darlin'. What the hell, Kristin, you're attractive, desirable, and available."

"Available!"

"You been complaining lately I don't spend as much time with you as you'd like."

"Are you telling me to go out with other men?"

"I don't want you getting bored, darlin'. Anyway, you never can tell, they might say something that could be very useful to me."

"You want me to sell myself in order to spy on your friends, is that it?"

"I want you to get as much out of life as you can." This time when he reached for her, she failed to avoid him. He drew her to him on the bed, his mouth smashing down on hers, his hands squeezing roughly at her breasts. She wondered what it would be like with Vaughn Leland. Or one of the others? Another man's lips on hers, another body, another voice. She tried to imagine it now and was very slowly drawn deeper into the dark imaginings, the fantasy enlarging as her excitement increased. She felt her clothes being stripped away and heard J.R.'s rough voice issuing commands, positioning her on the floor at his feet, giving a name to what he wanted her to do, naming her for what she was. And in that swirl of overheated crimson that enveloped her, she obeyed. It was exactly what she wanted, everything she wanted, at least for now.

The phone rang. Kristin groaned and reached for it in the dark. "Yes?" she said, and abruptly sat up. She shook J.R. awake. "Overseas call coming in, J.R., it's Hank Johnson."

He swung his feet to the floor and was instantly alert. Johnson was his man-in-charge of the Asian oil fields. "Hello, hello, is that you Hank? What in the hell's the matter, boy, calling me like this? You know I don't like to do too much of our business on the telephone."

Hank's voice faded in and out over the longwire from Southeast Asia. "This wouldn't wait, J.R."

"All right, let's have it."

"We got trouble," Hank said, as if shouting. "Big trouble. My contact inside the government here, he's come up with a piece of information I don't like, J.R."

"I'm listening, Hank."

"There's talk about an assassination plot."

"Against the Number One Honcho?"

"Exactly. J.R., I hate to tell you this, but there's revolution in the wind out here and it's not far away."

"What are the chances of it coming off?"

"Pretty damned good, from what my sources tell me. And if it explodes, J.R., it's gonna raise hell."

"Can the rebels win, Hank?"

"The way it looks, they can't lose. And if they do, without a cottonpicking doubt in the world, J.R., they are gonna nationalize the oil fields."

"They can't do that to me!"

"They'll take it all, J.R.—lock, stock, and every damned barrel of the stuff."

J.R.'s mind was spinning. "Are you sure of your information?"

"Mister," came Hank's solid Texas drawl, "one of the reasons you pay me all that money is because my sources are reliable. There's unrest throughout the area and more here than in most places. It's a matter of time. When the rebels make their move they'll take over the country fast—a week at most. Maybe less. When that's done, kiss those wells goodbye."

"There's a lot at stake, Hank," J.R. said, recalling his meeting with Vaughn Leland."

"Ewing Oil's got a fortune tied up out here, I know that."

It occurred to J.R. that he could lose all the points he'd made with his father. The good will, the trust, the license to run Ewing Oil the way he wanted to. But J.R. was nobody's fool; there was more than one string on his bow.

"Can you get to the rebel leaders, Hank?"

"What good's that gonna do, J.R.?"

"Money speaks all languages."

"Bribe them! J.R., you don't know these guys—they are fanatics."

Try it anyway. I'll have a man on a chartered plane with a suitcase full of good old American cash in the morning, Hank. In every pack of wolves there's bound to be one with a large appetite for the good life. Find him, Hank, show him the way to the lap of luxury without getting his tail shot off. Spend and spend, bribe and bribe. I am not ready to lose those wells. Not yet."

"No guarantees, J.R. But I'll give it my best shot."

"You do that, Hank, and stay in touch, hear."

3

When J.R. came tooling up to the garage area on Southfork the next morning, he was surprised to see luggage being loaded into a limousine, his parents preparing to depart. "Hey!" he said with forced joviality, "where's everybody going? No need to go off and leave just 'cause I let my manners slip a bit last night. Tell you what, apologies all around, okay."

"You give yourself too much credit." Jock said flatly. "Your momma and me, we've decided to take a little holiday up in Colorado and take care of some personal business at the same time."

"We won't be gone long, son," Miss Ellie said.

"Bobby and Pam are coming along," Jock said. "Which means you are in charge here. I expect to find Ewing Oil and Southfork in good condition when I get back. Understand?"

J.R., flooded by a sense of relief and anxious now for them to depart, put on his most reassuring smile—and reassured nobody. "Don't you fret about a thing, Daddy. You can count on me."

Bobby and Pam came out of the house and a phone began to ring behind them. Bobby made a move to return and answer it.

"Come on, Bobby," Jock called out. "Let's put the show out on the road."

Lucy came to the door, calling goodbye, motioning to J.R. "Phone for you, J.R."

20

He made his farewells, went into the den, and picked up the phone, turning his back to the door as if to exclude any casual eavesdropping. Even as he did, Sue Ellen appeared in the doorway, listening openly.

"J.R. Ewing here . . ."

"That you, J.R.?" came the familiar voice over all those thousands of miles.

"Hank! What's going on out there? What's the story, Hank?"

"It ain't good, J.R. The fish won't bite. And things are moving a lot faster than anybody anticipated. I mean to tell you, unless something happens we starve in 48 hours, maybe less."

"That doesn't give me much time."

"J.R., things are changing minute by minute. The way I see it, I got another day and a half before I got to skedaddle out of here."

"All right. Make your plans and keep calling in."

"Will do."

J.R. hung up, the instrument still in his big hand. He dialed a number. A secretary answered.

"J.R. Ewing here, is he there?"

"Just a moment, sir."

Seconds later Vaughn Leland came on. "That you, J.R.? How you this fine morning?"

"Just fine, Vaughn, and yourself?"

"Better'n ever, my friend. I been doing like you told me to and I've got some information for you."

"I'm listening."

"The news is good. Everybody's eager and ready to go, hot little checkbooks in hand. . . ."

"Well, now, that's what I like to hear. Why don't you round up every last one of them critters and herd 'em down to my office, say in two hours. I got an early meeting to take care of first. . . ."

"Be pleased to accommodate you, J.R. See you later."

"Yes," J.R. said, hanging up. "Later." He turned around and his eyes fell on Sue Ellen standing in the open doorway, a harsh, condemnatory expression on her otherwise lovely face.

"Same old J.R. Couldn't wait for your daddy and momma to get through the gates before you go wheeling and dealing behind their backs."

Before he could reply, she had whirled around and was gone.

An hour later J.R. was in his office, shaved and showered, dressed in a Western-tailored suit of pale blue gabardine. His boots were of glove-soft kangaroo leather, hand-worked in an intricate Mexican design. Kristin knocked and entered, a mug of steaming coffee in hand.

"Anything else I can get for you, J.R.?" Resentment over the way he had treated her last night still simmered, but she let nothing show. The obedient secretary, helpful, willing, subservient. Kristin was sure about one thing: her day would soon come.

"This is just fine, darlin'."

"Alan Beam is waiting."

"Well, by all means, show the man in."

She manufactured a cheerful smile of greeting and opened the door. "J.R. will see you now, Alan."

He went past her, hand extended. A slight, dark-haired man with the pinched look of ambition on his narrow face. His dark eyes were watchful and defensive, as if he felt out of his element, outclassed, yet desperate to play the game.

"Good morning, J.R. Must be real special for you to have me up here during business hours."

"It's early, Alan. Chances are nobody's going to notice you coming or going. I'll buzz if I need you, Kristin."

She pouted and left, closing the door behind her.

"Lovely girl," Alan said. The young attorney put what he hoped was a gracious smile on his face. J.R.'s relationship with his sister-in-law, no secret around Dallas, was an open subject of gossip in Barnes for Congress Headquarters where Beam was spending so much of his free time.

"And an excellent photographer," J.R. said, coming out from behind his desk. He handed Beam a single photograph. "Don't you agree, Alan?"

All color drained briefly out of the lawyer's face. He struggled for composure, mind turning over rapidly. "I can explain, J.R. It isn't what you think."

"What do I think, Alan?"

"That I—that your niece, Lucy, and me. Oh hell, J.R. We just kind of ran into each other . . . literally."

J.R. indicated half a dozen other photos on his desk. "I would say so, Alan—ran into each other and made love in some very unusual ways. If my daddy was to see these . . ."

"J.R. Let me tell you the truth. Lucy and I have been seeing a lot of each other. We are very much in love."

"You, in love! Spare me the hearts and flowers, Alan."

"I mean it. Lucy's pretty and smart and nice to be with an—"

"And rich."

For a moment, Beam almost gave it up. Then he dug in and drove forward. "Her money doesn't matter a hot damn to me, J.R. Not hers, not yours."

J.R. smiled, "You're a liar, Alan." He said it softly.

Beam filled his lungs with air. He hadn't expected the other man to accept his words at face value. In J.R.'s place, neither would he. In some ways, they were two of a kind, though Beam had a long way to go before attaining parity in power and wealth with the older man.

"I love Lucy," he insisted. "I am going to marry her. If you're thinking of buying me off, J.R., just forget it. I won't be bought."

"Buy you off . . ." Beam received the disturbing impression that J.R. was enjoying himself hugely. "What ever gave you that idea?"

"I'm not for sale," he said weakly. "No matter the price."

"Good. Be assured I won't try to undercut your ethical resolve. I won't buy you off."

"You won't!"

"Does my heart good to know that Lucy finally found herself a man. A real man, Alan. Congratulations."

"You don't mind?"

"Nothing could please me more. The day you two get married is the day I am going to set you up in your own law practice. No more doing errands for other people, Alan. You'll be your own boss. My wedding present to you both."

Beam was unable to believe this stroke of good luck. "You mean it, J.R.?"

"Well, sure. What'll it take to do it right? Quarter of a million sounds about right."

"If you really want to do it right, make that double."

"That's my boy, always thinking big. Half a million it is then. That will set you up in style in the shiniest new law office in Chicago."

"Chicago!"

"Chicago, Alan."

"But I have no intention of going to Chicago. Dallas is my home. I like it here. I want to stay."

"Of course you do. But you'll go to Chicago anyway. Lucy's inheritance and trusts have been set up and they're irrevocable. It should make no difference to you if you both live in Dallas or Chicago. But it does make a difference to me."

"I don't get it."

"You will—Lucy *and* the half-million. And this much of an explanation. Lucy's father—my brother, Gary—has abdicated his responsibility to Southfork and to the family. He's a weak and frightened man, unable to shoulder his share of the family burden. Well, all right. The only possible reason he could have for returning here to claim any share of Southfork is Lucy. With her gone, he won't try to cut in on my action. But if she stays in Dallas, Alan, if she stays on at Southfork, then you are never going to see her again. Or the half-million. Is that clear?"

"Very clear."

"Get on it at once, Alan."

The lawyer went to the door, looked back, his hand on the knob. "What if she doesn't want to marry me?"

J.R. indicated the series of photographs. "Love, Alan. Love and sex. Twin solutions to all the world's problems. Or so some people would like to believe. Do your number on her, Alan. I'm sure you've had lots of practice before this."

"I know just what you mean, J.R." He left, smiling and a lot happier than when he had come.

4

They gathered in J.R.'s office, a handful of middle-aged men. Physically they were a motley group: some well-padded in button-down shirts and suits by Brooks Brothers, one or two in dark and shiny silk by Neiman-Marcus, one in faded Levi's and scuffed boots, exactly what he had worn as a roustabout in his early days as a wildcatter. But all of them had one trait in common: behind the easy-going camaraderie, behind the booming laughs and friendly jibes, behind the carefully cultivated "good ole boy" personas each put forward, every one of them was rock-hard and ever alert for the big chance.

Never satisfied, they were men who had battled all their lives. For power and wealth, for prestige, for an edge over friend and enemy alike. No matter how large a slice of life's pie each acquired, he craved another helping. More land. More cows. More oil. More power. More money. It was the root cause of their being. What had brought them to this place on this morning. What each of them knew the other was after, what each of them ached for himself.

More.

Leather and chrome chairs had been brought into J.R.'s office, circling his desk like cowboys waiting around a campfire for beans and jerky to be burned up for eatin'. Tin plates and forks at the ready. Appetites larger than life. The hunger that could never be assuaged.

"Is this for real, J.R.?" Jordan Lee, frequently the spokesman for the cartel, said with a guileless expression on his open-as-all-outdoors Texas face.

J.R. spread his hands in supplication. "Did God make little green apples?"

Vaughn Leland shifted around in his chair. He was a banker, not an oilman, a man used to paper deals, used to clean hands and clean smells. He'd never had to scrub prairie dust out of his pores, never had to work the stink of a thousand bawling cows out of his clothes, never dug dry hole after dry hole in hopes of that one great gusher. He was a man who had always gotten his after the others did the tough and grimy work. But this deal—if indeed J.R. meant what he said—was too good to pass up.

"The thing is, J.R., you been keeping this Asian field all to yourself up to now. Can't blame the boys for feeling a mite uneasy at the sudden change of heart, now can you?"

J.R.'s lips lifted and spread to reveal large, perfect white teeth, tightly clenched. He dropped one hand on the thin pile of papers on his desk. "Boys, it is all right here. Facts, figures, geological assays, estimates of reserves, every last question answered, all legal and proper."

The man in Levi's, long, lean, hard-bitten, spoke without looking up. "What I want to know is how come you're finally letting us in?"

"That's the question every one of us is asking," one of the Neiman-Marcus types said. "There are no secrets in the oil business. We know to the penny how much all this is worth."

"Well, sure you do, Bradley. Give a looksee at these projections, decide for yourself if my figures ain't exactly the same or close enough to yours. Hell's bells, men, we all of us got sharp accountants, ain't nobody got here by being stupid."

An assenting murmur went round the circle.

"You still ain't answered my question," Stone said, studying the tips of his worn brown boots.

"Gratitude," J.R. said.

"Oh, come on, J.R."

"You can't be serious."

"J.R.," Stone said in that slow way of his. "I been around cows and horses all my life. I know the smell of shit and I know the smell of perfume—and I sure do smell shit now."

That elicited a round of laughter.

J.R. waited for them to quiet down. "Gratitude for all your loyalty when we needed you. When Ewing Oil

needed financial support, you boys were right there, on
the mark. I haven't forgotten that. But, of course," he
went on with a big grin, "those of you who know me well
probably suspect that is not the entire story."

This time no one laughed.

J.R. kept going. "Ewing Oil has had a couple of interesting propositions put to us these last few days. Nothing I
can talk to you about yet, but big deals. really big. Things
are moving fast, so fast that we have got to untie some of
our capital. *Fast*," he stressed. "Fast."

His eyes raked the serious faces watching him. These
were men who understood the sudden fluxes and flexes of
the oil maket. They understood the quick demands for
large amounts of cash, the need to close a deal on the
spot, to make swift and sometimes chancy decisions. Each
of them had been in that position, and would be again.

"All right," Jordan Lee said. "That makes sense. What's
it got to do with the Asian fields?"

"Simple. We need to liquify in order to swing these
other deals. Which is why Ewing Oil is prepared to sell off
75 percent of its Asian holdings to you boys."

Vaughn Leland asked the question each of them was
thinking. "How much, J.R.?"

"Ten million a point."

Somebody whistled.

"That's a hefty price, J.R."

"But worth it."

Seth Stone glanced sidelong at Leland. "What's the
bank say?"

"Those fields have always looked good to us."

Jordan Lee jerked around to face J.R. "Aside from the
price, what's the catch, pardner?"

They all laughed at that. Even J.R. was forced to smile.
Blind trust was not a commodity in large supply with this
group. Exactly what he'd been counting on. So skeptical
were they, so cynical and suspicious, it would never really
occur to them that they could be outsmarted, especially
by one of their own kind.

"You've got the numbers, men. The price is a bargain
when you consider the oil just waiting to be pumped in
those fields, and in a constantly rising market. Hell's bells,
we don't have to lift a finger about pricing. Just let those
A-rabs do it for us."

He hesitated, and allowed a slow grin to play across

his mouth. "But . . . you boys really do know me—there is a catch. Ewing Oil wants a 25 percent royalty on every barrel you take out of Asia."

A despairing groan went up and J.R. knew he had won; they had taken the bait. All he had to do was give the line a solid jerk, plant the hook. And he possessed the fine hand needed for that.

"Fair is fair, gentlemen. After all, who secured the leases? Who laid out the initial capital for drilling? I did. Ewing Oil took the risk. Now you people come in and it is a sure thing, a can't-miss deal. The oil is there in proven reserves. I know it, you know it. All you got to do is go in and take it out. These leases are worth a fortune."

"You're right about that, J.R.," Stone said.

"The only reason I'm opening the deal to you boys is I know you can come up with the cash in a hurry and I am in a bind. The question is—how fast?" He looked around.

Solemn faces confronted him.

"As long as it takes for me to get back to the bank," Leland said.

The others chuckled in approval.

"Think you can keep your head above water for a couple of hours, J.R.?"

"All joking aside, that's what you've got. A couple of hours until I go to those barracudas in New York. I need the money fast or I don't need it at all."

Ludlowe Apartment complex sprawled out on some choice acreage in the direction of the airport, not far from Stemmons Expressway. It was a convenient place to live for Alan Beam, allowing him ready access to central Dallas and providing the sort of privacy he required. Even more to the point, the complex included three swimming pools which gave him the opportunity to meet some of the loveliest girls in the world in his spare time, without ever leaving home. It seemed to Alan that he had the best of all possible lives and, thanks to J.R. Ewing, it could only get better.

He was on the phone attending to business when the doorbell rang. He finished his conversation and opened the door. Lucy, looking youthful and pristine in a lacy white blouse and a loose-flowing skirt, smiled up at him.

"Hi, honey." She wrapped her arms around his waist

and squeezed. Her body was full at breast and hip and he felt himself respond immediately. He wondered if J.R. and the rest of the rich and powerful Ewings knew much about little Lucy. Knew that instead of attending class as Southern Methodist University, she spent many of her days in Alan Beam's bed. For that matter, he asked himself, precisely how many beds had innocent Lucy crawled into during her young life? He remembered his first time with her, an overwhelming couple of hours. He had expected a girl relatively inexperienced and discovered himself in a tiger's lair—a scratching, biting wild creature, never still, never satisfied, and in her moist hot demands giving more than any woman had ever given him before. He was not without experience himself, but Alan had never had a lover as intense and sensual and imaginative as Lucy Ewing.

"What are you doing here?"

She ran her hands over his sides, onto his hips, and grasped his lean hard buttocks firmly, pressing tight against him. "Did you forget? We have a lunch date."

"It's only ten in the morning." He tried to work himself out of her grasp, remembering J.R.'s injunction, remembering the strategy he had plotted out.

"What I'm hungry for won't keep." She began unbuttoning his shirt.

"Lucy, wait."

"I can't." She licked his bare hairless chest, undid his belt.

"We have to talk."

"Say anything you want, honey. Anything. Go ahead, talk to me. Any words you want to use. There's nothing you can say or do or ask me to do that doesn't turn me on."

"I've got work to do."

"Ouoh," she cooed, drawing his pants down. "Look what I found."

"My work won't keep, Lucy."

"I want this beautiful thing . . ."

"Lucy, listen—"

"Yes . . ."

He drew back, rearranged his clothes.

"What's wrong?"

"I told you, I've got a busy day."

"Are you angry with me?"

"No."

"Because of the other night. Okay, so I was a little bitchy. A girl can't be loving all the time. I'll make up for it now, honey."

"I'm not angry. It isn't that."

"Then what?"

He put his back to her. "It's just that—well, dammit, Lucy," he came around. "I love you."

She began to giggle. "Is that all? Well, I love you, too, sweetheart. So let's finish what I started. I'll show you how much I love you, how good I can be for you."

"Uh-uh. No more."

"I don't understand."

"Okay, I'll spell it out. We're not a couple of kids. Making out every now and then. What do we do next—go steady?"

"What do you want to do?"

"I think we ought to get married."

"Married!" She wasn't sure whether to be pleased or troubled. "I didn't think you had it in mind . . ."

"Now you know better. But I see you're not of the same persuasion. Okay, but I can't go on this way, stealing moments. Sex isn't enough for me when I feel this way."

"Does that mean you don't want to have sex with me anymore?"

"Exactly. I think it will be best for us both if we stop seeing each other. I don't want you to get hurt, Lucy. I don't want to be hurt either."

"Oh, Alan, give me time to think."

"You do that," he said, directing her to the door. "Until then—"

"It will work out, Alan. All of it. I promise."

"That's not a promise you can keep."

"Alan, please . . ."

He opened the door. "Goodbye, Lucy."

She took a hesitant step outside, turned back and started to speak. Before she could, Alan had closed the door. She put her face in her hands and began to weep, not at all sure what was happening to her, not understanding the strange mix of emotions she was experiencing.

On the other side of the door, Alan Beam smiled with grim satisfaction. He was proud of the way he'd handled the situation, certain it would all work out.

Less than ten minutes later, Alan had a second visitor. This one even more of a surprise—Kristin Shepard. And yet, he told himself as he got her settled with some coffee in his comfortable living room, there were many reasons why she might have come. After all, as J.R.'s secretary and sister-in-law, Kristin was privy to many secrets, much information about Ewing Oil business and about J.R.'s personal shenanigans. Then a frightening thought struck him: what if she were here to extract some private price for what she knew about him and Lucy? But the fear lasted only briefly; he was going to make an honest woman out of young Lucy, marry her and ride off into the north to Chicago. Which was where he belonged, the city with Big Shoulders, a charged environment where he could shine, be his best, prove himself to everybody.

"You're wondering why I'm here," Kristin said, making it a statement rather than a question.

"Whatever the reason, it's my pleasure." He gave her his best smile.

Her mouth drew down, less in disapproval than regret that he felt compelled to function at such an ineffective and adolescent level.

"You're a nice looking young man, Alan, and I'm sure lots of women find that sufficient. Save the charm for them, save the sex appeal. I'm here for bigger things."

He sat down facing her, eager and serious, alert to her words, sure he was on the brink of something important to him.

"I'm listening, Kristin."

"We both belong to J.R., you know."

"Well, I wouldn't go that far. I work for—"

"He *owns* you."

He couldn't restrain his anger. "Don't put me in your class."

Her smile was aloof and forgiving. "Alan, each of us, each in his own way, is J.R.'s whore."

"Not me," Alan said with forced rage. But a bell of recognition had gone off in the rear lobe of his brain and he felt an undeniable logic to her words that left him weak and afraid.

"You'll marry Lucy because J.R. wants you to," she said. "You'll take his money because the money means more to you than your self-esteem, your pride, your manliness. You'll hide in Chicago, become moderately rich and successful and tell yourself you're free of him. Forget it. One day he'll call in the debt and when he snaps his finger you'll jump."

"That's not me."

"It's both of us. Unless we do something about it, and soon."

Alan wet his lips. "You really hate him?"

"I loathe him. I want to destroy him, if I can. Hurt him badly."

"As far as the eye can see, he's treated you very well. A solid job, a fancy condo, good clothes. What's he done wrong?"

"He has screwed me in every way possible," she said in a low, harsh voice. "In ways not permissible . . ."

Alan drew back inwardly, afraid and defensive. This was no woman to cross. Behind that sophisticated and glamorous facade was a diamond-hard core; Kristin, he decided, was a very dangerous adversary.

His mind kept turning over, looking to make capital of this encounter as of any other. Alan had long ago committed himself to never missing a chance. "Exactly what did he do?"

"Besides treating me badly in general, you mean? He led me on for months, promising to leave Sue Ellen, get a divorce, and marry me. And now . . ." She broke off.

He waited.

"And now he wants me to *entertain* his friends, turn me into a whore in fact as well as principle."

"But why?"

"To spy on them. Part of his private intelligence system. There never was a better place to collect information than a bedroom."

"Hard to believe but nothing surprises me about J.R. The man is ruthless, hard, mean. He deserves the worst in life."

"I want to see that he gets it."

"How, that's the question."

"That's why I'm here. You tell me, Alan."

He swallowed the protest that sprang to his lips. "I'm not sure," he said. "But all during Cliff Barnes' campaign for Congress I kept diaries on everything I did, every rotten trick J.R. ordered me to do. I kept duplicate records of every bribe made, of every one of J.R.'s dollars spent, to whom, for what purpose."

"Then we've got him!" she exulted.

"Not yet. But we have to stay on his tail. The man is always up to something and eventually we'll come up with some hard evidence to use against him. That, plus what I've got now . . . It won't take long."

"You're so right. He's up to something right this minute. He had a meeting this morning with Vaughn Leland and the members of the cartel. I tried to listen in but it was no use. Something's going down, something big, some way J.R. intends to shaft his pals and partners. They were supposed to get together again about now. Wait a minute! I'm getting an idea. What if I pretended to go along with his plan for me? Entertain his business friends, pump them for information. It shouldn't be too difficult to get that bunch of retrobates to open up. They all drink too much, they all have busy hands whenever I'm around."

"It might work."

"I'm sure it would. Let J.R. believe I'm doing it *for* him and all the time I could be enlarging a file that would— one way or another—hang J.R. Ewing."

"I love it . . . when do we start?"

Kristin's face was glowing hotly as she reached for the telephone. "No time like the present . . ."

J.R. bid the members of the cartel goodbye, thanking each one individually, assuring them that the transaction just completed would make them richer, their influence more far-reaching.

"Boys," he ended, "you will never regret this. I promise you that."

At the door, Vaughn Leland lingered, about to speak when the phone rang. J.R. went back behind his desk, almost too comfortable in his high-backed brown leather swivel chair.

"Yes, Connie?"

"Kristin on line two, J.R."

"Kristin?" He pushed the call button. "What is it, Kristin? I'm a busy man."

"Oh, I know that, J.R. Just wanted to let you know I've been pondering our discussion about my future *personal* activities. If I was short with you, J.R., I want you to know how sincerely sorry I am."

"Get to the point, Kristin."

"I want you to know that I'll do anything I can to help you, J.R. Anything at all."

He indicated to Leland that he would be with him shortly. "Why, that's real sweet of you, darlin', real sweet."

"I thought I might give Jordan Lee a call. That dear man has been at me for months wanting to take me out to dinner. You reckon I'd be safe with him, J.R.?"

"I'm sure you can handle yourself in any situation, honey. You do that, you give Jordan a call. His family's out of town and he'll enjoy your very good company. Now you be good, hear." He hung up and swung around to Leland, a big smile on his big face. "Got to tell you how pleased I am with the way things went, Vaughn."

"You look like the cat that swallowed the canary, J.R."

"Shoot, nobody ever thought I was a pussycat and those ole boys, they sure as hell ain't no yellow birds." He laughed until tears ran.

"Well, I wanted you to know I appreciate you letting me in on this deal. A man like me, making a profit is always a good thing."

J.R. held his smile as if afraid that relaxing his facial muscles might reveal too many of his emotions, too many of his thoughts. "I wasn't expecting you in on the deal, Vaughn. Didn't know you had that kind of money to throw around. I figured you'd just skim your portion off the top and let the others take the risks."

Leland laughed briefly. "Like you said, not really any risk, is there? Tell the truth, ain't often a man gets a chance to really make a fortune and I do know a good thing when it hits me in the face. I arranged a twenty million dollar personal loan from a drinking and diddling buddy of mine at another bank that shall remain nameless. Used my shares of the leases as collateral, along with a few other bits and pieces of personal property. Oh, I guess there always is a small risk. But this is a sure thing if ever I saw one. A sure thing, wouldn't you say, J.R.?"

J.R. looked him dead in the eye. "A sure thing, if anything is. And after all you've done for me, I can't think of anyone I'd rather have in on the ground floor of this deal than you. On this one, Vaughn, you are going to get everything that's coming to you. . . ."

"Well, I surely do thank you, J.R."

"Thank you."

Alone in his office, J.R. sat back with his eyes closed, aware that he had begun to tremble. He had taken so many chances, risked so much that was vital not only to him, but to the entire Ewing clan, and always landed right side up. Just one more time, he prayed. One more winner for J.R.

It frightened him to remember how close to total disaster he had come not so very long ago. Economic and professional disaster, personal disgrace and shame.

DamnBobbyalltohell! That sniveling sneak of a brother was constantly striving to do him in, undercut his position with Jock, shove him out as the operating head of Ewing Oil. He owed Bobby, owed a heavy debt that he meant to repay with painful interest one day. And soon.

His mind floated backwards in time to that night more than a year before. An all-encompassing darkness had settled over Southfork by the time J.R. arrived home and he did not notice Bobby seated on the patio, a condemnatory look on his face.

"J.R." came the perfunctory summons. "Let's talk."

There was an unaccustomed harshness in his brother's voice that alerted him to impending trouble. His defenses rose up in place. J.R. was always ready to do battle on his own ground, in his own good time. But he was dead set against fighting when his enemy could name the weapons and the rules.

"It's late, Bobby. I'd like to go to bed." He started past Bobby only to be grabbed in his brother's powerful grip, and swung around. "Take it easy, little brother . . ."

"I said let's talk."

"What the hell is this all about?" When in doubt, J.R. attacked. "I've got a busy day tomorrow, starting early. Somebody's got to look after Ewing interests, you know."

"Man, I got to tell you, J.R. Last year when you tried to turn Southfork into an oilfield, I figured that was your low point. J.R. had hit moral bottom. I see I was mistaken."

"That oilfield scheme is long gone, over and done with. I gave my word."

"Your word's worth about as much a pound of dried cow chips at roundup. Which is exactly nothing."

"I don't have to listen to this."

There was venom in Bobby's voice. "You've got some explaining to do."

"Explain what? It's you ought to be explaining. Poking

around my office, into my private papers. Dammit, man, you had poor Kristin in tears when you left. That girl works for me, my interests are her interests. Well, let me tell you, my business affairs are none of your concern."

Bobby reached back to a manila folder on the painted iron table. "This—" he raised the folder to shoulder level. "Do you know what this contains, J.R.?" He dumped the contents of the folder on the table. "Copies of the South-fork mortgages, J.R. Copies I had made at the Records Office."

J.R. felt his stomach turn over and he was afraid he'd be sick. He sucked cool night air into his lungs and braced himself to run a bluff.

He smiled and held his hands out disarmingly. "Bobby, Bobby, it was only a formality."

"A formality! Is that what you call mortgaging South-fork?"

"You don't understand . . ."

At that moment, Jock and Miss Ellie, wearing robes over their nightclothes, appeared. Miss Ellie seemed worried, almost frightened. Jock was angry and it showed.

"What's the ruckus, damnitall. Folks can't even get a good night's rest around here. What are you two fighting about now?"

"It's almost midnight," Miss Ellie said placatingly.

"Seems to me you boys were always scrapping, even as children," Jock broke in. "Scratching and screaming at each other, each one wanting what the other one had. Each one claiming he was getting the short end of the stick. More than once I had to separate you two fighting cocks and got punched out for my trouble, I don't mind telling you. Bobby, you won most of them wars with your brother. But you, J.R., you usually ended up getting exactly your own way. No matter, that's all past. Now what is this hootin' and a-hollerin' over?"

Bobby glared at J.R. "You going to tell them or am I?"

"What is it, J.R.?" Miss Ellie said.

"Just business, Momma, that's all."

"Don't lie to them," Bobby gritted out. "They'll find out soon enough."

"Nobody had to find out," J.R. shot back. "Nobody had a thing to worry about until you started snooping. I could have saved Ewing Oil and everything this family owns without Momma and Daddy losing a minute's sleep over it."

Jock frowned. "Well, since we lost more'n a minute's sleep already, supposin' you fill us in on all this."

J.R. knew a command when he heard one. Yet he could say nothing.

Bobby spoke up. "Cliff Barnes told Pamela that one of the reasons he would like to put the lid on Ewing Oil is to stop us from expanding into Southeast Asia."

"Southeast Asia!" The words rambled out of Jock with the weight of Holy Writ. "J.R., you said you weren't going into that."

"That's what I've been trying to tell Bobby. It's a good deal, Daddy."

"You gave your word, son," Miss Ellie said.

Jock made a gesture that drew all attention to him. "Where did you get money enough for the leases?"

"Mortgages," Bobby said. "About a hundred million dollars worth."

"A hundred million! How?" Jock's face was stony in the darkness, his legs planted solidly apart: a man standing his own ground, sure of himself, strong, unyielding, dangerous to cross. "How?" he said again.

"I had to go it alone, Daddy," J.R. replied nervously. "You would have done the same."

"How did you raise one hundred million?"

"We got a lot of assets when you add them up."

"Assets!" Jock said. "We have only one asset and that is Southfork."

Bobby indicated the mortgages on the table. Jock picked them up, his eyes on J.R. "What're these, boy?"

"Mortgages," Bobby said.

"With Southfork as collateral?"

"Try and understand, Daddy."

Miss Ellie's hand went to her mouth. "You mortgaged Southfork!" The words hung on the night air, a lingering accusation.

J.R. responded after a long interlude. "Those wells will come in and it will be as if nothing ever happened."

"When are the first loan payments due?" Jock said heavily.

"Next week, Daddy."

"How could you do this without talking to me first, J.R.? How could you involve Southfork?"

"This is our home," Miss Ellie said. "Your home."

"Daddy, you and Momma have your own problems. Your health . . ."

"Never mind my health, or your mother. We'll deal with that. But to mortgage Southfork—"

J.R. summoned up some aggressiveness. "You put me in charge of Ewing Oil. A decision had to be made and I made it. This deal was worth a calculated risk."

"Our home a *calculated risk!*" Miss Ellie said. "What kind of thinking is that?"

"Momma, there is no reason to worry. It's only business. A business deal."

Miss Ellie answered with unusual bite to her voice. "I'm capable of understanding what you call *business*. . . ."

"Momma, I didn't mean to offend you. Daddy," he was almost pleading, desperate now to have parental approval, understanding and, most of all, respect. "Daddy, I can handle it. I'll make it all all right."

Jock grunted, reviewing what he'd heard rapidly. "What're the chances of the oil coming in before the payments fall due?"

J.R. hesitated. "It's going to be close."

"How close?"

"Too close, I'm afraid. There's been some weather out there . . ."

"A typhoon," Bobby said. "Did a lot of damage."

"Then we've had it," Jock said, as if closing the book. He took Ellie by the hand. "Southfork has outlasted generations, won over squatters and land-grabbers, gunfighters and rustlers, oil swindlers—we've whipped 'em all and kept the land. But this—J.R., you've finished us . . ."

"Daddy!" J.R. cried to their retreating backs. "Momma! Give me a chance." He pivoted around to Bobby. "You did this to me, cost me Daddy's respect. I'll get even if its the last thing I do. I'll make you pay for this, I'll make you pay."

Bobby followed his parents inside, not giving his brother the satisfaction of an answer.

But now, J.R. thought, at ease in that high-backed brown leather chair of his, all would be made right. When his latest deal became known, when Jock understood what he had accomplished, what he had gained for Ewing Oil, he would understand at last that J.R. Ewing was indeed worthy to be head of the family. A true Ewing. Entitled to his father's respect.

Lucy couldn't get her last meeting with Alan Beam out of her mind. All night she had lain awake blaming herself for dealing badly with Alan, for not being worthy of him, for not being woman enough to please him.

Marry her! What kind of a wife would she make? Just a frightened, inadequate little girl. Not that she believed for a second that he meant the proposal. It was some kind of a trick designed to deceive and damage her. But why?

No answer came all that night as she turned and tossed. Finally she rose and lit a joint and padded downstairs, wearing only her very short, very sheer nightdress. A pale blonde wraith in the night moving swiftly and silently across the living room of the big house out onto the patio, going barefoot toward the barns.

"Who's that?"

The commanding voice brought her up short. In the dark someone came forward. Ray Krebbs, lean and tall, a very solid character and the foreman of Southfork.

"Lucy! What are you doing out here this time of night?" His eyes went over her, unable to miss the darker circles of her nipples under the sheer fabric.

She smiled up at him. Let him look. And all at once she wanted him to look, wanted him to see. Damn Alan Beam and his smooth city ways, his evasions and downright lies, his proposals that frightened and threatened. He wanted to rope and hogtie her and Lucy did not intend for any man to do that. Hell, no. As soon as they had you inside that marital corral they took liberties, owned rights to a girl; and, just like that, disappeared. All of them; run off without a word. Break up a marriage, destroy a family, ruin a child's life.

Not for Lucy Ewing.

"Ask yourself the same question," she said. She proffered the joint.

"Couldn't sleep." He shook his head.

"I'll tell you my bad dreams if you tell me yours," she crooned, and took a long hard drag.

"Come on," he said, taking her elbow. "I'll walk you back to the big house."

She avoided his grasp and leaned up against him. "Mmmm, you smell so good to me, Ray."

"Let's go, Lucy."

"I'm not ready to go back. Why don't you take me someplace."

"I'm tired, Lucy, I'm going to bed."

"I'll go with you." Another drag.

"Forget it. You belong in the big house, I belong in my place."

"Don't you like me, Ray?" She stepped back.

"I like you well enough."

"Look at me."

He kept his eyes straight ahead, the classic cowboy—forthright, pure, resolute. Also, not nearly as daring as cowboys were reputed to be. "I'll say goodnight, now, Lucy. Get yourself a good night's sleep." He disappeared into the darkness without another word.

She swore at the empty night that left her chilled and lonely and without reassurance. To Lucy it seemed she was always being rejected. Everyone turning away from her. Friends, family, lovers. Nothing ever came easy for her, nothing worked out the way she wanted it to be.

She had been only fifteen years old when she made up her mind it was time to lose her virginity. The decision was easier to come by than the fact. Every boy she turned to was reluctant, if not downright hostile. She enticed, suggested, seduced; nothing worked. Boys avoided her like the plague. Finally it broke through that they were as inexperienced and frightened by the prospect as she was; more so, in fact. She was willing to risk the consequences, the boys were not.

She understood she needed some one older, sophisticated, and horny as a bull rutting after a cow in season. Waite Walker was exactly such a man. He was twenty-five years old with big arms and shoulders and a swagger that announced he was all male and ready to prove it to man, woman or beast on command. Lucy made up her mind and went after Waite Walker.

The results were devasting. He misread her openness for knowledge, her sly flirtation for sexuality, her round adolescent body for a woman of experience. He took her down behind the silo on his daddy's farm and treated her no better than he might have treated a beast in the field. He left teeth marks on her buttocks and bruises on her breasts and arms, traces of blood on her thighs. And when he was done with her, he left her lying on the hard ground stunned and terrified and too uncertain to offer even a word of complaint.

Later, when she had time to reflect on it, she typically blamed herself. Obviously a man of his maturity and experience knew what sex was all about; and she didn't. Obviously she was naive and stupid to expect anything more, or better. Obviously she had been dealt exactly what she deserved.

So it was she came to expect very little from men, and received even less. She chose men certain to treat her badly and thus was never disappointed. She understood that they held her in low esteem, were using her, that she was good for very little else. But then she had never believed otherwise.

Used and cast aside. Mistreated and ignored afterwards. Mocked and shamed and left behind. It was the way her mother had treated her. And her father. Why not strangers?

Why not indeed?

5

The candles flickered gently, reflecting off the wine glasses as Jordan Lee and Kristin toasted each other. They drank and he refilled the glasses.

"It's a marvelous wine, Jordan," Kristin said, in a manner languid and provocative. She had dressed carefully for the occasion: a long black skirt, loose and flowing, and a lacy white blouse that made it evident that she wore no brassiere over her heavy young breasts. All during dinner, Jordan, from his place across the table, had found it impossible to keep his eyes off her. As the evening wore on, his desire increased and now he began to grow impatient.

"Yes," he answered, his oval Texas face pulled shut as if focused on a narrow, distant target. His eyes were slitted, his voice submerged back in his throat. "A good vintage." He pushed himself away from the table. "And so was the dinner, Kristin."

"I try, Jordan, I try."

He offered his hand and she took it.

"I'd say you succeed, little lady, at just about everything." He drew her to her feet. Her eyes were almost on a level with his and the sweet, heady scent of her filled his nostrils. Being this near made his pulse pound and heightened his senses. A sudden crotch-shift pulled his thoughts back in time; when was the last time a woman had affected him so much and so quickly, without touch or kiss? Too many years. Jordan had thought that kind of loving to be behind him, beyond his middle-aged capabilities. Yet here was this lush and lovely creature within easy reach. He warned himself to proceed slowly, not to give alarm, to lead her easily to a point satisfactory to him.

"How sweet of you to say so, kind sir." She curtsied.

"Nice of you to invite me," he said, leading her to the couch. This is a beautiful apartment."

"J.R. mentioned your family was out of town. It occurred to me you might enjoy some home cooking, Jordan. . . ."

He lifted her hand. "In my home, cooking was never like this." Her laughter was pitched high, brittle, went on too long. He brushed his lips against the back of her hand, directed one finger to his lips, holding, then very slowly drawing it into his mouth.

"Oh," she said. "Oh, dear."

"Shall I thank J.R. for the evening, or you, Kristin?"

"Oh, J.R., of course."

"A prince among men, isn't he?"

She placed herself in the center of the couch so that no matter where he sat they would be close, very close. She crossed her legs and adjusted her skirt unhurriedly. She kicked off her shoes and patted the place alongside.

"J.R. has certainly been wonderful to Sue Ellen and me. I can't help being fond of him . . ."

"How fond is that, Kristin?" He took up her hand again.

Her answer was an enigmatic smile. "Being fond of J.R.—they say it's not a universal emotion."

He shifted closer. "Not many people in Dallas find the man exactly likable."

"Is it true, does J.R. actually do dirty tricks on people? On his business associates?"

He put his arm behind her, across the back of the couch. As if in reaction, she leaned back, hair flaring out in a shining dark frame.

"Maybe so. But J.R. knows better than to cross me and the other boys in the cartel. Nobody messes with Jordan Lee, leastways nobody wants to stay around Dallas and in one piece."

She pursed her lips in response and Jordan bent over her, his mouth finding hers. For a long warm interval she made no reaction, then her lips went soft and slowly parted. He let his tongue drift against her teeth, feeling his way, aware that his desire had reached heights long dormant in him. When her teeth nibbled at him he moaned and pressed forward and was sure he was being accepted.

He reached for her breast. Weighted and firm with youth, the thrust of nipple hard and insistent in his palm. His senses reeled and his skin tingled. He stroked her side, bringing his hand down onto her ripe round buttock. Somehow, shifting and squirming, his hand made its way onto her knee and soon he realized that she wore nothing under the skirt. Electrified, he thrust his hand higher.

"Oh, no, please . . ."

"You're so beautiful."

"You mustn't do this to me."

He pulled back and she tried to sit up. One big, surprisingly strong hand held her in place.

"What game you playing, sister?"

"Game? No game, Jordan. I'm just not that easy. I like your company. I want to get to know you. Who knows, maybe, one day, we might even—"

"To hell with that!" He launched himself back down on her, those powerful hands everywhere, pinning her helpless on the couch.

She tried to shove him away. "Let go! Don't touch me *there!*"

"Lady, you are going to get exactly what you been asking for."

"No, you don't understand."

His laughter was raucous and harsh as he loomed over her. He tore her blouse open. "Beautiful," he said, sucking at one breast and the other, ignoring her protests, keeping her immobile under him. He licked her and bit her and when she screamed he slapped her across the face. Once was enough. She began to weep. Only then did he release her, and in that confused moment she thought it was over, that he had changed his mind. She was wrong.

She looked up and saw him stepping out of his trousers, his undershorts. She tried to slide past him but one big hand reached out to drag her face down to the floor. When she resisted, he punched her in the buttocks. Pain radiating along her spine, she moaned and went limp.

He tossed her skirt to one side and commanded her to spread her legs. Instead she crossed her ankles. He slapped her twice more and this time when he repeated the order she obeyed. "My," he muttered thickly, "my, my, that sweet little pussy. Just the desert ole Jordan has a taste for, little lady. . . ."

He went at her, rough and demanding. Taking heedlessly, giving pain and at the same time stimulating her in ways she'd never before known. In spite of the loathing she felt for him, her flesh grew taut, began to respond. Until her thighs locked around his head and she urged him on and on and on.

He shifted and she rose to meet him. Hands reaching, mouth gaping, she pleaded for release, pleaded for his flesh, and they rolled as one, a two-humped beast, never still, never quiet, begging and demanding, threatening and insisting, until each burst through beyond the translucent wall that kept them apart.

They lay without moving on the floor for a long time. The passion expended. The rage spent. The desire sated. Not touching, not kissing. Not sharing any intimacy. Until he sat up laughing in soft triumph.

"What's funny?" she heard herself say, wondering what was to become of her.

"Just thinking, little lady. That J.R. is indeed a true friend and a prince among men. Did me two good deeds in one day. The best lovin' a man ever had, for one."

"And the other?" she said with no special interest.

"He cut me in on the sweetest oil deal of my life, that's all."

And Kristin felt her brain labor back to normal. Every instinct cried out to her: find out all about that deal. Perhaps there lay the way to get even with J.R. Ewing. . . .

"You want to talk about it, sweetie?" she cooed.

J.R. returned to his office. At about the same time Jordan Lee and Kristin were getting up from the dinner table, he was sitting down behind his desk. At the same time that she gave herself to Jordan's kiss, J.R. began reviewing his day's activities. He had accomplished much, he reminded himself, would accomplish even more as the years went by. It was vital that each move he made advance his personal interests, the interests of the Ewing family, Ewing Oil and Southfork. He basked in the anticipated glory that would be his when this most recent deal became known. His Daddy would be proud of him, respect him, come to understand that J.R. was the hub around which family concerns revolved. One day, he knew in some secret place in his heart, it would be J.R. who took Jock's place.

The prospect made him shudder. With apprehension as well as anticipation. To take Jock's place, to fill those oversized manly boots, to be what Jock was and always had been. No man could properly aspire to more. No greater success could come to any man.

"I love you, Daddy," J.R. said aloud.

He recalled the time they had gone out looking for some bulls to buy. So long ago. A pair of strong studs to service the cows on Southfork. J.R. was twelve years old and this was the first time Jock had taken him along on one of his occasional forays beyond the fence line of Southfork.

They rode out past Amarillo up into the panhandle. North out of White Deer onto a bleak landscape. Father and son, on a pair of hired mounts, moving toward a single flickering light in the indigo darkness just before sunup. Coming up on a dozen cowboys wolfing down a hot breakfast around a roaring fire.

Greetings were exchanged and they were invited to dismount for eggs and bacon, hotcakes and coffee. Pretty soon Jock turned the talk to his quest and the foreman indicated he had a couple of bulls to sell.

Bored with the dry talk about weight and cost per pound, J.R. drifted off to the make-shift corral where a couple of youngsters his own age were trying to rope a horse.

They saw J.R. but said nothing, continuing their efforts in the slow rising dawn. Successful finally, one of them held the quivering horse while the other saddled him. Then, up onto the horse's back, and the big brown went stiff in the legs, humping crazily, head thrust down, eyes bulging, nostrils flaring, giving with heavy snorts and an occasional screaming whinny. In three seconds, it was over. The rider thrown heavily to the ground, the horse careening wildly around the corral. The two young cowboys ran for the fence. Astride the top rail, they glanced over at J.R.

"Care to try 'im?"

J.R. let his eyes go back to the horse. Now standing as if rooted in place, snorting softly and huffing hard, blacker than black eyes, the animal watched his tormentors warily. J.R. rode, and rode well, but he had always avoided the rigors of breaking horses. On Southfork that was left for mature men to do and the idea of climbing aboard some fear-crazed bucking horse filled J.R. with the terrors of hell on earth.

"No, thanks." He made his voice casual, gave his best winning grin.

The two boys were relentless, as if sensing a pure victim and unable to resist scoring a small victory over the newcomer.

"Scared?" said the first.

"Don't blame 'im," the second said. "I'm scared, too. But I've tried Buster a dozen times anyway."

"'Cause you got spine, Toby. This boy's plain yeller, down to the core."

J.R. felt himself stiffen in place. "Don't call me yeller," he snarled.

Both boys laughed.

J.R. took a step toward them when he sensed eyes watching. He jerked around to see Jock and some of the other cowboys a dozen yards away, waiting to see his response. He straightened his shoulders and confronted the two strange boys.

"Okay, I'll ride your damned horse for you."

He slipped into the corral and approached Buster without haste, circling to the rear, crooning softly to the big animal. Buster pawed dirt and J.R. leaped back as if struck.

He reached for the bridle. Buster jerked his head up and J.R. retreated again. Once more he advanced. Reins in place, hand on the pommel, he lifted his left foot into the stirrup. Buster, quivering, bared his teeth and flicked his tail. J.R. went spinning away, rolling in the dust. Buster reared up, front legs churning air, whinnying his displeasure. J.R. ran for the fence, diving between the split log rails to safety.

The laughter came from every direction. The boys at his rear, the men with his daddy to the front. J.R. dusted himself off and stood there wishing he were dead. Filled with shame and bitterness at his failure.

Later, alone with Jock, J.R. said, "I'm sorry, Daddy. Damned horse scared me half to death."

Jock stared him down. That sun-creased face unyielding, his manly voice unbending, flat. "Nobody put you in that corral, boy, except your own self."

"Those boys called me yeller."

Jock's eyes narrowed. "And you proved them out, I'd say."

J.R. felt his bones shrink, his skin tighten, his presence reduced to zero. "I ain't yeller, Daddy," he cried. "I ain't."

"Boy," Jock said coldly. "You goin' to have to prove it to me. Make us both forget what happened in that corral." Jock strode away, tall, implacable, so very strong and brave, so unreachable.

"But, Daddy," J.R. cried after that retreating figure, "I love you . . ."

The Ace Bar was a dark and noisy cave reeking of booze and stale tobacco. A three-piece combo pounded out a rock tune with neither verve nor passion. A topless dancer jerked and twisted along the small stage behind the bar, a clown's fixed smile plastered on her otherwise anguished face. Some men threw pennies at her as she moved, their mocking laughter announcing a throw that landed on target.

A few solitary drinkers at the tables paid no attention. Near the back door leading to an alley, two huskies in boots and Stetsons labored to beat a pinball machine that tilted too easily. Off to one side of the bar, Sue Ellen finished her drink and lifted a limp arm in signal to the barman for another. He refilled her glass and took her money.

Her large pale eyes lifted up to the topless dancer. A flood of sympathy brought tears to Sue Ellen's eyes. The woman up there—long past her prime—was a human being, deep pain etched on that frozen visage. Like the dancer, Sue Ellen felt she had nothing left: no strength, no courage, no real will to go on. Unlike the dancer she wore protective garments that saved her from the more obvious degradations life had to offer. She—God help her—was a Ewing.

She laughed aloud, a harsh, self-mocking eruption without humor or joy. A cowboy midway along the bar glanced her way, examined her with more than casual interest.

Sue Ellen threw back her drink and called for another.

There was a limit to how much a human being should be made to endure. An end to pain and problems. Everyone was entitled to affection and support and love. Except Sue Ellen.

Damn J.R. to hell and farther. Damn his mean, deceitful ways. Damn him and Kristin, her own ever loving by God sister. Damn her own self for failing as a wife, a mother, a woman. Damndamndamn.

She worked her way off the tall barstool and managed to misjudge the distance to the floor. She stumbled and almost fell, was bumped by a passer-by, dropped her shoulder bag—Sakewitz' best leather; Godalmightyhowmuchitcost!—to the floor. She staggered, having difficulty locating it, getting down on hands and knees, feeling for the elusive purse.

"This what you looking for, little lady?"

A pair of booted feet stood close by. She raised her eyes to see the cowboy, lean and tall, her bag in one great thorny hand. He helped her to her feet.

She allowed him to drape the strap across her shoulder. "Thank you, kind sir." She giggled, raised her eyes to his. His face was long and bony, the thin lips drawn back in what passed for a smile, the plainsman's eyes almost white in the dimness of the Ace Bar.

"Dusty?" she said. "Is that you, Dusty Farlow?"

"Does it matter?"

"Well, sure it does, but not all that much. If you're not Dusty, who are you?"

"Name is Josh, ma'am."

"Not Dusty."

"Hope you're not too disappointed."

"You sure do look like Dusty."

"Care to join me for a drink, ma'am. There's an empty booth along the wall."

He took her elbow in a firm grip, guiding her across the floor. Two cowboys sat in the booth drinking Lone Star beer.

Josh made a quick motion of one hand and they left, leaving a row of empty long necks behind. A waitress in a brief dance hall costume appeared.

"What'll you have?" Josh said.

"Bourbon and branch water. Very little branch," Sue Ellen said. "On the side, that is."

"Long neck for me."

She peered at the man next to her. "Is it really you, Dusty?"

"Josh is the name. What's yours?"

"Sue Ellen. But you know that Dusty."

Josh grinned at her and took her hand in his. "You're sure looking prettier than ever, Sue Ellen."

"Well, thank you, Dusty."

The barman brought the drinks, placed them on the table and hesitated. "You all right, ma'am?"

The cowboy stiffened in place. "What's your stake in this, mister? You did your job, now git."

"Just a concerned citizen is all," the barman said, backing off.

Josh drained half his glass. "Drink up."

She drank. She shook her head in wonderment, a pleased, blurred smile on her lovely face. "I just can't believe it . . ."

Josh looped his arm around her, moving closer. She was the best-looking woman he'd ever been this near, the best looking and the classiest. Look at those clothes, the fine gold chain around her graceful throat, the ring on her finger. Class and money. This time he'd really hit the mother-lode. All the goodies rolled up in one sweet-smelling package. He turned her face and kissed her long and hard.

"Why, Dusty, you just are overwhelming. Give a girl a chance to breathe . . ."

The two cowboys who had earlier occupied the booth slid into the seat opposite them, assessing Sue Ellen openly and hungrily.

"Hey, man, what's the good word?"

"Ride on, men," Josh said with a noticeable absence of good humor. "This one's all mine."

"Come on, Josh, spread the good times."

"There's enough to go 'round, buddyboy."

"Dusty," she murmured. "I thought you were gone forever."

"Who the hell's Dusty?" one of the cowboys said.

"I am," Josh growled. "I'm right here, darlin', at your side." He put his face against her hair, worked his way down to her neck, nibbling and kissing. One hand came to rest on her knee, the fingers closing hard and insistent.

"Ah, Dusty," Sue Ellen said vaguely, lost in a fogbank

of memories, "you mustn't . . . in front of your friends . . . you mustn't . ."

The barman went into the small room in the rear that served the Ace Bar as an office. He placed his call and waited until someone answered.

"This the Ewing residence?" he said.

Bobby Ewing, at work in the den at Southfork with Ray Krebbs, foreman of the ranch, picked up the phone on the first ring.

"This is Bobby Ewing, who's this?"

"I'm the bartender at the Ace Bar, Mr. Ewing. Now I don't want any trouble."

"Trouble! What kind of trouble is that?"

"It's Mrs. Ewing . . ."

"Mrs. Ewing!" Bobby's first thought was of Pam. "What is it? What's wrong?"

"I'm calling from over in Braddock . . ."

"Yes, I know the Ace Bar. What is the matter?"

"It's Mrs. Ewing, She's here now, with too many bourbons inside her, and it looks to me like she's going to need some kind of help. . . ."

"Which Mrs. Ewing?"

But the barman had hung up without answering.

6

$\mathcal{A}$t the same time that Sue Ellen was drinking with the cowboy, Josh, Pam Ewing paid a visit to her brother, Cliff Barnes, at his apartment. He wasted no time on preliminaries, his excitement evident as she entered.

"I've got some fantastic news for you!" he exulted by way of greeting her. "For us."

"Have you found something out about Momma?"

"Something much more important."

"Oh." Her disappointment was clear and she lowered herself into a chair, losing interest.

"I tried to call you in Colorado . . ."

"We were pretty busy, always on the move."

"But now you're back. Believe me, Pam, this is important. I've had the signatures verified and it is pluperfect proper and legal."

"The death certificate for Daddy . . ."

He shook his head impatiently. "No, nothing like that. This is a legal, bona fide, binding, *enforceable* contract . . ."

"Contract! What are you talking about, Cliff?"

"Here it is. Remember when you and I were going through Digger's belongings. I found it in one of those old beat-up trunks."

"I thought you got me over here to talk about Momma. Oh, Cliff, why are we wasting time over some old useless *contract?*"

He stared at her in disbelief. She hadn't understood

52

anything he'd said. Well, he'd spell it out, chapter and verse, give her a line reading.

"Sister, dear, listen closely. What I've got in my hand— this innocent looking piece of paper—it's what I've always dreamed about finding. A way of striking back at the Ewings, at J.R. Ewing in particular, and Jock Ewing, that old retrobate. It means I am about to get even for Daddy and for us."

Her eyes flashed. "There's something you keep forgetting, brother mine. I am a Ewing. I intend to remain a Ewing. Hurt that family and you hurt me."

"Don't jump the gun, Pam. Just hear me out."

"Let me see that paper—"

"I'll read it to you—'It is hereby agreed that all revenues and profits in the oil field now known as Ewing 23 will be shared equally by Jock Ewing and Willard Barnes and their heirs in perpetuity.'"

"So?"

"So! Can't you understand? This is dated February 26th, 1938 and signed by old man Ewing and by Digger."

"What's it got to do with you and me, Cliff?"

"This means . . ." He stopped and tried to regulate his breathing, to slow his heartbeat. "This means no more standing at the back door, hat in hand. It means we Barnes come in the front as *equal* partners with the Ewings. At least on this one field. For half-a-million dollars a year, maybe more. Can you picture the expression on J.R.'s face when I show him this. I can't wait."

She found it impossible to match his enthusiasm or his interest. "If the contract was any good, why was it hidden away for so long in that trunk?"

"Who knows? You knew Digger at least as well as I did. Our father was probably drunk when he signed this and forgot all about it. It wouldn't surprise me if Ewing got him drunk with just that purpose in mind. . . ."

"Oh, Cliff . . ."

"I mean it."

"Wouldn't Jock have remembered?"

"Maybe, maybe not. Anyway, this was signed more than forty years ago. Bobby only re-opened that field last month. Jock never gave this contract a thought. Why should he? It never entered his mind for forty years and since Digger was dead and buried—well, what if he did remember?—dead men make no demands."

"But you will."

"For Digger and for us. Bet your life on it."

"And what if J.R. turns his back on you?"

Cliff grinned in triumph. "Let him try. They'll listen, all right. they have to now. And I'm going to keep my promise to Daddy. His life won't be a waste. I'm going to see to it, one way or another. . . ."

The noise level in the Ace Bar was much higher now. More drinkers had bellied up to the bar and most of the tables and booths were occupied. The combo, as if inspired by a larger audience, played louder, if not better. The girl on the runway bounced and jiggled, always a step behind the beat. No one seemed to notice.

Nor did they notice Josh and his friends easing Sue Ellen toward the alley at the back of the bar. Her hair was disheveled now, her blouse gaped open. Her eyes were unfocused and her laughter was shrill and aimless, her attention leapfrogging from place to place, person to person. Two more cowboys joined the slow-moving group, staking their claim to any future goings-on. If Josh cared one way or another, he gave no sign.

"Where we goin'?" Sue Ellen wanted to know, not expecting an answer.

"Gonna have a party," somebody said. "You like parties, don'tcha?"

"Jus' love a party. Always did. Will all you handsome boys dance with Sue Ellen? Sue Ellen jus' loves dancing."

They moved out the rear exit into the alley, heading for a car parked nearby. At the same moment, Bobby and Ray entered the Ace Bar through the street entrance. The barman saw them and pointed toward the back door. Bobby and Ray picked their way through the boisterous crowd and out into the alley. Without a word, they separated. Bobby circled to the front of the five cowboys and Sue Ellen. Ray came up behind them.

Bobby held up one hand. "Hold it right there, fellas."

"What's this all about?" Josh said, shoving Sue Ellen behind him, taking up an aggressive stance a yard away from Bobby. "What's your stake in this, cowboy?"

"The lady's my sister-in-law. I want that understood from the start."

"Bobby! Is that you, Bobby?"

"Come on, Sue Ellen, We're going home."

"The hell you say," Josh drawled.

"Sue Ellen, I'm taking you home."

She shook her head. "No, I can't. I just found him."

Bobby was puzzled. "You know this man?"

"Don't you recognize him? Dusty Farlow."

"I see," Bobby said. He spread his hands. "Now we can do this peaceful, mister, or the hard way. Suit yourself."

"You heard the lady," Josh said. "She don't want to go."

"Let's not argue . . ."

"She stays with us."

"I told you, she's my—"

Josh took one long stride forward, throwing a right hand with surprising speed. But Bobby was already on the move, stepping inside, landing a quick short blow to the ribs and a right hand just above the belt. Josh doubled over. Bobby slugged him once behind the ear and the big cowboy went down and out.

Sue Ellen moaned in despair. "Look what you've done to Dusty."

"You've seen my work, men," Bobby said to the others. "Anybody else want a sample?"

They backed off without a word, Ray pulling aside to let them go.

Sue Ellen began to cry. "You hurt him."

"He'll be all right," Bobby said, guiding her away. "Everything's going to be all right now. Everything."

"You didn't have to hurt him." she cried. "You didn't have to."

The next morning J.R. was the first one up. Wearing a robe and slippers he made his way into the kitchen and poured coffee into a mug, then went out into the den. He switched on the television and stared at the picture fading into view. An announcer was reading the morning news:

"Three engine companies worked continuously through the night and the fire was finally knocked down at about five this morning. There are four reported injuries and estimated damage is put at—"

J.R. walked out of the den, the announcer droning on behind him. On the patio, he looked across the swimming pool to the fields beyond, a man with something on his mind. Behind him, Bobby, fully dressed, appeared.

"Morning, J.R."

"Morning, little brother."

"How's Sue Ellen this morning?"

"Sleeping it off, peaceful as a baby. Drunks do have a way about them."

"Be kind to her, J.R. That is one sad lady."

"Hell, she's got just about everything in the world she wants or needs. What's she unhappy about?"

"Ask her, J.R. The answer might surprise you."

"Maybe I'll do that, and then again maybe I won't. Still, I thank you for what you did, Bobby."

"We're all family here."

J.R. grunted softly. "Where you bound for at this early hour?"

"There's some fence down in Two Stick. Ray wants me to look it over. Seems it might have been cut."

"Rustlers again?"

"Don't know yet. We'll see. Take care . . ."

J.R. nodded and watched Bobby set off toward the barn. A moment later the phone began to ring. He hurried to answer.

"J.R. Ewing . . ."

It was an overseas call. He told the operator to put it through. He raised the hand holding the coffee mug and saw that it was trembling: how much he cared, how much he wanted this deal to go his way. How much he needed it.

The voice at the other end was faint. "Hello! Hello, you there, J.R.?"

"Hello, Hank. Can you hear me?"

Hank's voice came in stronger now. "That's better, J.R. I've been trying to get through for hours. It's a mess over here . . ."

"What's going on, ole buddy?" He placed the mug on the table, careful not to spill coffee. He rubbed his damp palm against his robe. "Let's have the news."

"Just like I said, J.R. All hell's broken loose. It's crazy in these parts. The revolution's in full swing. Shooting, bombing, fire and brimstone everywhere. Ain't worth a plugged nickle to be an American over here just this minute."

"What about your people?"

"I've sent them all across the border . . ."

"And you?"

"Time's running out. I'd best be on my way. I just wanted you to know . . ."

"Yes?"

"The oil fields have been nationalized, J.R. Every last well. Drilling platforms, ships, the whole cotton-eating shebang. All gone, J.R. I'm sorry."

"Well, now, don't you worry about a thing, Hank. Ain't your fault things went the way they did. You just get your welldigger's butt to a high ground, hear. Wouldn't want you getting killed on us."

"Don't aim to, J.R."

"Then take off. And thanks for calling, Hank. You did good work, buddy. There'll be a bonus coming your way . . ."

"A bonus?" the surprised and confused Hank Thompson said.

He received no reply. A smiling, cheerful J.R. had dropped the receiver back in place, breaking the connection. Everything, he crooned to himself, was going to be just fine. Perfect.

He went after some hot coffee and made his way back into the den. There, watching television, was Jock, fully dressed, all color drained out of his rugged face. The news announcer was saying:

". . . and White House Press Secretary Jody Powell had stated that such a reaction would be premature and unwarranted. He stressed the President's request for all citizens to remain calm. Most closely affected by the rebels' nationalization of foreign industries is the independent Ewing Oil Company with hundreds of millions of dollars tied up in exploration and drilling. The loss to the family-owned business can be calculated to be in the billions of dollars when it is all totaled up and will mean the end of one of Dallas' truly inspiring success stories. Ewing Oil came into being when—"

J.R. switched off the set and grinned at his father. Jock, his mouth flattened out, still pale, a spreading weakness in his joints, staggered and almost fell. J.R. helped him into a chair.

"Is it true, J.R.?"

"The nationalization? Yes, it is, Daddy. But—"

"Then we're wiped out."

A flush of uncertainty took hold of J.R. What if his daddy failed to understand what he had done? What if he'd acted too impulsively, too much the lone wolf? Yet that was the way Jock had begun, the way all the old wildcatters had started, freelancing no matter the odds or the obstacles. Real men, every one of them the kind of man J.R. had always aspired to become. And now. And now . . .

"It's all right, Daddy."

"How much have we lost?"

J.R. wet his lips and sucked up his guts. "Well, Daddy, the way I look at it . . . We have just made the killing of a lifetime. . . ."

PART II

The Ewings

YESTERDAY

$\mathcal{D}$awn is the best time. The sun flares up above prairie and hill, the heat already claiming the dew-kissed fields, sending long shadows across the cities of the flatlands. On honky-tonk row, the neon lamps have gone out. The brawls are over. The drunks sleeping it off. The girls are gone, having fled the daylight with the same speed and terror of revelation that Dracula might exhibit. The herds stir, the cows bawl, and cowboys crawl out of their sleeping bags to slosh down hot black coffee laced with just enough sipping whiskey to bring them fully awake.

On Southfork, Bobby Ewing galloped his horse up to the barn, swinging down as the big beast braced itself to a dusting halt.

"Way to go, Bobby!" Ray Krebbs cheered.

"Everything's going along in the east pasture, Ray. The Brahmas are coming in smooth as silk."

"I'll bet they are," the foreman kidded.

"Ain't nothin' to this cowboying, Mr. Krebbs. Just takes a little brains and hard work."

"Oh, yes sir, Mr. Ewing, sir." Krebbs' lean face broke into a pleased grin. Between him and Bobby there was a strong bond, a feeling that went beyond friendship. Understanding, empathy, a kind of masculine love that ranch hands seldom talked about. "Then there's no need for me to skedaddle out there, is there, Mr. Ewing, sir?"

"No need at all, foreman. Just take the morning off for rest and relaxation."

"I'll do that, Bobby, and tell your daddy you said so."

Bobby waved as he hurried on to the big house. He found his father and mother having their morning coffee on the patio, and joined them for a cup.

"Where's the rest of the clan? Nobody eating breakfast this morning?"

"Pam's upstairs," his mother said. "And J.R. and Sue

61

Ellen left for the airport to pick up her mother and sister."

"I forgot they're due today."

"What about you, Bobby?" Jock said. "Didn't you have a meeting scheduled with Senator Mulligan today?"

"In just about an hour, Daddy."

"Come down hard on the man, son. Remind him of past Ewing favors. That damned Cliff Barnes . . ."

"You're talking about my wife's brother, Daddy."

"I can't forget it," Jock said dryly. "I'm fond of Pam but that brother of hers . . ." He grimaced. "That man's done damage enough to this family."

"I'll see what I can do, Daddy." He swallowed some more coffee, climbed back to his feet, and went off in search of his wife.

He located Pam upstairs in the nursery, leaning over the crib. She was playing with John Ewing III, the infant watching her with wide eyes, tiny hands and feet waving in the air reflexively.

"You're going to spoil that child," he said from the doorway.

"All babies should be spoiled rotten."

"How about husbands?" He advanced into the room. "How about this husband?"

"That's an interesting idea."

He slipped his arms around her waist and she leaned back against him. "Look at you," he murmured against her cheek. "All dressed up for work and playing with another woman's baby. Can't have you being late and getting fired, can we? You know how much the Ewings depend on your salary."

She worked her way around to face him. "Bobby, what would you say if I told you the job at the Store isn't as important to me as it used to be?"

He blinked once before responding. "Would you feel that way . . . that strongly about the baby, if you didn't believe that your brother Cliff was the father?"

She disengaged herself. "I'm not responsible for my brother's behavior. Maybe if Sue Ellen really cared for the child . . . wanted him, loved him . . . maybe then I could accept what happened. She spends hardly any time at all with Little John."

"Sue Ellen's going through a bad time. But she'll come around. That doesn't make what happened between Sue

Ellen and Cliff your business or Little John your responsibility."

"I know." She gazed up from under her brows at him and he thought she'd never been lovelier. "Bobby, maybe we ought to start thinking seriously about having one of our own."

A quicksilver grin broke across his finely boned face. "Well, I thought that was exactly what we were doing. At least I've been trying my damnedest, in case you haven't noticed."

She touched his lips tenderly. "Oh, let me tell you, I noticed. Oh, yes, I have noticed . . ."

It sits out on State Highway 114 between Dallas and Fort Worth, the monstrous maze that is the Regional Airport, the world's largest, it is claimed. Especially by Texans. Seventeen miles from downtown Dallas, it services eleven counties and their three million citizens and gives baffled travelers nervous breakdowns trying to get from one airline to another.

Inside the first class waiting room sat a limited selection of Dallas' population. The rich and the very rich. Dressed in a variety of garb, they all had the comfortable look of men and women who knew exactly where their next meal was coming from. And that paying for it would never be a problem.

J.R. sat reading the Dallas Press and muttering under his breath. Until he could stand it no more. He turned to Sue Ellen alongside him and tapped the front page of the newspaper.

"Look at this, Man of the Year. Cliff Barnes named Man of the Year. Is that the most godawfulthingyoueverdidhear! I tell you, there aren't any civic standards these days, not-a-one. Cliff Barnes, would you believe it?"

Sue Ellen's eyes flowed into soft focus and her head swung toward him. "Did you say something, J.R.?"

He stared at her, choking back an angry retort. A woman slept with a man, committed adultery, became pregnant by a man not her husband and had his baby; how could she be so cool, so indifferent, so remote? He wondered if she still saw Cliff Barnes on the sly? Why not? She'd faked him out once, she might be foolish enough to try again. He made a mental note to have Sue Ellen watched, followed, her every move checked out.

Jesus H. Christ, how he loathed Cliff Barnes, that entire family. Including that damned sister-in-law of his, Bobby's pure-as-the-driven-snow wife. What a fraudulent bunch they were, starting with that dirty old man Digger and right on down the line. First chance he got he was going to get them out of his hair, once and for all.

J.R. manufactured a wide smile. He reached for his wife's hand and made no comment when she pulled away. "I think your mother's plane is running late, sweetheart."

She returned his smile, equally thin, equally cold. "It just landed, they made the announcement. You hate him, don't you?"

"Hate who, darlin'?"

"Cliff Barnes."

"He is not one of my dearest friends but I hate no man. Or woman."

"Who would have believed it?" she mused. "An insignificant little man like Cliff causing all that trouble for the omnipotent J.R. Ewing."

"About as much trouble as a fly causes a horse, Sue Ellen."

"Whatever you say, J.R."

"You know what a horse does when a fly bothers him, don't you? He swats it."

"Yes," she said, looking away. "I was right. The plane has landed."

Digger Barnes came out of the tourist exit into the terminal building looking exactly like what he was—an old wildcatter long gone to seed. Grizzled and rumpled in a J.C. Penney suit, his tie yanked off to one side, his collar unbuttoned, he moved with the remembered quick steps of someone still in a hurry, but not sure of his destination. He jerked around, scanning the waiting crowd, seeking some familiar face.

"Daddy! Digger, over here."

He located the caller. His son Cliff, too clean and too smooth looking like a man who has recently come into money. They hurried toward each other, embraced, until Digger in a flush of embarrassment at the intimacy pulled away.

"Daddy, you're looking fine."

"And feeling fine, Cliff. Now will you please tell me why I'm here. I was perfectly happy in California."

"I have a surprise for you."

"You could have written a letter, or telephoned me."

"Nope. I wanted you here, where I could see the expression on your face."

"Okay, what's the surprise?"

"Let's get your bags."

Digger indicated the single club bag he held. "This is my bag. Let's go."

They located Cliff's car in the parking lot, climbed in. "Is this the surprise?" Digger asked. "It's a fine car, a rich man's car. What are you doing with it?"

"Things are going my way."

"What's that supposed to mean?"

Cliff reached into his pocket, drew out a number of checks. "These are for you, Daddy."

"What is this?"

"Ewing Oil royalty checks."

"I don't get it."

"They're made out to you. Willard Barnes."

"And signed by J.R. Ewing . . ."

"Every couple of months, Ewing Oil pays out some of that oil money to Digger Barnes. How's that make you feel?"

Digger squinted at his son. "Boy, how'd you manage this?"

"I've become a bit of a power around Dallas, Daddy. The Office of Land Management—the O.L.M.—which I run, with no outside interference, the O.L.M. decides who drills for oil and who doesn't in the State of Texas."

"I'm impressed with that. But it doesn't explain these checks."

"I've got the Ewings boxed in. I am squeezing them. Hard. The only new field I let them drill in was Palo Seco and I arranged for you to own a piece. Not a big piece, but it is a start. Just a start."

Digger's gray-bearded face broke into a wide grin. "Well, now, that's worth coming back to Dallas for."

"It's only the beginning, Daddy. I've backed those Ewings into a corner. I'm gonna wipe them out . . . flat broke when I'm through with 'em."

Digger frowned. "I never asked for that."

"I can do it. J.R. has thrown every dirty trick he knows at me and failed to slow me down. No matter what he's tried, I've come out on top. He's fresh out of tricks."

Digger measured his son from out of those hollow, rheumy eyes. There was a gleeful intensity to Cliff he didn't appreciate. The desire for revenge could be carried too far and often backfired. He knew, he'd been there. Too many times.

"You sound a lot like them, Cliff. The Ewings. Never wanted to wipe them out, never wanted to see Jock Ewing broke and busted. All I wanted was that's rightly coming to me, what's mine honestly come by, honestly earned."

"I'll do better by you, Daddy. I'll make Jock Ewing pay for the way he treated you. An eye for an eye. Simple justice, that's all."

Digger felt himself sagging. "Let's get out of here, son."

"I thought you'd be proud of me, Daddy."

"I always have been proud of you, son. Of you and Pam. Don't do nothing to change that. Now I want to rest. It was a long flight and I am very tired."

J.R. drove the Mercedes in his usual controlled and careful manner. Next to him, Sue Ellen turned to face her mother and sister in the rear seat. Patricia Shepard looked younger than her years in traveling clothes that would have been at home in San Francisco, New York or Paris, France. Seldom was she taken to be the mother of two grown daughters. She was slender, crisp, with eyes that missed nothing. A woman stylish and still lovely, but lacking some essential warmth that might draw a man her own age to her. But men were of secondary interest to Patricia Shepard; her current plans centered on her still unmarried daughter, Kristin.

If Sue Ellen possessed a serene and maturing beauty, made tense and uncertain by her unsettled emotions, Kristin was brittle and slightly off-center. As if the unseen parts of her psyche had been strung carelessly, out of joint, bent in one or two places so that similarly bent people were drawn to her. And she to them. She never met anyone's glance straight-on, as if seeking to deflect close human contact, to shed those who would want to know her better.

She possessed a fine curved figure, her legs long, her bust high, her features perfectly etched and assembled. No compliment ever paid her told it all. No description ever fully captured her. She was a damned good-looking enigma, unfathomable to most, but to J.R. easy to read.

"I must say it, Sue Ellen," Mrs. Shepard said, "you are looking simply radiant. Motherhood suits you. Don't you agree, Kristin?"

Kristin's smile was crooked, not quite a smirk. "We were all so excited when we heard about the baby."

Mrs. Shepard went on. "J.R., look at you. The very ideal of a proud father."

"Welcome to Dallas, ladies. We are surely pleased to have you aboard."

"Oh, J.R., you certainly are a gentleman. I hope one day Kristin will find a man just like you."

"Well, sure she will, Momma," Sue Ellen drawled without emphasis. "You'll see to it, won't you?"

Before Patricia could reply, they pulled into the driveway of Southfork. "Here we are, folks!" J.R. announced.

"Oh, it's so good to be back here," Kristin said. "I just love this ranch."

Jock and Miss Ellie were waiting for them with warm and effusive greetings. Servants collected their luggage and disappeared with quiet efficiency. Drinks were served and gossip exchanged.

"What happened to architectural school, Kristin?" Jock wanted to know. "USC wasn't it?"

Kristin gave him her most winning smile. It was a smile no man had ever resisted for long, she knew, and she wanted Jock on her side no matter what the future held. "I can't get the classes I want until next term."

"Well, we are happy to have you and your momma back in Dallas. Ain't that right, J.R.?"

"Right as rain, Daddy. Anything you want, just you holler, Kristin."

"I'll do that, J.R."

After a while, the women went upstairs to see Sue Ellen's baby. One look sent Patricia into ecstatic raptures. "Will you look at that child! The size of him. I expected a tiny tot, Sue Ellen. When I heard he was born premature, I tell you I was worried."

Miss Ellie reassured her. "Oh, the baby is coming along just fine. Isn't he, Sue Ellen?"

"Just fine, Miss Ellie," came the answer without expression.

Patricia reached for the baby. "You don't mind if I hold him, do you, Sue Ellen?"

"I don't mind, Mother."

She cradled the infant in her arms, rocking gently. "John Ross Ewing the Third. How adorable. What a handsome boy you are. Sue Ellen, would you like to hold your son?"

"No, Momma, you hold him. I'm tired and I think I'll just lie down for a while."

"Looks just like J.R.," Patricia said. "Wouldn't you say, Sue Ellen?"

"Whatever you say, Momma."

"Well, you go and take your nap. New mothers need their rest, I can tell you. I still remember how weary I used to get after you were born."

Miss Ellie watched with some concern as Sue Ellen left the nursery. Then she brightened. "It's time for Little John's bottle. Let's go next door and you can give it to him in relative comfort, if you like."

"I would love that. Kristin, we're going next door." No answer came and Patricia's voice took on a thin cutting edge. "Kristin . . . you do want to watch Little John take his bottle?"

"Yes, Mother, I'm coming." But her mind was else-where, crowded with shifting thoughts about her sister's husband.

They gathered in J.R.'s office in the Ewing Building: Bobby, Jock and J.R. When they were all seated, Jock turned to Bobby.

"All right, son, let's have it. About your meet with Senator Mulligan. Is he coming down on our side or not?"

"He wants to help."

"Better believe it," J.R. exploded. "That old retrobate owes the Ewing family a lot, more than he'd like to make known."

Jock waved him quiet. "Go on, Bobby."

"Well, there are rumors that Cliff Barnes is on the take."

"Accepting bribes, you mean?"

"Damn his eyes!" J.R. exulted. "I knew that little pissant was too good to be true. We'll spike his ass to the barn door this time. What's Mulligan going to do?"

"First thing is to get the Senate to set up an investigating committee . . ."

"How long's that going to take?" Jock wanted to know.

Bobby frowned. "You know how it is up in Austin, Daddy. Those politicians don't move fast."

"Well, let's light a fire under them," Jock said.

"I'll do my best."

J.R. swore. "That's a waste of time. By the time those dinosaurs in the State House get around to stopping the O.L.M. Ewing Oil will be turned into one more Texas historical monument. We need action now."

"Why?" Jock said. "What's happening now?"

"There's a team of O.L.M. people poking at our wells up in the panhandle. They claim we're dumping too much salt water."

Bobby said, "They going to shut us down there, too?"

"They will if Barnes has his way," J.R. shot back. "That miserable specimen you have for a brother-in-law, Bobby, is making Ewing Oil an endangered species."

"Maybe not. Mulligan promised prompt action . . ."

"Action is what we need," J.R. gritted out. "The kind that gets results."

"Now J.R. . . ." Bobby warned.

"Don't you fret, little brother. Nothing violent. Wouldn't want to upset the ethical balance of your delicate character. Let's face it—every man has a weakness and Cliff Barnes is no exception. Ain't that a fact, Daddy?"

"I believe that."

J.R. grinned. "All's I got to do is find that flaw in Barnes' makeup. And push the right buttons . . ."

By the time they arrived at his son's apartment, Digger was worn out, his limbs heavy and weak, his head spinning. Too often lately he'd felt this way after even the least strenuous activities or if he came under unexpected stress. But he had never been a man to give in easily to inadequacies of the flesh. He never complained, never sought medical advice, never ceased pushing ahead. It was Digger's way.

He remembered how it had been when he was a young man. Strong, charged with energy, afraid of nothing, determined to carve an important place for himself in the world. With the help of his new partner, a big rawboned

Texan named Jock Ewing, he'd taken an option on some land northwest of Dallas and begun a drilling operation. It was hard work, hustling to round up enough cash to buy tools and equipment, to build a drilling rig, to do all the backbreaking labor by themselves. But Digger and Jock had kept at it, until one day while Digger was guiding a load of twenty-foot pipe into place, something went wrong. The ropes snagged and the pipe hung fifty feet above the ground, swaying in the breeze. There was a snag in the block-and-tackle and Jock went up the rig to break it loose. Trying to clear the line, Digger moved under the swinging load and without warning it tipped and began sliding.

"Look out below!" Jock yelled.

Digger skipped off to one side, jerking the guideline, making a desperate effort to tighten the bindings on the pipe, to right the load. Nothing worked and, too late, he saw the first long pipe slide out of the pack.

"Run, Digger!" Jock shouted.

Digger released the line and swung away, and tripped on a rock and went down. He scrambled frantically, slipping and sliding on the sandy surface. He rolled just as the pipes hit the ground. One twenty-foot length of pipe bounced, came up almost on end and flipped over, catching his left arm above the elbow, snapping it like a piece of kindling. Digger screamed and lost consciousness.

When he woke, he was in the hospital, his left arm in a cast to the shoulder. Jock Ewing stood at the bedside looking down at him with deep concern.

Digger blinked his eyes into focus. "What're you doin' here, pardner? Ain't you supposed to be out working at that damned rig? We got a well to drill, oil to find. Can't make no million dollars in this damned place."

Jock's mouth twitched. "What a deceitful old critter you are, Barnes. Here I thought you were damaged bad but you're just as mean and hard as ever. Guess I will be getting back to the well. One of us has got to do an honest day's work."

"I'll be back tomorrow after breakfast."

"The hell you will. Doctor tells me you'll be in that cast four, maybe five months. Arm won't be strong enough to use for close to a year. I'll hire me a helper."

"With what? Neither one of us got the money. Tomorrow after breakfast."

"You're crazy, Digger."

"With one arm, I'm more a man than most."

"Maybe you are at that."

"No one ever said Digger Barnes quit on a job, not ever."

But now, taking a few strides into his son's apartment, everything swam into a blur and his legs began to quiver. "Quite a place you got here," he said, hand going to his temple.

"I'm glad you like it, Daddy."

"How much do they pay you as head of that . . . what the hell is it you're head of?"

"Office of Land Management. They pay me very well."

"Enough to afford this fancy place? And that big shiny car you drive?"

"Daddy, I'm a frugal man. I have a very quiet life style."

"Don't bring the costs of this layout down. Looks to me like you've got some other source of income. You on the take, boy?"

Cliff glanced quickly over at his father and away. Digger was beginning to show his age and the hard life he'd lived, but he was still shrewd and sharp, allowing very little to slip past him.

"Daddy," Cliff said mildly. "If I was, and told you so, you'd be a party to it. The last thing I want is any trouble for you. . . ."

"Trouble! Me and trouble been pardners all of my days, boy, and don't you forget it. And I'm still hanging around. I don't go hunting trouble but I sure as hell ain't about to start running from it, either."

"Well, you take care of your troubles and I'll ride herd on mine. Now, what about something to eat, Daddy, or drink?"

"What I'd like to do is lie down for a while. I'm feeling a mite poorly."

"Are you all right? Maybe I'd better call a doctor."

"Just a few minutes rest is all I need. Where's the bedroom?"

"Right through that door, Daddy. What do you say to a bowl of soup or—"

"Nothing, son . . ."

Digger shuffled slowly across the floor toward the bedroom. He never made it, collapsing in a heap in the middle of the living room. Cliff ran to his side and called his name. But Digger made no response. His half-closed eyes glazed and unseeing, his breathing shallow—Digger Barnes was a very sick old man.

Sue Ellen was dressed in a very chic, very expensive pair of lounging pajamas, her hair precisely coiffed, her face carefully made up. She looked lovely and youthful, her fine boned face without anxiety or tension. But her hands lay coiled in her lap as if ready to strike out at an old adversary and she stared blankly ahead at some mid-point in space, seeing nothing, feeling nothing, thinking nothing.

She wasn't aware of her sister entering the bedroom. "Hi," Kristin said, "I'm not disturbing you, am I?" She received no response. "Sue Ellen! Is something wrong?"

Gradually Sue Ellen drifted back to the present. Her head swiveled toward Kristin, the pale eyes blinking, bringing the conflicting images inside her head down to focus.

"Oh, Kristin, it's you."

Kristin spoke brightly. "It's been months and we haven't had a chance to talk. After all, we are sisters."

"That's so, isn't it?"

"Are you well, Sue Ellen?"

"Quite well, thank you."

"You certainly look wonderful. It's just—when we heard about the accident."

Sue Ellen looked away. "I don't like to think about it. My mistake. I never saw that stop sign and the other car came out of nowhere. Ordinarily I'm a very careful driver."

"But now you're all right?"

"Do you have any doubts, sister?"

"Oh, no. Not a one." Kristin grew pensive. "That place must have been awful."

Sue Ellen's gaze was level and steady, forcing Kristin to look away this time. "What place is that, Kristin?"

"Why, the sanitarium, of course—"

A rising peal of laughter broke out of Sue Ellen, almost out of control. Gradually it dissolved into a coughing fit. Kristin hurried into the bathroom and returned with a glass of water. One sip and the coughing subsided.

"Thank you," Sue Ellen said. She put the glass aside.

"That place . . . oh, yes. That place was really wonderful," she went on with forced cheerfulness. "The best of care, the best of food, everything was simply super."

"Sis, why were you drinking so heavily? Miss Ellie told Momma and Momma told me."

"Sort of a family party line, isn't it? I think we've talked enough about me. How do you like California?"

Kristin straightened up. "We were at a lovely apartment hotel. Very lush, a swimming pool, all the fixings. Except the men."

"Oh, yes, the men . . ."

"The ones I met were either married or gay or in therapy. Or all three."

"Poor Kristin. Always on the prowl. Don't you know the best way to find a man is not to look so hard. The right one will find you. And for a woman these days, it's not so bad to live alone."

"Would you like to live alone?"

"There are times when I think single life would be very uncomplicated."

"I don't understand."

"Enjoy it while you can, sister dear. Think of it as a time when you can try new things, make your own mistakes and not have to answer to anyone for them."

"Oh, I don't know. Being married to J.R. Ewing, I would give up a little freedom and privacy for the position and power to be gained."

"You are very young in many ways, Kristin. But our Momma has trained you very well. Now, I'm suddenly very tired. . . ."

"Of course." She went to the door. "Miss Ellie has invited us for dinner this evening. Will you be coming down later?"

"How concerned you are, Kristin. Were you planning on occupying my chair?"

An angry glint came into Kristin's eyes. Her lips thinned out. "If you don't pull yourself together—someone surely will."

Paul Holliston's office was in the new Medical Arts Building, within sight of Reunion Tower. The waiting room was paneled, upholstered, with a soporific melody floating on the still air. All designed to allay fears, sedate anxieties, and prepare the patient for bad news; plus the physician's inflated bill. Poor people never passed through the portals of that waiting room. Poor people never encountered Dr. Holliston. For him, poor people didn't truly exist.

Cliff and Pam sat side-by-side without speaking on a deep sofa covered with tan glove-leather, their feet sinking into a silky pile carpet. A pretty young nurse appeared in the waiting room, padded over to them—her smile a thing of beauty, her voice low, cultivated, designed to provide support and reassurance.

"Doctor will see you now."

Paul Holliston was smooth and handsome, the kind of man welcome anywhere, a man who trod lightly through life, barely leaving footsteps. He looked, Cliff thought, just like his waiting room: expensive, carefully contrived, and without warmth.

"How is my father?" Pam asked.

"He's dressing. He'll be along in a minute."

"Is it serious?"

"Nothing that bed rest and staying off the bottle wouldn't help."

"Thank God," Pam breathed.

Digger appeared, still stuffing a shirt into his pants. He grinned crookedly at his two children. "Well, so you finally decided to pay your old man a visit," he said to Pam. "About time." He offered his cheek for a kiss. "Great looking gal, ain't she, doc?"

Holliston nodded carefully.

"Get me out of here, Cliff. This bonesetter's been lecturing me on the evils of demon rum since I got here. Worst time I had since I ended up in a Methodist mission in Houston twenty years ago."

"Daddy," Pam said. "Maybe you ought to pay attention."

"I have suffered enough indignities to my flesh and my mind for one day. Let's go home, folks."

"Mr. Barnes," Holliston said in a cool professional voice. "You have a virus, and that is what put you on your back. . . ."

"Well, okay," Digger said. "That'll pass."

"Yes, but that's not all. You have a liver which is badly absued. One more drinking bout could be your last. And, at your age, whatever you've been doing in those California oilfields, well, it is just too much work, Mr. Barnes."

"Man has to earn his living, doc."

"All right," Cliff said. "No more drinking and we keep him quiot."

"The hell you will, boy."

"I'm afraid that's not all of it," the doctor said.

Three sets of eyes swung his way. They waited.

"I wanted to talk to all of you, because this affects all of you. The thing that threw me initially is that I never detected it in you, Cliff, when you were in for your annual checkup. . . ."

"Detected what?"

Holliston addressed Digger. "Mr. Barnes, has any doctor ever told you that you have a genetic disorder called neurofibromatosis?"

Digger chuckled. "Last time I saw a doctor was maybe forty years ago, or more. Set a busted arm for me. That man couldn't have pronounced what you said and neither can I."

"Neurofibromatosis . . ."

"Is that what made him sick?" Pam said.

"No. When I examined your father I discovered six or seven café au lait spots. Discoloration of the pigment of the skin. I did a hearing test. Your father tells me his hearing has been getting worse. . . ."

Digger broke in heatedly. "At my age, what do you expect?"

Holliston went on without pause. "A neurological exam and x-rays confirmed my diagnosis."

Cliff shifted forward on his chair. "Exactly what are you saying, doctor?"

"Neurofibromatosis is an inherited genetic disease usually characterized by tumors that grow along parts of the nervous system."

"Inherited!" Cliff said.

"Does that mean that Cliff and I have it?" Pam said nervously.

"Yes," the doctor said bluntly. "Even though you may exhibit no symptoms. Every one of you is a carrier."

Pam looked from one to the other, back to the doctor. "But so far nothing has happened to Daddy or Cliff or me. Is there any reason for concern?"

"Mr. Barnes, did you have any other children."

"Yes," Digger replied slowly. "May the good Lord rest their souls."

Cliff explained. "I had an older brother. Tyler died when he was six months old. There was a girl, a little doll of a girl named Catherine. She died just before her first birthday. We never knew why."

Dr. Holliston pursed his handsome lips. "I was afraid of that. Cliff, Mrs. Ewing, you two were lucky. You survived. Your father survived. This is a disease passed from parent to child and so on down through the generations. Mrs. Ewing, do you have any children?"

Pam was unable to reply. She shook her head.

"And you, Cliff. Have you become a father since I last saw you?"

Cliff hesitated. "What if I had?"

"Then an immediate examination of the child would be in order to determine if it has detectable tumors. It's not uncommon for such tumors to turn cancerous in a child. We have to be frank—the family history here is a bad one."

"Are you saying that a child of mine could die . . . like my baby brother and sister did?"

"After only six months or a year?" Pam said, her fears rising sharply.

"To be blunt," Dr. Holliston said, "yes."

They rode back to Cliff's apartment in silence. Once inside Digger went directly to bed and minutes later was sound asleep. Pam made coffee, filled two mugs, and took her place across from Cliff at the kitchen counter. Her brother had not uttered a word since they left the doctor's office and still seemed lost in thought, unaware of her presence. Abruptly he went over to the bar and filled a water glass halfway up with Scotch, knocked it back without hesitation.

"Want one?"

Pam shook her head. "I know how you feel, but that won't help, Cliff."

"You don't know how I feel, how could you? Little John is my son and he's going to die."

"We can't be sure."

"I've got to get to Sue Ellen, tell her about Little John. About me . . ."

"No, Cliff . . ."

"You don't understand!"

"I understand this. Bobby and I want to have children more than anything else. We talk about it constantly and now—well, now maybe that's all over for us. For me. I know how that makes me feel."

"Sue Ellen has to be prepared."

"Sue Ellen is shaky enough, Cliff. A shock like this, it could put her over the edge."

"She has a right to know."

"Cliff, she feels so guilty about Little John already . . ."

"About me, you mean?"

"She's not well, Cliff. She's depressed. She drinks too much. If she finds out her baby may die there's no telling what might happen."

"I can't just sit around and wait."

"Take it easy. I'll handle it."

"How?"

"I'll think of something."

"You're going out of your way to prevent a scandal in the Ewing family," he snarled. "I hope you're not forgetting that your name was once Barnes, too."

"Don't be a fool, Cliff. I'm trying to help you and Sue Ellen. And most of all the baby."

"All right," he snapped through the flood of shame he experienced. "But I want to know exactly what's happening with my son."

"I'm your sister, Cliff. You can trust me."

"That's my wife you're staring at, J.R."

J.R., a Bloody Mary in hand, swung around and recovered his composure quickly. "Good morning, Bobby. Pam is a lovely young woman. You're a very fortunate man. I was wondering if Sue Ellen would like a bathing suit like the one Pam is wearing."

"Oh," Bobby said with thinly veiled sarcasm. "Is that what you were wondering?" He went back inside the house, J.R. trailing after him to join his parents in the dining room. Jock was just finishing his coffee.

"We're running late, Miss Ellie."

"Oh, Jock, after all these years—I always run late according to your watch and we always get wherever we have to go. Good morning, Bobby. Good morning, J.R."

"Where you folks headed for, Momma?" J.R. said, not really interested.

"Your Daddy is driving me to a D.O.A. breakfast. I haven't attended any meetings since Little John came home and to tell the truth I sort of miss it."

"Did you get Patricia and Kristin settled in town all right?" Jock said to J.R.

"Yes, Daddy."

"J.R.," Jock said, leaving the room. "Let's talk at the office later. About that young lawyer you've hired—what's his name?"

"Alan Beam, Daddy."

"He come up with anything we can use against Cliff Barnes? Time's running short on us, you know."

"I'm on top of it, Daddy."

"Well, if you need any help, just throw a rope over Bobby here. He'll give you his best."

"I can handle it, Daddy."

Pam appeared wearing a robe over her bathing suit, drying her hair with a towel.

"Would you like some breakfast, dear?" Miss Ellie asked.

"Just some coffee, please. I have to be on my way."

"That job at the Store keeping you busy?"

"I'm taking the day off. I'm carrying Little John to his pediatrician for his checkup."

"Why not Sue Ellen?" Bobby said.

"She was busy," Pam said casually. "I volunteered."

Without a word, J.R. left the room and went upstairs. He discovered Sue Ellen making up her eyes, wearing only a flimsy bra and panties. For a long moment it was almost as if he were looking at a woman he'd never seen before, never known before in any way. Her body was surprisingly lean, though full at the breasts and hips. Her buttocks were round and tilted perkily, visible in their perfection through the delicate fabric. J.R. became aware of his feelings, of his body response. He moved up behind her.

She peered at him in the dressing table mirror. "Don't tell me, J.R. You couldn't stand leaving for the office without one last adoring look at your wife."

"Believe it or not, Sue Ellen, that is true." He touched her shoulder, the skin warm and smooth. She shivered as he traced the curve of her spine with one stiff finger.

"Don't," she murmured.

"You are lovelier than ever, Sue Ellen."

"I don't know who you are, J.R."

"That's absurd, Sue Ellen. I'm the same man you fell in love with, the same man you married. Oh, I know things haven't always gone smoothly between us." His hands were at her waist, the fingers working at her flesh. He felt her stiffen in place and he pulled her back against himself. If she failed to give herself easily to the closeness, neither did she resist. "I have tried to change my ways, Sue Ellen, you know that. I have tried to be a loving and considerate husband ever since you came home from the accident." His hands rode over her buttocks and he whispered against her hair. "I got to admit it, Sue Ellen, you still have the greatest fanny north of the Rio Grande. . . ."

"I don't think you should touch me."

"I'm your husband."

"I feel as if I'm married to a stranger."

He cupped her breasts from behind and she gasped, made a feeble effort to free herself. "Is that what you need, another stranger. . . ?"

"You promised . . ."

"Never to mention Cliff Barnes to you, yes. Never to mention your lover."

"I made one mistake."

"Little John is the end product of that mistake, need I remind you of that?" He reached under the bra. "My Lord," he muttered, pushing himself hard against her bottom. "I believe you are better endowed than ever, darlin', and in better shape. Motherhood agrees with you."

"Let go of me."

"We did love each other once, Sue Ellen. I . . . still . . . love you . . ."

She broke free, wrenching around to confront him. For a microsecond her face was flushed and distorted with rage, then all emotion drained quickly away. "I make no call on you, J.R., for husbandly duties. None . . . at . . . all. Don't strain yourself for my sake. Your daddy's not around to see."

"This is what you kept asking for. More loving, more affection, more attention."

"I'm surprised you're up to even this much, J.R. With all your girl friends, I figured you'd be as dry as a water hole in summer."

He took a backward step and adjusted his clothes. "My mistake."

"That's right."

"But there is one thing we have to talk about."

She waited.

"I understand Pamela is taking Little John for his checkup. Seems only right that a mother take some interest in her son's welfare. Don't you care about the child?"

"The child is my punishment, the cross I have to bear. A reminder that I allowed myself to be used by two cruel and uncaring men, that I permitted my emotions to get in the way of my good sense."

"*I've* accepted the baby, why can't you?"

"That, J.R., is your punishment. As insufficient to your crimes as it is. Now if you'll excuse me, I'd like to continue dressing. In private, please."

El Rancho Chili sat northeast of downtown opposite a used car lot, sandwiched between a shopping center and a porno movie house. Scattered off to one side, a dozen outdoor tables under red and white umbrellas. Alan Beam, slender, intense and confident, sat at one drinking beer out of a bottle. He didn't stand when J.R. joined him, an omission silently noted and filed away.

"Dammit, Alan, I said let's have an out-of-the-way meeting place. Did you have to pick this dump? I am starving and there's nothing here worth eating, that's for damned sure."

A waitress in short shorts, a sequined shirt, boots and a ten-gallon hat, sidled up, order pad in hand. She looked to J.R. like a contestant in a beauty contest; not a winner, perhaps, but certainly one-two-three. There was that about living in Dallas, all those goodlooking young women.

"Hi yew," she drawled. "Whut'll yew have?"

"A bowl of Texas red for me and another ice-cold long neck, honey. Same for you, J.R.?"

He looked the girl over deliberately. She waited patiently; she'd been working at El Rancho Chili for a long time. "Tell you what, you got any chicken-fried steak, darlin', with white cream gravy?"

"Yew drinkin' anythang?"

"Iced tea, if you got it."

"We got it, mister."

They watched her leave, all moving parts meshing smoothly. "Hot damn!" Alan said. "How I do enjoy all of this. . . ."

"It's an acquired taste," J.R. offered without levity.

"Maybe you won't like the food, but you've got to admit there's a certain symbolism to this place."

"Spare me the philosophy."

"No philosophy. I've been doing some research into your particular circumstances, J.R., and this is all you're going to be able to afford if you don't stop Cliff Barnes. And do it soon."

"That's not funny."

"Wasn't meant to be."

The waitress returned with the food. They remained silent until she served them and left. Alan clucked admiringly at her swinging rear end.

"That is purely some of Texas' finest goods."

"Let's get to business. I hired you because I needed a sharp young lawyer. A man of ambition and drive . . ."

Alan preened and began spooning chili into his mouth. "From what I can find out about Cliff Barnes, and about you and your operations, J.R., what you really wanted was not a lawyer but a hatchet man. A hired gun."

J.R. tasted his steak and made a face. He pushed the plate away and swallowed half the tea. It was lukewarm and tasteless. Alan laughed at his discomfort.

"I admire your choice of words, Alan, if not your choice of eating places. Think you can handle the assignment."

"That depends."

"On what?"

"On what's in it for me."

"Nobody gets poor working for J.R. Ewing."

"Does that mean you want me to leave Smithfield and Bennett?"

"What put such an idea into your head? An established law firm makes for a good cover. It's just in certain matters you will report directly to me. You will reveal nothing of our activities on my behalf, nothing of what you learn or hear. Any questions?"

"I assume we are talking about Cliff Barnes?"

"You assume correctly. You go undercover on this job, a little discreet snooping and arranging."

"Cliff Barnes has been making noises like a redhot ecologist. Doesn't want the oil billionaires to continue defacing the landscape of our beloved Texas. It won't be hard for me to worm my way into that movement of his."

"That little sneak doesn't give a hoot and a holler about Texas or ecology. He's just got a bad hate on against us Ewings. That's his only motive."

"You don't believe that!"

"You work for me, Alan. Don't tell me what I believe."

"I wouldn't presume . . ."

J.R. shook him off like a minor annoyance. "Talk straight, boy. Don't put a show on for me. You're like a dog chasing his tail."

"If I talked straight," Alan said, meeting his gaze, "you wouldn't have any need for me. I'm a devious man, J.R. Just like you. I was born devious, shifty, always on the move. You had to fight for your place in your family, for your power. I had to fight my way out of the back of the yards in Chicago. And I don't intend to go back.

"You don't do all the fighting with your fists. Losers do that and I am not a loser. You fight with your head, your mouth, your cunning. If you can't beat up on the other guy, you verbally twist him like a pretzel and wash him down with a schooner of beer." He took a pull from the long neck.

J.R. measured him. "You figure you can wash Cliff Barnes down?"

"I reckon."

"What makes you so sure?"

"You think Barnes is driven by the desire for vengeance. Maybe he thinks so, too. I know better."

"Money?"

"Everybody wants money, but men who want only money get only money. Cliff Barnes craves power. Raw power that will turn him into a big man. And men who want power that badly are blind to everything else."

J.R. leaned back in his chair, thumbs hooked in his belt. "Just might be, Alan, that things will work out for you and me."

"It will be a privilege working with you."

"Not to mention the tax free cash bonuses coming your way." Alan offered his hand. J.R. took it briefly. "Then we got a deal."

"We're working together, from now on."

J.R.'s face hardened. "Get it straight from the start, boy. You work *for* me and always will, hear."

Alan felt as if the small cold finger of death had traced a path along his spine. "Whatever you say, J.R."

"And next time we meet, I'll choose the restaurant."

Pam was waiting in the chapel in Thanksgiving Square. In that quiet space, she was able to look inside herself with honesty and compassion for the first time in a long time. So many questions rose up; so few answers were presented. She wanted to weep but self-pity held no promise of better times. For her, now, it was vital to take hold of the reins of life and move with compassion toward a human solution to her difficulties. She became aware of someone taking the place beside her, and she reacted to the intrusion with resentment, as if this time and this place belonged to her alone. She looked up and saw Cliff, his face tense and disapproving.

"You didn't have to take the baby back to Southfork so quickly yesterday. I wanted to see him."

Her manner softened. "The way you sounded on the phone when I called ... frankly, Cliff, I didn't know what you might do."

"What makes you my guardian? Little John is my son."

"You're right, I'm not your guardian. But at the moment all you can think about is *your* pain. I can appreciate that, but it simply isn't primary just now."

"And what is, in your opinion?"

"Listen to me, Cliff. In the best of all possible worlds, your son would be with you. In this world, that's impossible. I'm concerned about Sue Ellen. . . ."

"You think I'm not?"

". . . *And* Jock *and* Miss Ellie. You know what this can do to them. They are not young any more."

He blew air out of his lungs and stood up. "Can we get out of here?"

He led the way into the daylight. The air was still and heavy, hotter than it should have been at this time of year. A weariness gripped Cliff and he wanted suddenly to give it all up, the worries, the problems, the endless struggle to attain his ends. What if he were wrong? What if revenge on the Ewings would bring him no satisfaction, would do

Digger no good? What if in the end he damaged all of them more than Jock Ewing had ever damaged his father?

"Tell me *exactly* what the doctor in Fort Worth had to say."

"Dr. Grovner," Pam said in recollection. "She was very nice. Dr. Grovner said Little John is fine, at the moment."

"At the moment."

"She did a thorough series of neurologic tests. She found no tumors, and there are none of those tell-tale café au lait spots on his body."

"Then he doesn't have neurofibromatosis. That's fantastic!"

"No, Cliff. He has it. Remember, Cliff, it's a genetic disease passed on from parent to child. If Daddy has it, you and I have it. If you have it, Little John has it."

"But if there are no symptoms—he's going to be all right." Cliff stopped walking and faced Pam, his features gathered tightly together, his voice penetrating and insistent. "Isn't he?"

"We don't know. The doctor said that in an adult the chances of fatality are rare. In an infant—well, apparently the tumors can show up at any time. Sometimes, frequently, Dr. Grovner said, they turn into neuroblastomas."

"What's that?"

"A malignancy. Cancer. The survival rate for babies is not very good, Cliff."

A moan dribbled across Cliff's lips and he swung away as if in pain. She caught up with him.

"Frequent checkups," she said. "That's the best we can do for him. . . ."

They went on for a while before Cliff spoke. "Have you told Bobby?"

"Not yet."

"How long do you think you can keep this a secret?"

"As long as I have to."

"You told me Bobby wants to have children."

"Very much."

"Then you have to tell him."

"That I can't give him what he wants most in the world—a family of his own. How do I tell my husband that I can't have a baby . . . ?"

That afternoon, in his office, Cliff met with Alan Beam. He'd been impressed with the young lawyer ever since first meeting him at the Save the Landscape rally. Alan was bright, ambitious, and a hard worker. And most of all, he seemed sincerely to want to do something to prevent the continued rape of the land by uncaring industry in Texas, mainly the oil business. He was exactly the sort of person Cliff wanted on his team.

"Alan," he began, "I want to tell you how pleased I am to have you aboard. There's no shortage of people who agree with our goals, but there are very few who can get things done."

Alan laughed. "You know what they say about Dallas— it's the 'can-do' city. Well, I'm the can-do boy."

"Good enough. There'll be plenty you can do. What I'm aiming at is a state wide crusade to oppose indiscriminate drilling by the oil companies. The stench of oil and oil money has got to be countered. We've got to clear the landscape, clean the air, purge Texas politics of oil influence."

"Anything you want me to do, Cliff, I will. It's why I am here."

"Give me a couple of days to ponder on it and we'll really put you to work."

"As a matter of fact, Cliff, I've been giving all this a great deal of thought. I've grown to appreciate what you've accomplished, virtually on your own. As head of the O.L.M. and as an individual. But it's time to move to another plane."

"Meaning what, Alan?"

"The state, the nation, need decent, intelligent fighting men to see that the right laws are passed, that government does in fact serve the people's interests, the big business doesn't kill the goose that lays the golden egg. Government needs men like Cliff Barnes."

Cliff made a steeple with his fingers, peered across the apex at the other man. He considered his answer carefully. "I'd be a liar if I claimed not to have considered elective office for myself."

"Then you know I'm right," Alan enthused.

"I'm not sure running for public office is the right thing to do."

"It is precisely the right thing. How else can you exercise all your talents, all your strengths in behalf of the people? Not only do I believe you should run, I believe you are obliged to run."

"I'm still young, with comparatively little experience. . . ."

"The House of Representatives is where you belong. For now. You'd stand out up in D.C., a jewel among rough stones. Cliff, the good you can do at O.L.M. is sharply limited. In Washington—well, that would be just a start, a launching pad to bigger and better things. Remember, LBJ was just a country schoolteacher when he got himself elected to Congress. He ended up in the White House."

Cliff didn't want to consider such dreams of ultimate glory. And yet. And yet. "Running for office, the Congress, it requires an organization . . ."

"The ecology group can be the core of that. Just turn me loose and I'll round up some of the best young minds in Dallas, the hardest workers, the most dedicated followers any candidate could have. . . ."

"Maybe you're right, Alan."

"I'm sure I am."

"There's one thing bothering me. The money. An effective campaign costs a fortune these days. I don't have the money myself and I lack the sources of supply."

"Leave that to me. I know how to raise funds. I know where to reach out for the big contributors."

"You really believe people will back me?"

"Believe it! I'm convinced of it. Cliff, you'd make a terribly attractive candidate. Qualified, committed, charismatic. You've got everything it takes and the voters will have to respond to you. Just give me the word, Cliff, and I'll start the ball rolling. . . ."

One word, Cliff thought. One word and he would be on his way, straight to the top. Everything he ever wanted; fame, wealth, power. He opened his mouth to speak and the word came out loud and clear.

"Go," he said. "Do it, Alan. Do it for me and you'll never be sorry."

Smiling widely, Alan offered his hand. Cliff sounded exactly right—a man who had thoroughly convinced himself, a man open to manipulation, a man doomed to defeat.

A few nights later, the Ewing family attended a play at the Dallas Theater Center. It was a pleasant evening—

dinner first beneath a six-ton metal sculpture in the Fairmont Hotel's Pyramid Room. Beluga caviar, Maine lobster, beef Wellington, two excellent French wines, desert and coffee.

Only Sue Ellen didn't seem to be having a good time. Picking without appetite at her food, she responded only to direct questions with monosyllabic answers. And during the first act of the play she sat with her hands clenched in her lap, her knees pressed together. At intermission, Miss Ellie took her aside.

"Are you all right, Sue Ellen?"

"I'm having another one of my dizzy spells, Miss Ellie."

"You poor thing. Let me get you some water."

"I think I'd better go home."

"Of course. J.R. will drive you."

And he did. Swiftly and competently out over the flat miles to Southfork. Kristin insisted on coming along, attending her sister in the back seat. None of them talked all the way back to the ranch.

Sue Ellen led them out of the car. Her strength seemed to have returned and her color was good. She smiled too sweetly at her sister.

"Kristin, there was no reason you couldn't stay on through the play and come home with the others."

"I thought I could help. Are you still dizzy?"

"I'm much better, thank you. It was so warm and airless in the theater."

"I thought the air conditioning was exactly right," J.R. said tightly.

"I'll be going to bed now," Sue Ellen said. "J.R., why don't you and Kristin drive on back into town. There's still time to see the last act."

"I'll come up and help you," Kristin said.

"You needn't do that."

"That's right, Kristin," J.R. said. "I'll take care of Sue Ellen."

"How kind you all are to me. It's just a bit overwhelming, you know."

J.R. trailed her up the stairs and into their bedroom. She began taking off her clothes at once. He watched narrowly, again stimulated by the piece-by-piece display of fine womanly flesh.

"What do you think you're doing?" he said finally, remembering his annoyance with her performance all during the evening, remembering how much difficulty she was giving him, how angry he was.

"Getting ready for bed, husband dear, can't you tell?"

"I've had about enough of your complaining ways, Sue Ellen. Your disruptive habits. What is it you are after? Can you tell me that?"

She put her back to him and took off her bra, stepped out of her panties. Watching her, J.R.'s breath caught in his throat. Each time he saw her like this it sent his memory reeling back to when they were lovers, to how it had been in the beginning. That warm, lush body, the silent demands she made, the pleasure she gave. Yet somehow it had never been sufficient for him and his interest had waned, his passion paling, going limp eventually. He'd seen the rage begin to build in her, the confusion and the fear. And if, for the shortest of intervals, he had cared, he soon put such indications of weakness behind him. She donned a nightgown and he was startled at the sudden disappearance of the naked woman he had so enjoyed looking at. The change brought him rudely back to the present.

"Answer me, dammit! What is it you want?"

She came around gracefully to face him. "To go to bed, of course. By myself."

"You are a bitch. You're after something and I want to know what it is."

Her laughter was brittle, mirthless, directed at him like a serrated blade. He shuddered, unable to let go of what he had begun, unable to change his ways, not wishing to change. "J.R., the first thing that would enter that nasty little mind of yours is that I am after something. But I am after nothing."

He knew she was telling the truth. He couldn't tolerate it; everybody, *everybody* had to be after something. "Oh, don't hand me that, Sue Ellen. The time you spend up here in your bed playing at being sick. Those sad wife's eyes you turn on the family. The way you play on Momma and Daddy's sympathies. I read you like a book. That little scene in the theater tonight—'I'm having another of my dizzy spells, Miss Ellie,' You are not sick, sugar. There is nothing at all wrong with you except that you're feeling sorry for yourself. Except that you are a goddamn useless-as-tits-on-a-boar drunk."

"Why thank you, J.R. How good you are to me."

"This whole thing is an act," he roared at the top of his voice. "*You are not sick!*"

"Now you practice medicine, J.R. How cunning of you. Another one of your secrets? So many secrets, so many crimes . . ."

"Don't talk to me about crimes, lady. That meeting of yours with Cliff Barnes . . ."

"Meeting with Cliff Barnes . . . ?" Time stood still while she struggled to recollect.

"That's right, at the Gardens Restaurant."

"I'd forgotten all about it."

"Sure you did. Don't tell me that was an accident."

"It certainly was, at least on my part. I was with my mother and sister. Do you think I'd arrange an assignation under those conditions? Anyway, I despise Cliff Barnes only slightly less than I despise you, J.R. There. Does that make you feel better?"

"Why should I believe anything you say about Barnes? Your mutual history doesn't create any confidence in your word."

"Now it's my turn. What is it you want, J.R.? Are you jealous because you think Cliff and I are seeing each other again? Why should that bother you? After all, it will relieve you of all those odious husbandly duties you find so difficult to fulfill."

"I am not jealous."

"Or are you interested in me simply because you think another man wants me? It's the chase that always mattered to you, always has been. Anything or anyone you possess you quickly lose interest in."

"You're still carrying the torch for that misbegotten opportunist like a lovesick schoolgirl."

She got into bed, pulling the sheet up to her waist. "As long as my actions and my emotions are under discussion, J.R., let's give equal time to yours. You can stop putting on your Mr. Nice Guy act whenever your father and mother are around. Because, J.R., I no longer give a damn about you. What you want or think doesn't matter. What you do doesn't matter. Now get out of my bedroom and let me alone."

For an extended apprehensive interlude he stood poised as if about to launch himself in violent attack. Until the tension left his body with a spasmodic twist and he strode away, slamming the door behind him.

She slumped back on her pillow, eyes closed, the tears beginning to flow.

J.R. came storming out of the house, heading for his car. The cool night air did nothing to diminish his anger. The high sky dotted with chips of brilliance was lost on him as he bulled along, neck bowed, fists clenched. He swore revenge against Sue Ellen, against every one of his enemies, against every one who opposed him. He swore . . .

"J.R. . . ."

A soft feminine voice brought him up short. Kristin, behind him in the darkness.

"Yes," he said without turning. "What is it?"

"Is Sue Ellen all right?"

"Yes," he said curtly. "She's fine."

"I was worried."

He came around slowly, chin down almost to his chest, assessing Kristin. Gliding through the darkness in a short black gown cut low and bloused at the waist, she resembled a startling night creature, pale, lovely and immensely desirable.

"You're a good sister to Sue Ellen."

"I care about people."

"All people?"

She threw back her head and laughed softly. "Those I know and like. Those I'm close to."

"Does that include me?"

She swayed forward, in no hurry to get where she was going. "I have a deep and abiding appreciation for you, J.R. Sue Ellen doesn't fully comprehend what a fine and unique man you are."

"But you do?"

"I believe so."

She was little more than an arm's length away and the heady scent of her unloosed waves of undisguised passion flooding his middle. He wanted to reach for her, crush her under his mouth, touch every part of her, perform unspeakable acts on her flesh. He smiled.

"I was just going for a drive."

"What a nice idea."

"Care to come along?"

"I wouldn't want to intrude."

"Be my pleasure, Kristin, darlin'."

"In that case, I'd love to come along."

"Sure you wouldn't rather go off to bed?"

"Oh, no, it's much too early for sleep."

They drove straight out for nearly ten minutes, neither speaking. With an abrupt wrench of the wheel, J.R. put the Mercedes onto a dirt road that took them past scrub pine up into the low hills.

"Is all this part of Southfork?" she asked.

"All this and more." He switched on the car radio and a whisky voice came on singing "Sweet Memories."

> My world is like a river,
> as dark as it is deep . . .

"Willie Nelson," J.R. said.

"You really love this ranch, don't you, J.R.?"

"All us Ewings love the place, Kristin. Fall's the best time—roundup. All the stock is driven in from the far pastures to the holding pens."

"Do you actually do some of the cowboying, J.R.?"

Her naïveté made him laugh. "It's the land I love, Kristin." He patted her thigh and squeezed gently, unhurriedly, then directed his attention back to his driving. "I'm no cowboy, never have been. Sun and dust, hawks planing in the sky, twisting canyons, the smell of the herds. No, Kristin, honey, that's not my style. I like shiny new things. Clean offices and air conditioning. Big deals, big victories, big money."

"You know, J.R., I have always had a secret admiration for the movers and doers of this world, the men who make things happen. And you are surely one of those."

He pulled the Mercedes into a stand of tall pines and parked, then shifted around, one arm on the back of her seat. "You're a very pretty girl, Kristin."

"In case you haven't noticed, I'm a woman."

"I'm beginning to notice." He stroked her hair and she pressed her head back against his hand.

"Hmmm, that's good." His fingers went down to her neck, working the muscles under the soft skin. "Ah, that is so nice, makes me want to go all loosey-goosey."

"I suppose you heard it all, Kristin. What went on between Sue Ellen and me."

"All lovers have quarrels."

"Your sister and I have not been lovers for a very long time."

"Poor J.R."

"I wouldn't want you to think I am some kind of angel—I'm not."

"I have never believed that, J.R., not for a minute. But I surely do admire the way you handle youself."

His hand was on her bare back holding firm, easing her closer. She offered no resistance. He guided his other hand onto the gentle roundness of her belly.

"I surely do admire the way you look. . . ." he said.

"And feel?"

His answer was to slide his hand onto one breast, full and sensually heavy under black crepe. She moaned and her head arched back. He bent over her, mouth tasting the delicate skin under her ear, his hand going beneath the dress.

"You are just about the sweetest little piece J.R.'s laid eyes on in a mighty long time."

"I'm glad I please you, sir."

"You sure you know what you're up to, Kristin?"

"Has something happened to make you change your mind?"

In answer, he worked the narrow shoulder straps loose, tugging at the dress.

"Gently," she cautioned. "Wouldn't want you to tear my nice new dress."

"I'll buy you a dozen more." He undid his belt. "And lots of other pretty things."

"You don't have to promise me anything, J.R." Somehow, with swift sure movements, she got the dress off. She was wearing nothing else.

He gasped and struggled with his pants.

"Here," she murmured. "Let me do that." She leaned down and kissed him gently as he came into view. "Ah, J.R., what a real man you are!"

"I want you to know," he husked out, "that I am not going to let you get away from Dallas. I'll put you on an allowance . . ."

Her lips were everywhere, warm, wet, insistent. "Whatever you say, sweetheart."

". . . An apartment."

"If you want it that way . . ."

"I want . . . I want you where I can get my hands on you."

"Whenever you say the word, lover." She maneuvered around to accommodate him and he entered her from behind. She sucked air and gasped and told him she wasn't sure she could deal with a man so big and powerful. He thrust mightily in answer and she cried out in pleasure and pain as he pulled her closer, fingers digging into her soft breasts. "I will be an absolute beast for you, J.R."

"Anything I want . . . ?"

"Anything . . ."

"Tell me what you want."

She twisted and writhed and rode him with youthful vigor. "You, lover. And one more thing." She held still.

"What . . . is . . . that?"

"A job with Ewing Oil."

"Well, I don't know."

"So I can be with you always, darlin'."

It seemed like one very fine idea. He envisioned afternoons with Kristin in her apartment, evenings in his office. When he traveled, he might take her along. Hell's bells, if a man couldn't get what he wanted at home why not keep it all in the family?

"Whatever you want," he muttered and drove up against her. "Now give me what I want . . ."

And she did with a skill and passion that he feared might do him in before his time.

Southfork was at peace. The other members of the family had gone to bed. The barns were quiet, the corrals empty. Crickets chirped and somewhere off on the prairie a cow bawled. Everything was as it should be.

On the patio, Bobby and Pam, enjoying the clear night air before retiring. He glanced over at his wife. All evening he had experienced a distressing uneasiness in Pam, some subtle change in style and attitude that troubled him. He could restrain himself no longer.

"Are you sure you told me the whole story about Digger?"

She answered without looking at him. "Yes, why?"

"That play tonight, that was a comedy we sat through.

And a pretty good one, in my opinion. You didn't crack a smile once."

"I guess my mind was elsewhere."

He hesitated. "Want to tell me about it?"

A chill made her shudder. "Bobby, please hold me."

"Nothing finer I can think of doing, ma'am."

She rested her cheek on his chest. He was so solid, strong, dependable. His love was a tangible support, the one certain thing she'd found in her life, the one thing she needed more than any other. To lose Bobby would be to lose the meaning of life.

"You're trembling," he said.

"There's something I want to say."

"About Digger?"

"About us."

She felt him stiffen, make a conscious effort to relax. "What about us?"

"Bobby, I've made up my mind. I can't go through with having a baby."

He dropped his arms as if they had been yanked away. He stepped back, an expression of dismay and anguish on his handsome face. Anger rose in crimson cloud around him.

"I don't understand . . ."

"Please don't ask me to explain."

"Yesterday you were happy about the idea. What happened after you went back to the Store? What made you change your mind?"

"Bobby, I can't stand it when you're angry with me. I love you so very much."

"I think I have a right to be angry. Are you going to get off on that identity trip of yours again? Is that it? Good Lord, Pam. Having a baby doesn't make you any less of a person. Certainly no less than hanging markdown tags on dresses at The Store does. What are you thinking about? You know how much I want us to be a family, to have children, to live normal, healthy lives."

"I see. It's what you want that counts. Your needs only. What about me and my needs?"

"You want children too. I know you do."

"You seem to have settled the whole matter. You are speaking for me now."

"Am I wrong?"

"Forget it, Bobby!" she cried in a low breaking voice. "Just forget it!"

He watched her run off into the darkness knowing that he would never forget it. Neither of them would. Neither of them could.

PART III

The Ewings

TODAY

7

$\mathcal{B}$obby heard the news of the nationalization while shaving that morning. Ewing Oil, the network announcer said, sole owner of record of the Asian oilfields. Losses up in the hundreds of millions, maybe billions. No chance of salvaging anything.

"It means," the announcer went on, "the dramatic end of one of the largest most active independent oil companies in the United States. Jock Ewing, a legend in the fields of Texas and Louisiana, started over forty years ago as a wildcatter and—"

Bobby switched off the radio, mind careening wildly from fact to conclusion to possibility. The report was devastating and if accurate would create havoc in the oil business. Interlocking financial interests would bring down the entire Ewing structure, every business, every holding, the varied investments. And Southfork! The ranch was the centerpiece of it all, the pride and the joy of all the Ewings, the solid base which made everything they did possible. He pulled on a pair of faded jeans over worn ranch boots, threw on an old shirt, and hurried downstairs.

The dining room was empty but he found Miss Ellie having coffee alone on the patio. He kissed his mother and filled a cup.

"Where is everybody?"

"Sit down, Bobby, have some breakfast."

"I think I'd better get on downtown, Momma."

She raised her eyes to him. "I heard the report, Bobby. I know what happened. What will it mean to us Ewings, son?"

He shook his head in wonderment. All his life, no matter the problem no matter how large and painful the difficulties, Miss Ellie remained strong, solid, supportive of the others. Jock was the tough one, the hunter stalking his prey, bringing home the meat. But when true strength was required, Miss Ellie was always on hand; unruffled, clear in her mind, cutting through to the heart of the matter with only a few words. His mother, he acknowledged, was a remarkable woman.

"If the radio report is true," he said, honoring her too much to dissemble, "we'll end up losing everything. . . ."

"Southfork—?"

"I'm afraid so, Momma."

She raised her cup but did not drink. Her hand, he noted, was shaking.

"The Asian deal, it wasn't supposed to be ours. He kept it to himself."

"That sounds like J.R. Always after the big score. Your daddy was a lot like that when he was a young man. . . ."

"But Daddy was a free-lancer. He could afford to take chances. Now Ewing Oil is a family affair. Certain risks are unacceptable." He looked around. "Where is J.R.? Where's Daddy?"

"Down at the office, they left without stopping for breakfast."

"Which is what I should be doing, Momma."

"Keep your temper, son, It's no time for losing control."

"I'd like to tell J.R. exactly . . ."

"Bobby!" The hard edge in her voice brought him up short. "J.R.'s your brother and this is a family matter. Work it out. Do what needs doing, hear. Keep the recriminations at a minimum."

"I'll do my best, Momma." He kissed her on the top of the head. "Don't you worry about a thing."

She smiled at his retreating back. "What else do I have to do?"

A crowd of reporters were jammed into the reception area of Ewing Oil when Bobby arrived. He forced his way inside, located one of the secretaries.

"Where'd all these people come from?"

She made a face. "They were waiting when I opened up. Thank goodness your Daddy and J.R. got here early. I could never deal with this pack of wolves."

"Where are they?"

"In J.R.'s office, popping questions and hardly waiting for good answers."

Bobby worked his way to a place just inside the entrance to J.R.'s office. His father and brother stood behind the desk, braced against the onslaught of the press. Flashbulbs kept going off and a dozen television cameras were rolling, their bright lights washing all color out of the room.

"Now, boys," Jock was saying, "seems to me you got what you came for. Why'n't you just ride on out of here and let us get some work done?"

"One more question, sir," a reporter said. "What isn't clear to me is whether or not Ewing Oil invested all of its capital in those oil leases and does this nationalization mean the end of the Ewing empire as reported elsewhere? Further . . ."

J.R. raised one hand and turned on that wheeler-dealer's grin of his. "That's two questions, Mr. Carleton, but we'll let that pass. I will say this—Ewing investments are diversified in order to protect our interests against just such a dramatic turnaround as we see happening in Asia today. . . ."

"What about the claims that Ewing's losses were total, adding up to billions?"

"Highly exaggerated. There are some losses, naturally. In this business . . ."

"Can you tell us what other investments you're into at this time?"

"No. I can't tell you that. Nor should I."

"Isn't it true that despite your disclaimer of total investment in the Asian fields, Ewing was in fact completely and solely involved? Isn't it true . . ."

J.R.'s annoyance showed on his face. "Same answer as before. This is a business and we seek to make prudent investments based on sufficient knowledge. Our situation is always fluid and flexible. We make our moves according to various market factors and nothing, as in all areas of life, gentlemen and ladies, is forever. Next question."

"Can you tell us this—did you suffer *any* losses?"

J.R.'s manner was casual. "Well, certainly. We took a beating, no different than anybody else in that situation. But we're still in business. Ewing Oil has survived, will continue to survive . . ."

"Mr. Ewing . . . ?"

"I think that does it for now," J.R. said. "My father and I have answered all your questions to the best of our ability. There's nothing else I can add now. If anything comes up in the future, we'll let you know. Thanks for coming, everybody."

Bobby stood to one side and watched the members of the press file out. When the last one was going, he closed the door to the office and put his back against the portal as if to close out the rest of the world.

"How bad is it?" he said.

Jock put his arm around J.R.'s shoulders. "Ewing Oil is alive and well, thanks to J.R. here."

"I don't undertand—"

"Tell him," Jock said.

"We're in good shape, little brother."

"Those leases . . . ?"

J.R.'s grin widened and his eyes glittered. This was what he lived for, the moments of sweet triumph before his daddy that were his alone. No credit to share with Bobby, or anyone else. Standing alongside Jock he felt himself swelling with pride and delight at the uncertain look on his brother's face.

"I sold those leases a couple of days ago, little brother. Seventy-five percent of our Asian holdings."

"Sold them . . . ?"

"At ten million a point!" J.R. was literally beaming.

"Somebody's looking out for us," Jock said, clapping his oldest son on the back. "That's for sure."

"For damned sure," J.R. added.

Bobby was having difficulty assimilating what he'd just heard. "Are you telling me Ewing Oil got lucky . . . ?"

"You could say that. I'd say I made some very good moves. I had a chance to buy into those gas fields off the East Coast. Daddy and I talked it over more'n a year ago. But I needed a lot of cash before those folks'd even talk to me."

"Who bought the leases?"

"Would you believe—Vaughn Leland bought some of them, for one. That old barracuda's finally going to get what's coming to him."

Jock rocked back and forth, that weathered face furrowed. "J.R., when you going to learn, a man's misery is nothing to make fun of."

"Sorry, Daddy."

"Who else is involved?" Bobby wanted to know.

"Some of the boys have been pestering me to get in on the deal from the beginning, you know."

"The boys? Does that mean the cartel?"

"Andy Bradley, Jordan Lee, Seth Stone . . ."

Bobby shook his head in disbelief. "Our friends—wiped out."

Jock, who had turned away, came around. "Business is a gamble, Bobby. They know that."

"You knew about this deal, Daddy?"

"Can't say as I did." Jock returned to his desk.

Bobby jerked around to J.R. "Why weren't we told about it? You are supposed to clear it with us before you do anything."

"No time." J.R.'s annoyance was evident. He hated explaining to his brother, hated having his judgment questioned. "You and Daddy were off somewhere. Colorado, maybe . . ."

"There are telephones. Or you could have waited."

"I had to move fast and, as things turned out, it's a good thing I did."

Bobby couldn't believe any of it. Despite J.R.'s attempt to appear sincere and conciliatory, there was a note of duplicity in his voice. But then, Bobby remarked to himself bitterly, duplicity was mother's milk to J.R. "You accept that version, Daddy?"

A crimson flush suffused J.R.'s face. "You calling me a liar, little brother?"

A stuttering memory flashed across Bobby's brain, a picture brought up vivid out of the buried past. Elusive. Charged with animosity and bad feelings. And from the expression in J.R.'s cold eyes he knew his brother was recalling the same moment in their lives. The same incident, the same deadly emotions. Then it was gone. Bobby opened his mouth to speak but before he could the door to the office burst open and Jordan Lee charged toward J.R.

His face was livid, his eyes bulging, spittle running at the corner of his mouth.

"J.R. you rotten motherfucker . . ."

"Hold it right there, Jordan," Jock said.

Jordan kept coming, fists clenched, the angle of his body suggesting swift and immediate trouble. Jock, all his old instincts alert, started around the desk toward the intruder. J.R. pulled back in clear retreat. But it was Bobby who stepped into Jordan's path, bringing the other man up short.

"Stay cool, Jordan," he said gently, holding his open hands at shoulder level as a peace offering.

"Cool! You must be mighty proud of yourself, J.R. You must be on top of the world."

"We all got to take the good with the bad, old buddy," J.R. said.

"You bastard," Jordan said, making another forward move. Bobby, positioned solidly between him and J.R., moved with him.

Jock said, "Now hold on, Jordan. J.R. didn't know what was going to happen when he sold you boys those leases. He couldn't know about the nationalization. Just dumb good luck on our part, bad on yours . . ."

"The hell you say." Jordan's breathing was harsh and uneven. "Months ago we begged him to let us in on the deal, this was no new thing, Jock. He wouldn't dicsuss it, wouldn't return calls. All of a sudden he wants to sell. But quick. Too damned quick, Jock. Immediately . . ."

"I told you, Jordan, I needed the cash for other deals."

Jordan fixed him with a baleful glance. "You knew those wells were going to be worthless. You knew about the revolt, the nationalization. It's all too easy, J.R. You suckered your friends into buying the leases."

J.R. talked fast, more for his father's ear than Jordan's. "We still own twenty-five percent of those leases. That means we took a bath for two hundred and fifty million dollars, plus all the royalties on your share. Hell, man, would I do that if I knew what was coming?"

"The way you work—yes."

"Why?" Jock said.

"To make himself look good. Most of that loss can be absorbed in tax write-offs against profits, which means you will end up with a very tidy profit. You really pulled a raw deal this time, J.R."

"Come on," Jock said. "This business, it's a crapshoot. Always has been. You pick up the dice you can win or lose."

"Sure, and that's okay. Only J.R. plays with loaded dice."

The words rumbled angrily out of Jock. "You gambled, you lost. That's business. Take it like a man. You made plenty of money with us before, you will again. We take care of our friends, always have."

Jordan backed off, suddenly subdued. He seemed much older than when he'd first appeared. Pale and drawn, his lower jaw was quavering as if unhinged. "I am very happy to hear that, Jock. Real happy. And I'll pass that good information on to Marilee Stone. I'm sure she'll appreciate your good wishes."

"What the hell is that supposed to mean?" Jock shot back.

"It means," Jordan said before he left, "that Seth Stone killed himself about an hour ago."

Jordan Lee. That man... another ... buttoned to in ... angry. He never was one to hide ... with a ... keep ...

8

J ock, Bobby and J.R. were seated in J.R.'s office, drinking coffee, speaking only occasionally. More than the others, Bobby was withdrawn, functioning ponderously and with concern within himself. J.R. was his brother, and the family ties were strong, but Bobby understood him in ways his father did not. The dark impulses that drove J.R. had been passed down from father to son, but the son lacked the judgment, the ethical core to soften and control his obsessive need to win. Bobby also enjoyed winning, but he did not *have* to win. It was a distinction lost on the older sibling.

"We've got to do something to help them," he said.

"What!" J.R.'s alarm was clear for both of them to see. "What are you suggesting? Business is business. Nothing wrong with swinging a good deal, with making a profit. That's the American way."

"There's a difference between free enterprise and the freedom to steal."

J.R. was on his feet. "Are you saying I robbed those boys?"

"I'm saying I don't like any of this. Seth Stone killing himself, that ain't good business practice."

"He was always a weak man," J.R. said.

"Speak no evil of the dead," Jock intoned, as if coming from some buried past.

"Well, I am not about to stand for . . ."

Bobby cut him off. "I was you, brother, I'd worry about

Jordan Lee. That man is carrying a deep hurt and he is angry. He never was one to take things lying down. Keep your eyes open."

"I don't need you to protect me, Bobby."

Again ancient images flashed onto the screen of Bobby's mind, white hot, searing, uncomfortable to look at. He forced them aside.

The intercom buzzed, a welcome interruption. "J.R.," came Louella's voice. "Marilee Stone's on the wire, would like to talk to you."

All color drained out of J.R.'s face. "What am I supposed to do, Daddy? I can't talk to that woman, not now."

Bobby heaved himself erect, started out. "Relax, J.R. I'll take care of it for you."

J.R.'s eyes skittered over to one side, seeking Jock's reaction. "I don't need you to—"

Just then the door opened and Vaughn Leland stormed in. He put one hand against Bobby's chest, shoved him out of the way, crossed the office to J.R.'s desk.

He jabbed one straight, strong finger in J.R.'s direction. "Better talk fast—"

"What's there to say? You want me to say I'm sorry? Well, I am. That satisfy you?"

"Sorry doesn't cut it, J.R. I want an explanation, and an apology, and restitution . . ."

"Restitution! Forget it."

Jock shuffled his feet and rubbed his chin. "Not one penny, Leland. That was a fair deal, fairly made. You gambled, you lost. That's all there is to it."

"The hell it was! J.R. knew nationalization was coming."

"You can't prove that."

"I don't have to prove it. I believe it and that's enough for me, Jock. Your son lied to us, he cheated us . . ."

Jock's voice came out of his chest! "I'd be careful, if I was you, about tossing words like cheat and liar around. That don't sit well here, Leland."

Leland spoke to Bobby. "How do you stand on this?"

Bobby's gaze was level, giving nothing. "You know better'n to ask. I'm a member of this family. I'm a Ewing."

"I see." He looked back at Jock. "I want that money

back. I borrowed twenty million dollars to pay for those leases and as a result I'm wiped out. Everything is gone, everything. No way I can repay that loan."

J.R. shrugged.

"Jock," Leland said, "we've known each other a long time, go back down the long hard road together. Twenty million dollars. You have got to help me."

Jock faced him down. "Appears I came to you not so long ago when I was about to lose Southfork, maybe you recollect, Leland. I asked for an extension on the loan. A deal's a deal you said. I believed it then, I believe it now."

Leland went from face to face as if in search of succor. He lighted on Bobby. "It was crooked, you know it was. J.R., you will regret this, I promise you."

J.R. blustered. "Are you threatening me?"

"Threat! No, this is a promise. One way or another, I'm going to get you for this, take it out of your scummy hide." He jerked around to Jock, his face flushed and distorted, his fingers flexing. "He's your boy, a chip off the old block. There are ways to handle your kind and nobody knows that better'n you, Jock. Chickens always come home to roost."

Jock forced the words out, one by one. "Better be on your way, before I do something we'll all be sorry for."

Without another word, Leland slammed out of there. His enraged presence lingered behind. It was Bobby who ended the ominous silence. "J.R., did you know Leland had to borrow all that money?"

"How would I know that? This deal went fast. I gave them twenty-four hours to come up with the money."

"Why the rush?"

"I told you. I—"

"I don't like it. Deals this size—they usually take time."

"I can't make you believe the truth."

"The truth! J.R. you don't know the meaning of the word."

"Look here, I don't have to take that from you. You been sniping at me for too long now. Just back off, little brother, or—"

Bobby came around the desk fast. "Or what?"

"Cut it out!" Jock roared. "Dammit, this is family business. Y'all remember that."

"Daddy," Bobby said, "I think Leland is right. J.R. knew about the nationalization and dumped the leases on our friends. All that speed to do business, no time for questions, no time for research. Take it or leave it. Just your conniving style, J.R."

"That's your rich imagination at work, Bobby."

Bobby took an aggressive step forward.

Jock stepped in. "I'm gonna ask you something, J.R. I'm gonna ask it one time and you are gonna answer—and we're never gonna mention it again."

"Yes, Daddy?"

"Did you know up front the wells were going to be nationalized?"

"Daddy, I swear it. I had no advance information. You know I would never do anything deliberate to hurt my friends. Never."

Walking was not Jock Ewing's style. He was a man at home behind the wheel of a powerful car, eating up the endless Texas miles. Or in the saddle on a strong horse. He went almost nowhere on foot. And wandering the streets of Dallas in boots suited more to stirrups than concrete sidewalks made little sense to his orderly mind. Yet wander is what he did. Alone, without urgency, relatively oblivious to his surroundings. Trying to create future order out of current chaos, to gain a perspective on what he had heard, what he knew, and mostly what he felt.

He'd lived a rough life, doing rough work among rough men. Fighting with fist and boot had been a daily occurrence back in his young days. Killing, by knife and by gun, was not unknown. And though the years had gentled Texas and Texans down, the strain of violence ran deep and true. Hardly a man he knew didn't own three or four guns: handguns, rifles, a good shotgun for hunting. Hardly a man he knew wouldn't use his weapons if circumstance dictated. Only the right motive was necessary.

The loss of two-hundred fifty million dollars was one by goddamn hell of a good motive.

A friend's suicide was another.

The dissipation of a lifetime's work was a third.

Anger. Insult. Revenge.

Jock had seen men killed for lesser reasons. And greater ones. He'd been in the crowd in Elm Street on the day the President of the United States had come riding through with his young wife and Governor Connally. He'd heard the gunshots from the Texas School Book Depository, seen the young President's head lurch forward, already a dead man.

And now tacky souvenirs were sold on the site. Postcard maps marked the spot of the murder. Nickel and dime memories of that awful event washed thin in Dallas.

Jock had taken human life himself, but never lightly and never without regret. Dallas would always be remembered as the place where John F. Kennedy was assassinated, yet Dallas hadn't killed him. Not Dallas anymore than Los Angeles or Detroit or Boston. But the stigma always remained. . . .

A man had to be careful about the enemies he made. J.R. was building an unmanageable roster of them, men who he'd done wrong in one way or another, men who felt cheated, deprived, deceived. Men who ached to strike back, to hurt him in any way possible. J.R. was in need of protection, someone or something to shield him from danger. What was it he had said to Bobby back in the office? The words came leaping back, a crackle of memory.

"I don't need you to protect me, Bobby."

A reminiscent lens opened up in Jock's mind and he squinted down the long tunnel of memory to when J.R. was still a boy, big for his age but pudgy and already antagonizing people for no good reason. Trying to stake a claim on space that wasn't always his.

"I don't need you to protect me, Bobby."

They had attended a Friday night game of Bobby's high school football team. J.R., bigger and older, had been unable to make the team. But Bobby, in his sophomore year of high school, was a valued member of the squad. Hard-hitting, quick on his feet, in on every play. The game was over and the crowd milling around the field when the trouble started.

Too much beer drunk, too many disappointments; for every winner there was a loser. Some remarks were made, an insult or two, a threat, a shove, a sudden movement that sent someone reeling, blood running.

Jock tried to lead J.R. out of the melee. It was not his fight, not their trouble. Without warning, two rawhide hard boys, all bone and muscle, confronted them, mocking

J.R., telling him what they thought of his school's victory. J.R. couldn't keep from replying.

Words were exchanged and before Jock could react punches were thrown. J.R. went down, both boys pounding at him. Jock tried to separate them, took a powerful shot in the jaw that sent him onto his back, stunned and unable to move.

From out of nowhere Bobby, still in uniform, exploded on the scene. His punches were short, swift, and on target. In seconds both boys went fleeing into the crowd. Bobby helped Jock to his feet and made sure he was all right before turning to J.R.

"Let me help you," he said.

J.R. knocked his hand aside. "Get away," he had snarled. "I don't need you to protect me, Bobby."

It occurred to Jock that his oldest boy was meaner than he was strong, tougher than he was brave. Always trying to prove something. For J.R., winning wasn't ever enough; his friends had to fail. Jock wondered how he had failed his son, what he could do to help. One thing was very clear: J.R. needed someone to protect him.

9

$\mathcal{B}$obby spent the remainder of the day privately debating his next move. Torn between loyalty to his family and his need to act in a correct ethical manner, he finally left the office without telling anyone his destination. He rode around for an hour before heading back to Southfork, anxious to tell Pam of his dilemma, listen to her reaction. Like himself, Pam was also subjected daily to parallel obligations and loyalties. Married to a Ewing, she could never forget she'd been born a Barnes and that her father and Jock had become enemies.

He drove up to the big house and went inside. He found his mother reading in the den, kissed her on the cheek.

"You're home early, son."

"I want to discuss something with Pam."

"Oh, dear. She isn't here. Pam tried to phone you but you'd left the office. You must have been on your way back here."

"Is she okay!"

"Fine. She decided to fly over to Corpus after all."

"I was afraid of that."

"Don't you fret, she'll be all right. Pam is a good girl, she knows how to take care of herself."

"It's this business about her mother. She's going so fast . . ."

"I can understand her need to find out about her mother. None of us knew Rebecca very well. There are un-

112

spoken ties, Bobby, between daughter and mother. Strong ties."

"I know, but she's becoming compulsive about it. Obsessed, as if on a profound quest."

"In a way, that's what it is."

"I don't like it. She's still in shock from Digger's death."

"Do you intend to try and stop her!"

"You don't think I should!"

"If you do it might cause more harm than good."

"Well, under the circumstances, there's not a lot I can do about it now."

"Good thinking. I've never held with banging your head against a wall."

"It surely does smart," he said, grinning. "Think I'll go upstairs and freshen up. See you after a while, Momma."

Miss Ellie returned to her book.

As he started upstairs, he encountered Sue Ellen coming down. He waited for her to descend.

He kissed her on the cheek and took hold of her shoulders, peered into that once open unlined face. All girlish freshness had been eroded by time and trouble, the large washed-blue eyes no longer clear and full of joy. When she smiled, it was purely an exercise of her facial muscles, without pleasure or happiness.

It made him wonder. His family. What dark, brooding elements turned its members away from their better selves. Created a league of the living dead where before there had been excitement and energy and a surging life-force. What elements moved them from love and understanding to conflict and pain and the erosion of their most human aspects?

Seeing Sue Ellen standing before him, her anguish etched in every plane of that lovely face, knowing the pervading sense of inadequacy and defeat that she experienced—it made him think of his second brother Gary, Lucy's father. Unable to sustain his marriage to the beautiful and perfectly fine woman, Valene. Unable to be a proper father to Lucy. Unable to remain at home with his family, unable to remain in Dallas or even the remotest corner of Texas. Unable to manage the daily pressures of dealing with J.R. and with Jock. Perhaps with himself, Bobby thought ruefully. What manner of family had they become?

Enemies everywhere. Blood relations. By marriage and by association. Business partners and employees, friends, servants and lovers. There was no kindness anywhere, no compassion, no one offering a helping hand.

Was it all J.R.'s doing? He could not accept that. Or some bad seed passed on from his earliest forebears through Jock and Miss Ellie? Or did it leap full-blown out of the land, out of a Texan's rush to build bigger farms, bigger ranches, to rape the land for its buried wealth, out of the lack of regard and respect for people unlike themselves in even the slightest way. The sleekness of Dallas, the glass and steel high rise buildings, the long lines of the interstates traversing the prairies; Houston, El Paso, Fort Worth, once ramshackle towns, now centers of—of what? —of raw wheeling and dealing for profit. Some win, most lose. And the winners are the better men, yes?

No. The logic didn't work. Not in practice. A lucky strike a generation or two earlier had turned roughnecks into multi-millionaries, given them inflated visions of their own importance. Transformed an extraordinary lust for riches into the American equivalent of a moral crusade. Turned their sons and daughters into wild living, wilder spending profligates who bought his-and-hers Rolls Royces and swimming pools in the shape of cowboy boots.

The cowboy was a creature of the past. No John Wayne he. No Gary Cooper. More like an embittered Gabby Hayes, used up by hard work, hard times and low pay. Men with only their bodies and their courage to sustain them, men with no other marketable skills, men destined to live out their lives with the stench of cow droppings in their nostrils.

And their women. Burned out by poverty and neglect and too many babies before they were thirty. Pain etched into once beautiful faces that set them apart, a special race. No leggy Texas girls among them. No buxom cheerleaders jiggling and bouncing for the TV audience. No drawling models prowling Fifth Avenue in the latest fashions. All part of the myth, the Texas legend, the Lone Star lie. And the tortured expression in his sister-in-law's eyes brought it all home to him vividly, in widescreen living pain.

"You're looking good," he said with more sincerity than he felt.

"I don't feel so good. That business at the Ace Bar—I owe you an explanation . . ."

"You owe me nothing, Sue Ellen."

She rocked her head as if to clear away old wounds, old memories. "I thought that cowboy was Dusty Farlow."

"I know. You said his name."

"Bobby." She braced herself, as if about to walk into a den of vipers, afraid of what lay ahead and more afraid of what awaited her if she failed to advance. "Bobby, I loved Dusty Farlow."

"You don't have to tell me these things."

"That's just it, I do. I have to tell someone at last. Dusty loved me. In a way I never knew a man could love a woman. Tenderly. With gentle concern. Passionately, without anger or bitterness. Those hours I spent with him—sometimes just being together, not talking very much, not doing anything special, not touching—he made me feel so very very good, Bobby.

"Maybe I shouldn't have let it happen. Me being a married woman, and all. But I needed somebody in my life, somebody who cared for me alone. Not for me as J.R.'s wife. Not for me as a rich Ewing. Just Sue Ellen, lonely, sad lady."

"I hear what you're saying."

"J.R. is not an easy man to be married to."

A wry smile tilted his soft mouth. "J.R. is not easy in any way, in case you haven't noticed."

Her smile matched his. "When Dusty and I made love it was something special and very sweet, Bobby. He *appreciated* me. He *wanted* me and he wanted me to be pleased, fulfilled, gratified in *every* possible way. And I was. I was. I loved him very much."

"I'm sorry."

"About the plane crash, you mean?" She cocked her head, eyeing him obliquely. "He's not dead, you know."

Bobby hesitated. "The plane was found, Sue Ellen."

"That doesn't mean he's dead."

"Sue Ellen. About Dusty, I mean."

"He's coming back for me, Bobby. I just know it. He loved me too much to leave me this way, to desert me, to sentence me to a life with J.R. for all those years ahead."

"Sue Ellen—"

"I'm not crazy, Bobby. I *know* Dusty. All he ever wanted was for us to be together for always. Just the two of us. That was his deepest desire. He vowed he would take me away one day. Pluck me from J.R.'s savagery and meanness. Take me away, one way or another. That's what he said, *one way or another*. He wanted to confront J.R. To punish him. Dusty was a gentle and kind man but he wasn't soft. He was not afraid of J.R. He was strong and smart and I am convinced that all this—the plane disappearing, people thinking it crashed—all this is part of Dusty's plan. He's out there, waiting for his chance, for our chance. When it happens it will happen fast. Perhaps I won't even have time to say goodbye, Bobby. Dusty will materialize and take me away. But first—"

"First?"

"First he'll punish J.R."

"Punish him how?"

"One way or another," she murmured. "One way or another." She shook her head again, this time as if to bring herself back to the present. A trace of a childish smile appeared on her lips. "Anyway, I did want to thank you . . ."

"Hey, you're family."

"There's some around here don't act as if that's so, Bobby."

"There's some that's less smart than others. But give it time, all things change."

"Not always for the better. Anyway, I appreciate what you did, I want you to know."

"I know without your saying."

She cocked her head as if trying to look past his dark warm eyes. "I believe you do, Bobby. I think you must be a very special man."

"Just an ordinary Ewing." He laughed.

She didn't. "My experience tells me otherwise."

He didn't choose to pursue that line of talk. "Why don't you get some coffee, take it easy today."

"Has J.R. said anything?"

"About what happened, you mean? Not a word."

"I'm sure he's given it some profound consideration. I seem to have supplied my darlin' husband with exactly the ammunition he needs to get rid of me. . . ."

"You're wrong about that."

"You're J.R.'s brother, I'm his wife. Believe me, I've seen sides of him you may not know exist. Nothing would please him more than to put me away for good. . . ."

"He won't . . . he can't . . ."

"Look what he caused Seth Stone to do. J.R. can always find a way."

"Then you have to keep from providing him with a way. You must stop drinking, keep away from places like the Ace . . ."

"I want to, I really do. Something set me off. It was a shock and it came just when I thought I had the drinking under control. I swear it, Bobby, I am not going to touch another drink as long as I live."

"Anytime you need somebody to talk to—I'll be around."

"I know that."

"Now go in and have that coffee. Talk to Momma. She'd like that, I'm sure."

"Not after the way I've disgraced myself."

"You've got to face her sometime. Do it now."

She hesitated, smiled up at him, then lifted her chin and went into the den.

About that same time, Alan Beam presented himself at Kristin's apartment. She, wearing a floor-length hostess gown of some filmy fabric that manged to reveal and conceal simultaneously, admitted him.

"Would you care for a drink, Alan?"

He turned on his most charming leer. "Around a beautiful lady like you, Kristin, I have to keep my head clear."

"My, aren't you the flatterer! Come in. sit down, tell me why you called."

He handed her a copy of the afternoon paper. She scanned the headline:

EWING OIL EMPIRE COLLAPSES
Oil Fields Nationalized

She returned the paper to him without a word.

"You're taking it very well."

A twinge of unrest slithered through him. Something was wrong here. He'd come expecting to find a woman distraught and concerned for her future. Kristin was calm and controlled, seemingly untouched by the disaster that had enveloped the Ewings.

"It can't be true."

"What do you mean?" He raised the paper as if it were gospel, sworn and attested to. "It says—"

"The Ewings haven't been hurt at all."

He had come to offer his help; at once he understood he needed her help. "I'll have that drink now, if you don't mind."

He watched her go to the bar, her movements lithe and feline, suggestions of her fine flesh giving form to her gown quickly dropping away. J.R. was a lucky man in so many ways. Alan wondered what it would be like to make love to a woman of such dramatic beauty, of such apparent sensuality. He wonderd what she would do if he were to put a move on her.

She returned with the drink, and one for herself. She curled up on the sofa next to him, raised her glass in a silent toast and drank. A wicked smile lifted the corners of her voluptuous mouth.

"Men like you, Alan, always make a mistake about men like J.R. Ewing."

He resented the implication even as he recognized its validity. "In what way?"

"J.R. knows how to protect his fanny. Whatever else he is—and he is one of the world's most monumental sons of a bitch—he is shrewd and ruthless and about a mile smarter than just about everybody else."

"Meaning what?"

"Meaning J.R. peddled those leases."

He made a gesture toward the newspaper. "That isn't true?"

"Not a bit of it."

"When?"

She lifted her perfect shoulders, let hem drop. Alan's eyes flickered downward to where her breasts—free of any brassiere—shimmered into view under the thin fabric, her fine hard nipples thrusting forward. She let him look in silence until, embarrassed at having been found out, he raised his eyes. She smiled at his discomfort. Kristin was a woman who enjoyed having men admire her, wanted them to want her, found pleasure and—she hoped— eventual profit in her desirability. Alan was young, good-looking, and ambitious, a combination she treasured in a man. Right now he was just another lawyer of no particular importance; but you never could tell how things would turn out.

"A couple of days ago," she answered.

Alan pushed aside the panic that surfaced in his mind, trying to make sense out of what he knew. He had assumed the press stories were accurate, a naive assumption apparently. He had been ready to forge new alliances for himself, embark on a new path to Success and Glory. That now seemed premature. What he had to do was strengthen his current hand; he'd been dealt cards that let him participate in the game, but the stakes were high and he needed help to win. In this game, two pair brought you in second; Alan needed a full house. Kristin, he assured himself, looked like a winner's card to him. "But the revolution took place forty-eight hours ago. Nationalization was announced only last night . . . ."

She went over to the bookcase against the far wall and picked up a micro-recorder. "I have had guests," she said soberly. "Most men like to talk to a pretty young woman, especially older men, successful men."

"And you taped what they said. Ah, Kristin, you are a girl after my own heart."

"I taped this particular conversation. Of course, you're not interested, you don't want to hear what was said."

He grinned with joyful maliciousness. "Play the damn thing." He was beginning to feel more at home, comfortable in the company of a kindred spirit.

She pressed the playback button and a moment later a male voice was heard, slightly muffled and distant, but every word distinct.

"We finally done it, sugar. We got J.R. to let go of some of that Asian black gold."

"That's Andy Bradley," Kristin said quickly. "One of the members of the cartel."

On the recorder, her voice said: "Is that good, Andy?"

"Good! Hell, it is great! Those fields out there are rich, enough oil to flood the market. . . . I tell you, no matter what the price, we came away with a bargain. I'm beginning to believe J.R. Ewing is only half as clever as he thinks he is."

"How come he let you boys in on the deal?"

"He needs the cash. Some kind of a deal in the works. Dumbass cowboy, no matter what he's got cookin' it can't measure up to those fields. Now, Kristin, honey, get your sweet little fanny over here where I can—" She pushed the "off" button, and returned to her place on the sofa.

Alan touched her cheek lightly. "I believe I am in your debt, Kristin."

She chose her words carefully. "We are both working for J.R., aren't we?"

"Are we?" He took her face between his hands and kissed her. For a fraction of time he was afraid he'd made another mistake, until her lips parted and she accepted his tongue. Her hand stroked his chest, across his flat hard' belly, fingers hooking under his belt. He reached for her breast.

Breathing hard, she pulled away, staring up at him. "I think we might be very good together."

"I'm sure of it." He shifted closer and this time she held him off. "What's wrong?"

"Nothing. But it occurs to me that we have so much more to discuss."

She was right and he knew it. More to the point, she remained in control of herself no matter what was happening. He, on the other hand, was acting as if his brains were between his legs, risking everything for what appeared to be an easy matinee. "I just wanted you to know how I feel."

"Your feelings will keep. First, back to J.R. and the Asian deal. It all went off so smoothly, too smoothly. J.R. dumps his holdings and boom. Just like that, nationalization."

"A coincidence?"

"Not where so many millions of dollars are concerned. J.R. and the Ewing Oil comes out a winner and the rest of the members of the cartel take a dirty bath."

"You think there was some kind of a conspiracy?"

"I am convinced that J.R. had to have advance information. He knew what was happening and unloaded on his pals."

"But how?"

"Hank Johnson is the key."

"Who's Hank Johnson?"

"J.R.'s man in the Far East. A first-class oilman with a nose for what's going down. Hank had to know there was a revolution brewing and if he did, you can bet he found out what the rebels were after, what they intended to do."

"Besides Bradley, who else bought the leases?"

"I told you, J.R.'s closest friends and business asociates —the cartel."

"If you're right," Alan mused, "wouldn't they like to know it?"

"Some of those boys—they'd string J.R. up. Literally. Rumor has it more than one of them walks around with a .38 under his well-tailored jacket and from what I hear they all have used guns in the past. Bang, bang."

"The old wild West."

"These boys are the genuine article."

Alan felt a twinge of fear. "I'd just as soon not get involved with any old gunfighters."

"They'd pay plenty to know the truth."

"We have no proof. Anyway, J.R. would pay plenty to keep them from knowing."

Kristin grew thoughtful. "J.R.'s smart, too smart to leave any evidence lying around."

"Maybe." Alan felt compelled to pursue the matter, seeing it as the key to the door to his future. "What if we talked to Hank Johnson? What if he had proof of what took place? Records, phone calls, plane tickets; the kind of stuff that would prove he was in close touch with J.R. just before the rebellion blew up."

"The kind of records a man on an expense account would keep."

"Exactly."

She slowly rose, swaying in front of him. "I think," she said in a low, penetrating voice, "you are going to be a lot of fun to have around, Alan."

His arms circled her, hands reaching for her backside, face going forward between her thighs. The acrid female scent of her clogged the cavities of his skull, made him faint and weak.

"Not yet, lover, not quite yet. First there's a call to be made." She disengaged and dialed, spoke to the overseas operator. She waited.

"Hank Johnson, please? Is that you, Hank? Kristin Shepard here. J.R.'s just fine, riding herd on the whole outfit like the ramrod he is. That's right, that's J.R. for you. Listen, Hank, J.R. wanted me to call to tell you to send us all the records of plane tickets, phone calls, hotel receipts —that's right, anything that shows where you were just before the takeover. Sort of a subterranean insurance policy, you might say. No, Hank, send them to the condo by special courier. To me, that's the way J.R. wants it. He's not a man who ever thinks in a straight line, now does he? Yes, he wants to destroy the evidence himself, okay. Get on it at once, Hank. I'll tell J.R. how cooperative you've been. Bye, Hank."

She hung up and put the phone down.

He stood up and went to her. "You are good, Kristin."

Her arms went around his neck. "Not too good, I hope."

"Good enough," he said, just before he kissed her. But definitely not good, he thought. Not even very nice.

10

"*D*octor Ellby, I'm frightened."

He gave off strong reassuring vibrations, as if he possessed the power to make everything all right. No matter the problem. The furnishings and decorations of his office supported that impression. Soft dark leather chairs, accented with stained wood. An antique chaise tufted and inviting, easy to settle on, easy to relate from. Walls lined with books suggesting all that information now resided inside the doctor's large, active brain.

"Fear is an inevitable satellite for a human animal, my dear. Those who do not try do not fear."

Sue Ellen nodded gravely. Every instinct in her protested against these sessions, against revelations of her private self, of her secrets. Yet Doctor Ellby seemed to be her sole link to sanity and continued freedom. Either she continued visiting him four times each week or J.R. would certainly make sure she was again institutionalized. And that she could not endure. To be shut behind those wire cages as if she were insane, some wild creature not to be trusted, not to be allowed her freedom. A great cold spasm held her body in thrall for a long moment; and passed at last.

"If Bobby hadn't come along—"

"The Ace Bar, you mean?"

She nodded. "I barely remember the place, the incident. Yet I know it happened. Me, with a total stranger, more than one man. My God, what if—? I am so ashamed of myself, so filled with loathing. Disgust."

123

"Ah. We come close now." Doctor Ellby was Texas born and bred, yet managed somehow to suggest a faint Viennese accent in his speech. As if no psychiatrist worth his salt could possibly be native to Dallas. "So, you will tell me what is the worst that might have happened?"

She was unable to meet his gaze. "But you know. I was drunk."

"The root cause of your problem, no?"

"My mind was a blank."

"Drink enough alcohol and it will subvert many of your bodily functions. Balance, vision, memory. Blackouts are not uncommon."

"No more," she said. "No more, no more. It's going to be all right. I'll never take another drink—ever again. Bobby is going to help me. He'll keep me straight. He won't let J.R. mistreat me anymore. He won't let J.R. send me back to that place."

"Fletcher's Sanitarium. Ah, yes. All institutions tend to be depressive. They exist to perform a function. A drunken woman is an embarrassment to everyone, herself included."

"My husband would like to get rid of me, once and for all."

"Your husband loves you, Mrs. Ewing. He told me so. Hasn't he told you so?"

"Many times. But my husband is one of the champion liars of all time. Anyway, it doesn't matter what he says. He treats me like a piece of filth."

"So you turn to your brother-in-law for assistance, no?"

"What's wrong with that?"

"You hand over control of your life to another human being. You put your welfare into somebody else's hands."

"I trust Bobby."

"More than you trust yourself?"

"What if I do?"

J.R. sat behind the desk in his office when his secretary buzzed to say Hank Johnson was on the phone. He picked up the instrument at once.

"Hank! That you, boy? Where you calling from? Anything wrong? Anything I ought to know about?"

There was an angry note in the oilman's voice. "Just called to tell you I am putting you on notice, J.R. A man don't trust me, I don't have to work for that man."

"Hank, what in hell are you going on about? Who put that bird in your ear—that I don't trust you?"

Hank came rasping back, a crackling bite to his voice. "Okay, J.R. I'm sending the stuff. But I'm mad as hell."

"Mad? Look here, Hank, somebody slipped a burr under your saddle, okay. But it wasn't me. I—"

Hank broke in. "You want those records destroyed, you can trust me to do it, after all these years. But have it your way. And one more thing—why'n hell did you spill your guts out to Kristin? Dammit, J.R. This operation was yours and mine alone and supposed to stay that way."

"Whoa! Slow down, boy. There's something fishy here. Kristin doesn't get much more'n the time of day from ole J.R. She works for me. But . . . that's . . . all. Now what's this stuff you keep talking about? Hank, what in hell's going on?"

"The records, J.R. You had Kristin call me to send 'em on so's you could destroy them by yourself. Didn't you do that, J.R.?"

"Hell, no! You ought to know me better'n that. Whatever else I am, I am not dumb. You talking about records that will show you and I were in touch about the time—"

"Not about, J.R. All sorts of records to show we were constant communication just before, during and immediately after the rebels started their big push. Hell, I did like you told me, recorded every damned conversation. . . ."

"You sent that stuff back here?"

"Kristin called me. Said you wanted to take care of everything your own self, J.R. The lady said to send *everything* on to her at the condo by special courier, like you said."

The line crackled ominously.

"J.R., you still there?"

"I'm here, Hank. Now listen, ole buddy. There's been a mistake. I told Kristin nothing about those records. *Nothing.*"

"You mean she was acting on her own? Well, hot damn! Ain't she a little ballbuster, that one!"

"You can say that again. Hank, you go off somewhere private and burn those records, tapes, everything. Get rid of it now. And stay where you are until you hear from me again. That suit you, pal?"

"That sounds about right to me, J.R."

"There's going to be a substantially larger bonus on the way to you, Hank. You did real good."

"What about Kristin, J.R.?"

"That bitch better get down on her knees and give her soul to God 'cause her ass sure as shit belongs to J.R. Ewing the Second. . . ."

Pam Ewing was bent over a large ledger at a massive oak table in the Corpus Christi Hall of Records. For hours she'd been studying that book and others just like it, reading off the endless roster of names of the dead. Now the print on the pages was beginning to blur and her eyes to burn. She squeezed them shut. What was it the clerk in charge had said? Oh, yes—"If your mother died in Corpus Christi, she'd be listed in our files." In the darkness behind her eyelids; Pam let her mind reach back to that hospital room where Digger, her father, lay dying. Finally that abused body could take no more. Miss Ellie and Bobby had been there, and Cliff and their Aunt Maggie. Digger, so feeble and pale, fading fast, had seemed so much smaller than he actually was, a diminished reminder of the man he had once been dying of age and alcohol, wasted in flesh and spirit.

"Ellie," he had husked. "I'm glad you came."

"Digger, there's always been feelings in my heart for you."

"I know that." His eyes had sought out Cliff. "Son, I got to talk to you. I want you all to know how it really happened."

"Daddy, you better rest."

"What for!" he had said with surprising strength and anger. He sagged back, breathing hard. "Ain't like this raggedy-ass range bum is going anyplace. Listen—a deathbed statement, that's all legal and binding."

"Daddy," Pam had said, unable to keep back the tears.

"Ellie, I want to clear the air. I wanted to deliver one last hurt to Jock for hurting me, for taking you away from me so long ago, Ellie. I always loved you, Ellie."

"And in my way I loved you, too."

"Ain't what I mean, but it don't matter none anymore. I want to set matters right, is all. That body they found buried on Southfork, that Hutch McKinney . . ."

Ellie had grown tense. "They think Jock shot that man, murdered him."

"Daddy," Cliff had said quickly. "You better try to sleep."

"Lots of sleeping time to come. Ah, what the hell, I still love you, Ellie. Always did. But all along you've been Jock's girl, right from the beginning. I can't let Cliff or anybody else hurt you by hurting Jock."

"What is it, Digger?"

"You know me—even back in 1952—I was on one of my three-day toots. Drank an ocean of liquor, feeling no pain. We were living over in Braddock back then. Maybe a mile from Southfork, no more. I came home finally to your momma, Cliff, Pam, like I sooner or later always did. Only this time it was different.

"Rebecca was a pretty woman, I tell you. And next to you, Ellie, I loved her in my way. Only it seems likely I never treated her real good. She was carrying that night . . ."

"Pregnant!" Pam had exclaimed.

"That's right, pregnant with you, Pam. She wasn't alone that night. That sneak Hutch McKinney was there with my wife. I said what was he doing in my house and he sassed me. Then Rebecca spoke up:

" 'Digger,' she said just as plain as could be, 'Digger, Jock fired Hutch and he's putting Dallas behind him. And I'm going with him. We're taking Cliff along.'

"I didn't understand none of it at first. Until your momma told me that she loved with Hutch McKinney.

"I said I wouldn't let her go, that she was my wife, that she was pregnant with my baby. That's when McKinney spoke out—'Not your baby, Digger, mine!'

" 'Digger, Hutch is the father,' your momma told me.

"Whore! Whore! *Whore!*" Lying in his hospital bed, Digger, reliving it all, was yelling it out.

"Hush, Digger," Miss Ellie said, trying to calm him. "None of it matters much anymore."

"I hit her and Hutch swung at me and I beat him, beat him bad until he was bleeding and near killed. I dragged him outside and he went for his gun. Later I found out it was Jock Ewing's gun, stole by Hutch. I kicked the gun out of his hand and shot the filthy bastard right between the eyes . . . I carted him away and planted him in the first open space I come to. It was a section of Southfork.

"A few days after I took Rebecca and Cliff and we

moved to Corpus and when Rebecca died we went back to Dallas to stay with Aunt Maggie. . . ."

"And I was glad to have you all," Maggie said.

"Daddy!" Pam said, trying not to scream in the hospital room. "Daddy, what about the baby?"

"Baby?" Digger muttered.

"The baby Hutch McKinney fathered," Bobby put in.

Digger's eyes fluttered shut, his breathing harsh and labored.

Pam leaned over him. "Was that baby me, Daddy? Was Hutch McKinney my real father?"

"I always loved you, Pam. Just like you were my own," Digger had muttered just before he died. Remembering brought tears to Pam's eyes. She closed the last ledger and brought it back to the checkout desk. The clerk said: "Did you find what you were looking for?"

"I'm afraid not."

"Then your mother did not die in Corpus." It was the voice of ultimate authority.

Had Digger lied about that too? For what reason? She could think of none and that made her smile, for if Rebecca Barnes had not in fact died in Corpus Christi she might very well be alive and thriving somewhere else. Waiting for her daughter, Pam, to track her down.

"That's the best news I've had in a long time," she said to the clerk and left, beginning to plot her next move.

11

"That was nice," Lucy Ewing said automatically that same morning. She lay in the bed, the conditioned air cooling her naked body, looking up at the ceiling. She imagined that via hidden cameras or two-way mirror a group of vicious and lecherous men and women had observed her and Greg Forrester performing in his bedroom. She imagined she could hear their derogatory comments about the way she looked, the inadequacies of her face and body, the way she had performed; always a failure as a woman, not deserving of anyone's affection or continuing attention. How long before Greg would tire of her, ask her to leave?

His hand came to rest on her thigh, squeezing, as if trying to tell her something. The absence of language distressed her, made her believe that once again she had failed to come up to some man's standards.

"You want me to leave?" she said, sitting up.

His eyes squeezed open. "Don't be silly."

"You're just saying it to be kind."

"Hey, little beauty, we're just getting warmed up."

She hovered over him, examining his face for some indication of duplicity, deceit, a hint of the easy lies that men told. "You think I'm a pushover don't you?"

He laughed with genuine pleasure. Naked he looked even thinner, his body bony and angular, though owning a kind of sinewy grace. His belly was ridged and flat, his thighs surprisingly heavy and muscular. He was, he had told her, an experienced and expert skier.

"Neither one of us held out for very long," he said.

"The man isn't supposed to."

"Where's it written? Are only women the protectors of virtue, keepers of the moral line? I think not. No. Shall I tell you why I succumbed so quickly to your lustful and indecent proposals, Miss Ewing?"

"Because I'm rich." She tried to keep it light, but the undertone of uncertainty seeped into her voice.

"Because you're cute and smart and possessed of a body beyond perfection. You turned me on and against all my cerebral convictions I gave in. Mainly because I've had the hots for you ever since you registered for my class at the university."

"Well. That's better. Even if it's not so."

"Oh, it's true, all right. But I can't figure out why you're here. Why me?"

She kissed his left nipple and he shivered. She kissed his right nipple and rested her cheek on his broad flat chest. Why him? Why not him. Why not any man who happened to be handy. For so long she'd operated on that basis—well, almost. Love seemed to be only an extended passion, little different in the long run than a one-night stand. And how many of those had there been? Too many to count at her young age. An inward shudder wracked her psyche.

"Why?" Greg said again. "I'm twice your age. A used up middle-aged college professor. A dispenser of useless knowledge to uninterested young people who'd rather be out playing basketball or shooting quail or getting each other into trouble. Yes, why me, Lucy?"

"Well, I never had one of my teachers before."

"A conquest!"

"In a manner of speaking. Am I your first student?"

"Ah, the pursuit of knowledge. Seek and ye shall be rewarded—my dear, women students trot in and out of here as if it were Grand Central Station in New York City. I barely have time for reflection."

"You pig."

"Absolutely correct."

"And you reward them with honors in your course."

"I give them what they're entitled to—no more than they offer. A fleeting sensual reward, ephemeral pleasure that fades quickly enough in the memory since it takes place without meaning or hope. A quick roll in the hay never got anybody to academic heaven, Lucy Ewing."

"Is that what I am—a quickie?"

"You're still here."

She slid out of the bed. "Not for long. I wouldn't want to keep you from your next appointment ..." She located her panties on the floor.

He reached for her arm, yanked her back onto the bed. "I'm not finished with you yet."

She spread her legs. "Okay. Do it, get it over with, and let me get on my way."

"I think you mean it, and that's too bad. Because I truly like you, Lucy, and enjoy your company. Yes, I want to make love to you again. but I also want to talk to you, get to know you as a human being not a student. As for the sex, tell you what. Suppose we swear off for the rest of the day. Kind of a penance for hurting each other. Let's get acquainted. I'm Greg Forrester, teacher, dreamer, fantasizer of a dozen novels and plays that will never get written. In other words, your typical intellectual playing it safe and sorry in the groves of academe. There. Now what's your sad story?"

"Must I have one?"

"We all do, people like us."

She constructed a fable to satisfy him, to make herself sound glamorous, exciting, a woman of the world. But when the words came out she felt tears welling up behind her eyes and she needed to be held and comforted.

"I ... feel so ... alone."

"You're with me." There was the sound of genuine concern in his cultured voice.

"I barely know you. It's always that way, men I don't know making love to me, men I don't want to see again."

"You don't like it—why do it?"

She shrugged and wiped at her eyes. A wry smile turned her pretty mouth. "I've sworn off drugs. I can't tolerate the taste of liquor. So what else is there—sex."

She expected him to laugh, he didn't, nodding solemnly. "And you always choose the wrong ones."

"Unerringly."

"Why is that?"

"Oh, I've figured it out, I think. I'm the traditional

poor-little-rich girl. I've got everything, I've got nothing. No momma, no poppa, nothing."

"Your parents are dead?"

"My mother is a tramp who ran off and left me," she said bitterly. "My father did the same. He's a drunk."

"But the Ewings, the rest of them . . . ?"

A harsh exclamatory sound burst out of her. "It's a human zoo out at Southfork with everybody doing dirt to everybody else. Every one of them's got troubles, real troubles, real pain. Anything bothering me—well, it's always minimized, or shoved aside."

"You feel unloved?"

"I sure as hell am *under*-loved."

"So you let men get to you too easily. Can't you tell the difference between fake feelings and the real thing?"

"I don't know. Maybe not. There's Alan . . ."

"Alan?"

"Alan Beam. He's been after me . . ."

"I thought . . ."

"Not for sex, silly. I give him more than he can handle from the looks of it. No, to marry him. Now he says he won't sleep with me any more unless I do marry him."

"Do you want to marry him?"

"I don't know."

"Why not?"

She searched for the answer that had been eluding her for so long. "I—I don't think I love him!" She began to weep.

He held her for a long time until the crying ceased and she lay warm and at ease in his arms. "I'm sorry," she murmured presently.

"For what?"

"For spoiling your good time."

"Don't be stupid. You have no idea how rewarding it is to encounter real emotion for a change, valid pain, authentic desire. So large a part of my life is filled with posturing, masks, an ongoing charade without commitment or meaning."

She yawned. "I'm sorry."

"You know what it means, when a girl yawns in bed?"

"What?"

"That she either wants to fuck or fight."

She thought it over. "I don't want to fight," she said. And they didn't.

Late for work, Kristin had rushed Alan Beam out of her apartment, showered and hurriedly dressed. Just about ready to depart, she was brought up short by the sound of the doorbell. She was expecting no one. She opened the door and saw J.R. standing there, looking ominious in his white Stetson, his brows pulled down in an angry scowl.

"I don't want to talk to you, J.R." She started to close the door.

He leaned against it, barged past her into the apartment.

"You have no right to come pushing and shoving in here like that. You don't own me, J.R."

"You need a reminder, honey, I *own* this condo."

He was right, she had forgotten. Accepting her presence as possession. She decided to brazen it out: all her life Kristin had bent men and boys alike to her will. A smile, a frown, a bit of attention; they leaped at her command. She knew what J.R. enjoyed most, knew how to win him over.

"J.R., you angry because I didn't come in this morning? I am sorry, sugar. I overslept, that's all. I'm on my way this instant and I'll work overtime, if you say so, hear."

"Tell me about you and Alan Beam, to begin with."

"Alan—You must be mistaken. There is nothing to tell."

"Do you take me for a fool! He was here and not for conversation, if I know you."

"Why J.R.! I do believe you're jealous."

"You are a fool. I don't care what you do or who you do it with, just so long as I get what I pay for. And what I pay you for is loyalty and a modicum of smarts, lady. You have not been loyal and you have shown yourself to be stupid."

A spasm of fear went through her. If he had learned so swiftly about her and Alan then he must certainly know much more about her activities. *That* was something to be frightened about. She took a step toward him, one hand reaching. He knocked it aside.

"I think you've got something to tell me," he declared forcefully.

"About Alan, all right. It was a mistake. I was foolish. It won't happen again. I was lonely, annoyed with you, J.R. After all, you've been practically ignoring me lately and—"

"Don't you understand, Alan Beam belongs to me, body and soul, and so do you, darlin'. I buy and sell the Beams of this world and believe me they come cheap. Now talk."

The fear increased. What *did* he know? What did he want of her?

"About what, J.R.?"

"Tell me about Hank Johnson."

Her extremities went cold, became leaden. Her mind revved, gradually picking up speed, operating at close to normal after a moment or two. She took off her coat, knowing that the skirt and sweater she wore displayed her full figure to advantage. She watched J.R.'s eyes taking it in, knew exactly what he was thinking. What he was remembering.

"J.R., it's so good to have you here. Can't we talk later? Much later."

"Talk to me, tramp."

"You filthy bastard." She charged forward, raking at his face. He hit her again and she went skidding down to the floor. He took up a position above her, placed his boot across her throat and let her feel the full weight of his big body.

"What could you have possibly have in mind? Did you actually believe you could get the best of me in any way? Did you think J.R. Ewing was so dense and innocent as to trust a person of your caliber? What did you intend, Kristin? Answer."

She groaned, hands pawing helplessly at his boot. "J.R., you are killing me"

"What a good idea. Better start spilling your guts."

"Alan," she gasped. "Alan made me do it."

"Alan? How could he force you to do anything?"

"He said he would tell Jock about our love affair, yours and mine. I slept with him to protect you."

"Well, bust my ass!" he said admiringly. "You are good."

"It's true. He made me call Hank. He wanted to have some hold on you. You see—"

"Oh, yes, I see. I see that Alan Beam couldn't make you walk across the room if the place was on fire. He's weak, hungry, ambitious, but a smarmy little leach without brains or guts enough to trouble a dying calf. Don't lie to me anymore, Kristin. It just gets me mad.

"Now I'll tell you. You were the brains behind this. The

idea was simple—get your hands on those records. Use them against me with the boys in the cartel. Make me look bad, even worse. Maybe even blackmail me—extract a lifetime of tribute in order to prevent those records from falling into the wrong hands. Let me tell you, sweetheart," he said, stepping back, motioning for her to rise. "You are out of your league, you and Beam. A couple of small-time claim jumpers, outreaching yourselves. You are going to be very sorry you ever thought of doing this and sorrier yet that you tried it."

She was on her feet, massaging the pain out of her throat. She walked directly into the kitchen, returned almost at once with a ten-inch bread knife in her hand. "Touch me again, J.R., and I'll kill you."

"Not you, sugar. You haven't got the heart for it."

"Don't be too sure. You don't scare me."

"It takes brains to be scared. Since that's something in short supply around here. I'll put it into perspective for you, Kristin. Now *is* the time for you to be scared."

He reached into his pocket and she jerked backwards, eyes widening. He laughed grimly. He removed his hand from his pocket, holding a thick fold of bills.

"They tell me," he said, counting off hundreds, "that Rio is lovely this time of year. You go there. Hit the Copacabana beach in one of those itty-bitty string bikinis of yours. Swing your sweet little butt around, wiggle your fine boobs and you won't be alone for long. Do what you do best and you should be good for at least a year with some rich married Brazilian businessman."

She brandished the knife. "I ought to stick you good."

He tossed the money on the coffee table. "Take it and get out of Dallas. While you can, Kristin."

"Some day someone's going to stop you, J.R."

"Not you, sugar."

"You always told me—never underestimate your enemies. I am your enemy, J.R. For now and forever."

"Take the money and go. By this time tomorrow. Or else I'll have one of my bigger friends come around to see you. Maybe two or three of them. They could have a lot of fun with you, Kristin, use every orifice in that magnificent body of yours, before they break your kneecaps."

"I won't be scared!" she shouted as he started to leave. "I won't be bought off."

J.R.'s mouth curled as he walked out, leaving the door

ajar behind him. Anyone seeing him would have been horrified at the expression on his face, and terribly afraid.

Pam went from the Corpus Christi Hall of Records to a working-class street across town. She examined the dilapidated houses running down the block with a degree of affection, as if she had stood here before, as if she belonged here and had squirreled away warm memories of this place. One house in particular drew her attention and it was with some displeasure that her concentration was broken when a woman appeared out of the house next door.

A woman in her seventies, she picked her way carefully down the few crooked steps fronting her house. Once safe on the sidewalk, she looked up and spied Pam coming across the street as if to intercept her. She turned one way then the other, as if trying to escape and going nowhere. Confusion and dismay on her wrinkled face, the look of a woman who preferred her own company to that of strangers. She worked her back around to Pam and shuffled slowly down the street. Pam hurried after her.

"Oh, please, ma'am, I'd like to talk to you for a minute."

The older woman stopped, head down. "What'daya want?"

"Have you lived around here long?"

"Long! Guess so, a long time. Most of my life and that's long."

Relief flooded through Pam. Perhaps she had struck it rich out of pure good luck. "My name is Pamela Ewing. I'm trying to locate someone who used to live here, in the house next door to yours. Maybe you remember her— Rebecca Barnes."

The old woman came around to face Pam, eyeing her obliquely. "Name's Odette," she mumbled. "Odette Billings. Once was young like you, and purty. Maybe purtier than you are."

Pam smiled. "I'm sure you were very pretty."

"Can't understand it, how it happened to me. The way I look. I mean. Gettin' old and crinkled. Had a husband once, only he up and died on me. Before him, had lots of boy friends. Lots. But that was a long time ago. What I want to know is how'd it happened, getting so old so quick? I jes can't understand it . . ." Her moist eyes fixed on Pam. "What was that name you said?"

"Rebecca Barnes."

"My memory ain't too good these days. She was your momma, you say?"

"Yes."

"Yup, I guess she was at that. There's a resemblance."

Pam felt her heart begin to pound wildly and her palms grew moist. "You knew her?"

"She had a little boy, I reckon. About five, I'd say. Maybe six."

"My brother, Cliff."

"If you say so. I don't recollect no girl, though."

"She would have been pregnant with me at the time."

Odette Billings tried to penetrate the scrim that blurred the past. "Yup. Wait a minute, she was pregnant. Big with it, she was. Yup, full up and about to bust with a child." She cackled happily.

"Yes, yes, she was carrying me."

Her head nodded loosely, Odette started to walk away. Pam fell into step beside her.

"Please, is there anything else you can think of? Anything at all?"

"Sorry. It was so long ago. Wait . . ."

"Yes?"

"One thing, one Christmas I think it was. I went to visit my brother, Phil. He lived in Galveston in those days. Worked the docks, made good money. Course it was right hard labor and Phil finally ruint hisself as a man, you know what I mean, and that put him off the docks for good and all."

"You visited Phil that Christmas?"

"Huh? Oh, right, I went to see ole Phil. He's gone now, too. All gone, all my family, all my friends, I'm the only one left."

"What about Rebecca Barnes?"

"Huh? Well, I stayed on for a couple of weeks with Phil and then I came back. She was gone, Rebecca was gone."

"Just my mother?"

"No, the whole family. Gone."

"Where? Do you know where they went?"

"Nobody knew. Never left an address or word or nothing. Just took off without a word goodbye." She paused. "I got to go now."

"Thank you, very much."

Odette started down the street. "Nice woman, that Rebecca," she muttered. "Nice. Beautiful like you, ma'am. Only she could've said goodbye, you know. She could've . . ."

That evening after dinner, Sue Ellen excused herself and went right up to her room. A quiet exultation suffused her as if she had accomplished a great deal, done what she had seldom before done. She had just donned her nightclothes when J.R. arrived. He stripped off his jacket, shirt and tie, and slipped on a freshly laundered shirt. Buttoning it, he watched Sue Ellen.

"You surprised me this evening," he said.

"How could that be, husband? I was under the impression that you read me so clear and so deep that nothing I did or said could surprise you."

He tucked his shirt tails into his pants, began knotting his tie. "You managed to maintain a certain decorum through dinner, beginning to end."

"Sorry to disappoint you."

"I was pleased."

"Is that right? You expected me to act the fool in front of your family, to be embarrassed about what happened to me, to shame myself. But it didn't work that way, did it? I was the perfect lady—charming, witty and cold sober."

He checked himself in the mirror, his mouth emphatic and downturned. His eyes still and icy. The knot of his tie was precise, perfect, exactly as he wanted it. "Sue Ellen, I do believe you are heading straight for a nervous breakdown, at ninety miles an hour. We are going to have to do something about your inarticulate ravings, sugar."

"J.R., get this straight. I am not raving. I am not drunk. I am in total control of myself."

"You are not going to put me away again."

"We'll see about that."

"I will not permit it. Bobby will not permit it."

"Remember, darlin'—" He put on his jacket. "I always get what I want. Always." He turned to go.

"Tell me, J.R. You planning on sleeping with my sister, Kristin, tonight?"

He remained silent, staring at her.

"Poor Kristin. In that case, which slut are you staying with tonight?"

He came around fully. "Whoever the slut is you better believe she'll be more of a woman than the slut I'm seeing at this minute."

He left, slamming the door behind him. In a rage, Sue Ellen threw a pillow at the door. She went to J.R.'s chest, pulled open a drawer, began to scatter clothes around the floor. Suddenly she stopped, reached into the drawer and brought out a loaded .38 caliber revolver. It was heavy in her hand, yet oddly satisfying. She raised it up and stared down the lethal black barrel. Soon she brought it up to her lips and slowly, so very slowly, guided it into her mouth, her thumb on the trigger. The metallic taste made her grimace and she separated herself from the weapon.

She pointed it at the door, to where she had last seen her husband. Her straight arm began to quiver, the muscles straining. "Bang," she said softly. "Bang. BANG. BANG!"

She collapsed to the floor, still pointing the gun. "Die, damn you, die."

PART IV

The Ewings

YESTERDAY

Only a few months before the nationalization of the oil fields in Asia, J.R. rose early. He dressed swiftly, taking a long lustful look at his sleeping wife. Nothing like a sleeping woman to turn a man on, to get the old adrenaline up, to untap the libido. Even a wife as cold and distant as Sue Ellen. J.R. made a silent vow; he would woo her as he had before their marriage, win her affections once again, make her yearn to feel him again between those luscious thighs of hers. Remembering how it was, the kind of low-down, slightly mean and dirty lover Sue Ellen had been, roused his simmering passion even more. Women like that were hard to find; oh, yes, there were plenty anxious to bed down with J.R. Ewing, but few as beautiful and sensual as his own wife. To sleep next to a woman and not possess her was a foolish and counterproductive activity. Especially early in the morning, before breakfast, when both of them were thick with sleep, warm and slow-moving.

His practiced eye traced the line of Sue Ellen's back and hip under the sheets. What a superb body still; strong and supple. Made to give and get pleasure. J.R. failed to comprehend how she could possibly turn him down. Hell's bells, it wasn't necessary to love someone in order to hump 'em. Wasn't even necessary to *like* 'em. J.R. knew that for a fact.

Having reluctantly resisted the impulse to wake his wife, he went downstairs, helped himself to a tall glass of orange juice and stepped outside. The sun cast long graceful shadows, already heating up Southfork for what he sensed would be a thick, hot day. A typical Dallas day. Thank the Good Lord for air conditioning; the way J.R. figured it, air conditioning had to be invented by a Texas boy. Somebody fed-up to here with sweating all during his work day.

The sound of a splashing swimmer drew him over to

the pool area in time to see Kristin Shepard come out of
the water, sleek and full-busted in a tight black tank suit
that displayed her magificent body in all its lovely detail.
J.R. licked the edge of his glass and watched as she
climbed up on the diving board, the effort drawing the
seat of the suit tightly over her full bottom, now in sharp
relief. For an unbearable interlude she posed, a straight
slender shaft against the blue sky, then she ran lightly
forward and executed a fine quick jacknife, slicing into the
water with hardly a ripple to mark her entry.

J.R. cooled his suddenly warm throat with some of the
orange juice until Kristin climbed out of the pool again.
This time she spied him, smiled and waved.

"Lookin' good, Kristin," he called.

"Why, thank you, J.R." She leaned forward and shook
water out of her hair, and in that split moment her superb
breasts fell heavily forward leaving J.R. breathless. He
advanced a step or two instinctively.

"More, J.R. . . . ?"

The subdued but clear summons in that unexpected
voice brought him around, guilty and ashamed. His mother, as always looking fresh and pretty and under complete
control, was at the breakfast table on the patio, pitcher in
hand. Two servants were bringing food out in warming
pans and covered dishes.

"What's that, Momma?" He joined her, not looking
back, hearing the sound of Kristin's next dive, shoving the
image of that sweet young body out of his mind.

"I said, 'More juice, J.R.?'" A fixed smile lifted her
mouth, a watchful expression in those cool blue eyes.

"No, I don't think so, Momma. I'm just fine, Momma.
Just fine."

"Pretty, isn't she?" Miss Ellie said, checking the prepa-
rations for the family's breakfast.

"You mean Kristin, Momma? I reckon she is, though I
hardly noticed."

"Of course, son. A married man doesn't pay much
attention to his wife's little sister. Wouldn't be fit,
wouldn't be right, wouldn't be moral."

"I guess that's so, Momma."

"I guess it is, son." Miss Ellie, discovering something
not to her liking, disappeared inside the big house, heading for the kitchen.

J.R. returned to the pool. Kristin swam over to the near

side and pulled herself languidly out of the water. One shoulder strap had slipped low, the suit falling away, exposing a considerable portion of one ample white breast. If she noticed, she gave no indication. J.R. picked up a towel and tossed it in her direction. She caught it deftly and smiled her thanks, began drying her hair. J.R., breathing shallowly, waited for her breast to come into full view.

As if in direct silent reply, Kristin wrapped herself in the towel, smiling sweetly at him. "How you this fine morning, J.R.?"

"Just as chipper as a man could be, Kristin, honey. And you?"

"Never better."

"I got to admit you surely do look fetching today. You must have slept well."

"I always do, sleep well, that is. I just love it out here at Southfork. Makes me feel like one of the family."

"You are one of the family."

"One or two steps removed."

"Nothing stays the same, sugar."

Kristin ducked her head as if not to confront the implication. "Momma's gonna be so jealous when I tell her what a good time I've had. She'll be sorry she spent her last Texas evening at the apartment in Dallas."

"I imagine she had loads of packing to do for that European trip of hers. You've got some packing, too, I reckon. Going to miss you, Kristin, when you go home."

"Well, J.R., I am certainly going to miss you, all of the Ewings." She arranged herself on a chaise under the sun and stretched out. It took all of J.R.'s will-power not to put himself down with her. He turned away in time to see Sue Ellen come out of the house. Like her sister, she was wearing a very tight, very revealing swimsuit. And J.R. was struck again by what a fine figure his wife possessed. Taller than Kristin, more amply proportioned, larger at the shoulder and hip, she made a more womanly appearance, less of that pared down girlish look. It occurred to J.R. that a man couldn't go wrong working both sides of that street.

"You planning on taking a swim, Sue Ellen?"

Her eyes went from him to Kristin and back again. "Sort of keep the pool in the family. Unless you have some objection, J.R.?"

There was a hint of irony in her manner and he refused

to believe that she knew what he was thinking. And feeling. "Might be a bit too intense out there in the sun for you, Sue Ellen. Your skin is so fair and sensitive."

"I'm touched by your consideration."

"Maybe we ought to go upstairs."

Her gaze was unrelenting. Those bleached eyes looking almost white and all-seeing. "Why what in the world for, J.R.? You're all duded up and ready for your office and I just this minute got out of bed, well-rested and anxious to face the day."

He put a smile on, the bright cheerful facade that masked off the dark and brooding underside of J.R. "Plenty of time before work. What the hell, I am the boss. It's early."

"You haven't answered my question. What for?"

The smile was locked in place. "Well, now, Sue Ellen, sweetheart. Remember how it was after we first got married. Those mornings. Seems to be we like to never got up and out of bed. Bed was the place to be, a real old-fashioned playground, you might say."

"And you'd like to crawl back in that playground right now?"

"I've got some mighty damp and dirty ideas to put to work, for your pleasure, sugar."

Her eyes flicked over to Kristin. "Your bedroom urges are so sudden, J.R. Inexplicable almost. And about as romantic as one of Jock's—breeding bulls . . ."

She left him standing there speechless as she dove gracefully into the pool. It was, he remarked to himself, a pisspoor way to start the day!

An hour later J.R. strode into the reception room of Ewing Oil, the great white Stetson sitting squarely on his head, his jaw equally square, his mouth firmed up and disapproving. One of his secretaries, a pleasant looking woman named Connie, recognized the expression. Don't cross the boss this morning, she warned herself, rising at his entrance, forgoing her usual morning smile, all business and corporate efficiency.

"Good morning, J.R. I've got the nighttime memos that were on the service and Wade Luce has called in twice already this morning."

"Can't talk to him. Too busy."

"So I said. He's on his way over."

"Damn that man. All right, move him in and out—a couple of minutes. If it goes over five, break in with an overseas call. Saudi Arabia will do."

"You used the sheik last time Mr. Luce was here. What about Indonesia? That—"

"Yes. Excellent. Indonesia fits in with everything." He checked out the empty desk with the covered typewriter. "Louella not in this morning?" A hint of displeasure lined his voice.

Connie hesitated. "You did say she could have the day off, J.R."

"Did I? Why'd I say that?"

"So she could shop."

"Oh, yes, I think I remember now."

"She's getting married."

"So she is. Well, find out if she's picked out a pattern and order something nice from Neiman in silver. Brides still like silver these days, don't they, Connie?"

"Yes, sir."

"Do it then." He went into his office and deposited his attaché case on the desk, sailed his hat onto the leather sofa. He began going through his mail. Something caught his eye and he reread it, scowling. "Didn't need *that* today!" he muttered.

The intercom buzzed and he flicked a switch. "What is it, Connie?"

"Jordan Lee just came in."

"Damn. Doesn't the man understand the meaning of the word appointment? All right, send him through." He turned back to the letter in his hand.

Jordan Lee appeared. Not as large a man as J.R., he had the well-padded appearance of one who dined well and had for many years. Yet beneath the flab of riches and easy living was a steely structure of a self-made man: tough, aggressive, without a great deal of feeling.

"Morning, J.R."

"Morning, Jordan. What brings you here without warning?"

"Sorry to bust in on you this way." He clearly was not sorry. "You seen that O.L.M. notice yet?"

"I was just reading it."

"That Cliff Barnes is out of his mind."

"The man is out to ruin us oil people, Jordan."

"No way we can meet those emission standards at the Kilgore field."

"Barnes knows that. Which is why he's setting up these stricter requirements, the way he is."

"If he's trying to keep us out of those fields, he's sure as hell going to succeed, J.R."

"He's already succeeded, looks to me."

"Damn his eyes. I'd like to put a knife in his back."

"Seems like that's what he's doing to us."

"J.R., I can't speak for you, but I cannot afford to fight the O.L.M. in court for five years on this one. My outfit hasn't got the capital and my stockholders ain't gonna sit still for an end to dividends and capital growth both over such a long period."

"Seems to me we have no other choice. Fight or go under, Jordan."

"Is that the best you've got for me, J.R.? Because if it is, I am pulling out of the cartel and you'll find that goes for Luce and the other boys in this thing, too. We have got to have that new oil, the higher prices, the quality crude. Way things are happening over in Arabia and all, no telling when supplies are just gonna dry up overseas. We have to find new sources."

"Tell that to Barnes."

"I have and he told me a few things."

"Such as?"

"Such as it seems it is Ewing Oil he's after. You and your daddy. I got the feeling—though he never said as much—that if we was to form a new cartel without you, J.R., O.L.M. would climb down off'n our backs."

"But not mine?"

Jordan Lee lifted his thick shoulders, let them fall. "That's the only way Barnes is gonna leave us be, J.R."

"Now, Jordan, I want you to consider what you are saying. Don't do anything hasty, anything you'll regret." He pushed the intercom. "Connie, would you ask brother Bobby to step in her a minute?"

"Yes, sir."

Jordan Lee spoke regretfully. "J.R. don't think you're gonna pull any rabbits out of a hat on this one. There ain't no rabbits in your hat this time. Matter of fact, the way I see it, you ain't even got much of a hat."

"You wouldn't want to sell Ewing Oil short, Jordan. Or

understimate my feats of legerdemain. Ah," he said standing, "here's Bobby."

"Morning, J.R." Bobby said. "Hey, Jordan, how you been, pardner? Long time no see."

"You're looking good, Bobby. How's your daddy?"

"Just fine."

"Say hello for me, and to your momma, hear."

"Will do, Jordan. Now how can I help you fellas?"

Jordan edged toward the door. "I'll leave you boys to talk this over. Remember what I said, J.R. Time's running out on some of us. And we can't afford to go under."

Jordan waved and departed, closing the door behind him.

"What was that all about?" Bobby inquired, taking a chair across from his brother, heaving his booted feet up to the edge of the big desk.

"Bobby, I got to level with you, little brother. The way things are happening right this minute around here you just ain't pulling your weight."

Bobby frowned. His tanned athlete's face seemed to shift and alter, less angry than confused, less resentful than annoyed. He had lived in close promimity to J.R. all of his life and had never gotten quite used to the hostile ways of the other man. Attack and destroy, undercut, subvert, deal from the bottom of the deck, or from out of his sleeve. Always the wheeler-dealer, always on the edge of disaster, always prepared to cut an enemy or destroy a friend. It was an approach to life and business Bobby had never found to his taste.

"J.R." he drawled, struggling to maintain his emotional balance, "say what's on your mind. I make a very rapt audience." He smiled to take the edge of his words.

"Okay, here it is then. You are going to have to step up the pressure on your people up in Austin. Those senators are sitting around with their thumbs up their asses doing us absolutely no good. That damned committee of theirs ain't shoving the appropriate legislation through nearly fast enough. Tell 'em to get in gear and I do mean today."

Bobby chose his words with care. "J.R., the wheels grind slowly in politics, you know that."

"To hell with that. We need action."

"I was talking to our friends yesterday. They know what our needs are. They understand the urgency of the situation. They are trying, J.R. Nothing more to be done."

"Horsecrap, little brother. There's always something more to be done. Another palm to be greased. Another back to be scratched. Another weak sister to be shored up."

"Bribes are not my style."

"Maybe if you spent a little more time in the state capitol you could light a fire under those boys."

Bobby let his breath out slowly. "J.R., do I have to remind you? I have responsibilities here and at Southfork. I have a ranch to run. . . ."

J.R. was on his feet, prowling restlessly. He reminded Bobby of a big mountain cat, tawny, sleek, and more dangerous than he looked. "Nothing," J.R. gritted out. "Nothing is more important to a Ewing than plucking that damned brother-in-law of yours out of the Office of Land Management. Cliff Barnes is squeezing hard, you see, real hard. He is squeezing me and Daddy and Ewing Oil, which means you and Momma and even brother Gary, wherever the hell that one is. We are talking here about the family business."

"You surprise me, J.R. Remembering that it is the *family* business."

"What's that supposed to mean?"

"It means up till now you've been just as happy to have me out of the family business."

J.R. whirled around, finger pointing, body leaning in as if about to pounce. "You gonna let Barnes wreck everything I've worked for? All the years, the sweat, the money. You gonna let it all go down the drain?"

Bobby responded calmly. "I was under the impression Daddy had something to do with making Ewing Oil into what it is. Not to mention Momma, and my own little contributions . . ."

"Well, there you have it. Just what I was trying to get across to you—the family business. You gonna let us all down?"

"Damnit, J.R., why is it I always get he feeling you're working a game on me, trying to get me out of the way?"

"Little brother, you are becoming paranoid, as those shrinks say. I am simply reminding you, you just have got to keep the pressure on those lardass senators up in Austin, make them do the job for us."

Bobby put his hands flat on the desk and pushed himself erect. "I'll do what I can, J.R. But remember, the name is Bobby Ewing and I do things my own way."

J.R. was grinning. "Why, of course you do. And that'll be good enough, I just know it will, little brother."

He waited until Bobby had left before glancing at his watch. He went to the closet and pulled out a black vinyl-covered attaché case. It felt solid in his hand, heavy with the important goods of life. He went out into the reception room.

"I'll be back after a while, Connie," he told the secretary.

"But, J.R., you've forgotten about Wade Luce. He should be here any minute."

He swore softly. "Tell him to wait, this won't. Otherwise he can try me again." He marched out without another word, the Stetson squarely perched on his head, his jaw tilted bravely and aggressively, a man of important concerns, a man in charge of his world, right smack on top of things.

J.R. strolled with increasing discomfort alongside Alan Beam down the broad corridor of North Park Mall past fresh flowers, to the strains of a Tchaikovsky symphony. J.R. was oblivious to both, his eyes searching ahead for a familiar face. Any familiar face. He did not want to be seen with the young lawyer.

"Goddamn, Alan," he finally said, "you sure do pick the god-awfulest places for us to meet."

"Nothing so anonymous as a crowded public shopping mall, J.R."

"You been watching too many of those detective shows on TV. Half this town knows who I am on sight and the other half's heard of me. Can't you get it through your head, we are not supposed to be known to each other."

"J.R., I know what I'm doing."

"You byGodbetter know. Else I'll skin you alive, boy."

There were times when Alan thought J.R. was funny. What he failed to understand was that J.R. Ewing was never intentionally funny, didn't see much humor in the world, didn't enjoy people laughing at him. But Alan Beam was swelled up with a sense of his own growing importance, failing to realize how much he depended on the good graces of men like J.R.

"There is nothing to worry about," he said in the syrupy tones of a new mother cooing to her infant.

J.R. glanced his way. "Let me worry and you do things right. Do things right and all my concerns will be in vain. And both of us will be happy. Let's get to the Barnes for Congress campaign."

"We're getting nibbles. It looks good."

"Not from my perch. That man is costing Ewing Oil a fortune. Light a fire under his ambition, Alan, get him on the road to Washington."

"These things take time, J.R. Patience is in order."

"I have no time and less patience."

"We have to convince Cliff that he has a solid shot at a seat in Congress."

"That's what I'm paying you for."

"He has to believe that it's worth quitting O.L.M. in order to make a run for it."

"You'll convince him, I'm sure of it. And when you do he'll throw O.L.M. away like an old used candy wrapper. Just make him think he can be elected. That's what that boy is after, a seat in Washington. And after that the Senate, who knows the White House one day. Plant the bug in his ear, Alan."

Alan felt a tide of uneasiness sifting under his skin. He wasn't sure J.R. grasped the full possibilities of the plot. "J.R., we've got to be careful. Nobody actually wants to elect Barnes to Congress."

J.R. put on his most terrible smile. "Not if you enjoy practicing law in Texas, they don't."

"We are treading a very thin line here."

J.R. tapped the vinyl attaché case. "What's in here will make the cheese a little more binding."

"I'm not sure I get it."

"You don't, Barnes does. This case is full up with hundred dollar bills, Alan. Contributions from all of Cliff Barnes' secret admirers, all those hundreds of little people who just can't wait to vote him into Congress."

"Are you serious?"

"If you believe I am, then you're not the man for me."

"You scared me for a minute."

"This money is all Ewing money. What's here will buy a lot of posters, take care of a lot of rallies, maybe even be a little left over. Make sure to use it all, Alan. Don't get sticky fingers."

"Oh, you can trust me, J.R."

"Sure I can."

"I know how to use that money, how to make the most of it."

"Do whatever you have to do with it. And make sure you get some crowds to stomp it up for Cliff Barnes. And pay for everything, everyone, in cash. . . ."

"Cash on the line. I get it. No records. No receipts."

"No trail back to me."

"Of course not. When we get a little enthusiasm cranked up, I'll be able to raise money elsewhere."

J.R. stopped and took Beam's slender bicep in hand and squeezed. "Boy, use your head. I want Barnes totally dependent on Ewing funds for his campaign. Totally. Nobody else gets in on this one."

Pain rippled down into the lawyer's elbow and he was relieved when J.R. turned him loose. "A solid campaign will use up a great deal of money, I'm afraid."

"Exactly. And once Barnes is committed—once he resigns from O.L.M. and takes this thing seriously, all funds will stop flowing. The money tree will die. The campaign will have only one way to go. No congressional seat for that smug, smarmy little shitkicker. No office in Washington. No power. No job. No O.L.M. Nothing . . ."

"I get it."

"Good. Glad you're finally tuned in. Because when I get Barnes down and out, bleeding from the eyes, nose and ears, I will then bring my boot down on that little insect and absolutely, positively wipe . . . him . . . out. . . ."

Listening, Alan Bean went cold. He had never been as afraid for himself as he was for Cliff Barnes at that moment.

That night the Ewings gathered around the dining room table in a farewell dinner for Patricia Shepard, mother of Kristin and Sue Ellen. A sharp-featured, perky woman in her middle years, she was declaring her excitement over the upcoming trip to Europe.

"I envy you," Miss Ellie said. "It's been a long time since Jock and I have taken such a trip."

"That's a fact," Jock agreed. "As soon as we get these

piddling little business problems of ours straightened away, maybe we ought to do just that—take an extended trip, a real holiday."

"Oh, yes," Mrs. Shepard enthused. "There is so much to share in Europe. Music, art, ballet, all those ancient churches and ruins . . ."

"Personally," Jock said, "I prefer new buildings myself."

Mrs. Shepard wasn't sure whether or not to be amused. She never could tell the rancher's intentions from that dry, plains voice, that never-changing outdoorsman's face. She decided a warm smile would suffice. "Mr. Markward loves to travel."

"He sounds like a mighty unusual farm machinery man. . . ."

"He is quite unusual. We are strongly drawn to each other. . . ." Her eyes went quickly round the table. "Spiritually attracted," she amended.

Lucy, from her place near the far end, giggled. "I am so relieved that it isn't physical, Mrs. Shepard. Or anything else weird and gross."

Mrs. Shepard, not sure how to take that, ignored the comment. Miss Ellie, having no doubts, took Lucy's hand in her own, squeezing gently. "Now, Lucy . . ."

"Well," Lucy went on, eyes round and innocent, her manner disingenuous. "I bet Mrs. Shepard is relieved, too. I mean, traveling can be such a trial, can't it? If a man *expected* something of a woman—well, it would be simply unbearable, I should think."

"Lucy," Miss Ellie repeated.

"Yes . . ." Mrs. Shepard said, with forced cheerfulness. "Oh, I do wish you would come with us, Kristin. But of course you have plans of your own."

"What plans are those?" J.R. said, trying not to seem too curious.

Lucy watched and listened with heightened interest. Hers was a skepticism born and shaped by hard experience and she tended to see other people's actions in a clear and unencumbered manner, missing very little, misreading nothing.

"I might go back to Sante Fe," Kristin said. "Or perhaps California. It depends."

"On who?" Lucy put in sweetly.

Kristin stared at the little blonde, then away. "Time will tell," she murmured.

Bobby, listening to all this, found his mind reaching back to a time when he and Kristin had been alone before his marriage to Pam. How lovely she had looked that night, and how desirable. Yet something had put him off, made him hesitate and wonder. Again that same sense of wariness took hold of him. Kristin was after something, but what?

"I can understand your desire to go back," he said. "All your friends are back there."

Pam, seated next to her husband, reacted in an almost identical manner. She felt a surge of animosity toward Kristin and an undertow of guilt about it.

"I'm sure you'll want to see your friends again before you leave for architectural school," she said. "That's going to be very exciting for you, Kristin. . . ."

"I suppose so. But I wonder if I've missed something. Maybe I'm rushing into this architecture thing too fast."

Mrs. Shepard spoke up. "My idea of what a girl like Kristin should do is to get married. To the right man, of course. That's my favorite dream, to have my baby married and well taken care of."

J.R. smiled at Mrs. Shepard. "I'm sure that dream will be fulfilled one day soon, Patricia. As lovely as Kristin is, what young man could resist?"

"I'd even settle for some kind of a mundane job until next term," Kristin said.

"A job!" Mrs. Shepard seemed surprised.

Sue Ellen avoided her sister's eyes, avoided her husband's eyes. In the silence of her mind she anticipated J.R.'s response. She was not disappointed.

"A job," he said thoughtfully. "You really mean that, Kristin?"

"I really do, J.R."

Sue Ellen put a wide-eyed look on her face. "Why, J.R., I'll bet you can find some way to help little Kristin out. That way we can keep her around Dallas for a while longer, and won't that be nice for everybody?"

"A job," J.R. said again. "I'm sure something can be worked out. Hey, Bobby, what do you think? Maybe Kristin can fill in for Louella on a temporary basis. My secretary is getting married," he said to Mrs. Shepard.

Bobby wanted to object, to put an end to it. All at once he found the prospect of having Kristin in the office every day disturbing, an alien influence that was bound to cause unrest and conflict. "I'm sure Kristin would find office work dull and much too confining," he said.

Kristin brightened. "From what I've heard around here, Ewing Oil sounds fascinating."

"Yes," Sue Ellen said, "fascinating."

"Well, then," J.R. said, "Want to give it a try?"

"I'd love it, J.R. If it's all right with Bobby and your father."

"Makes me no never-mind," Jock said.

"Bobby?" J.R. said.

"Suit yourself, J.R."

J.R. looked over at Kristin's mother. "How about it, Patricia, darlin', that sound good to you? Have your little girl spend her summer with us. Under the watchful eye of big sister and all the Ewings."

"If that's what Kristin wants. But where would she live? I've already surrendered the lease on my apartment in Dallas."

Lucy couldn't stay out of it. "I don't think Kristin would be happy out here on Southfork. Much too isolated for someone so worldly and sophisticated."

"I wouldn't want to impose," Kristin said carefully.

J.R. smiled one of his broadest, most reassuring smiles. "Don't you worry about that. I think Ewing Oil can scare up someplace fit and proper for Kristin to stay in. What do you think, Daddy? The Oakside condo? That's available."

"Sounds good to me, son."

"Kristin, there you are," J.R. said. "Looks like you have a place of your own right in Dallas proper."

"My," Mrs. Shepard said, as if unable to accept what was taking place. "I don't know. It's all so fast. I'm grateful, but it's all so fast. Sue Ellen, what do you think? Is Kristin doing the right thing?"

All eyes shifted over to Sue Ellen. She measured her words, issuing them deliberately. "I am sure that Kristin knows exactly what she is doing. As always."

J.R. leaned back in his chair. "There," he said expansively. "Everything's settled. Kristin, you start work for me tomorrow."

"Oh, J.R.," Kristin enthused. "I don't know how I'll ever thank you."

Lucy was about to speak again when Miss Ellie squeezed the girl's hand. Lucy clamped her mouth shut. After all, she too was a Ewing and had learned early how to recognize a danger signal when it was flashed.

Later that same night, Mrs. Shepard and Kristin had an opportunity to talk privately. Kristin listened attentively. She had learned that though her mother was not a direct woman, there was always a clear message delivered in what she had to say. Kristin had also learned that even if her mother was not truly supportive, she provided strong guidance in matters that were practical and ultimately rewarding to a young woman struggling to find her direction in an essentially hostile world. Patricia Shepard, Kristin had discovered, never permitted emotional litter to slow her forward path.

"J.R.," Mrs. Shepard began, over hot chocolate and a last cigarette, "is such a fine man. The way he stands behind Sue Ellen, though lately that can't have been easy for him. Someday, Kristin, you're going to find a man like that yourself. If you're lucky."

Luck, Kristin had long ago decided, had nothing to do with it. "I think it's possible, Momma."

Mrs. Shepard grew reflective. "I'll be leaving tomorrow and you'll be entirely on your own. I know I can trust you to always remember the things I taught you. Be alert to the right opportunity. Life offers only a certain number of such chances and it is vital, *vital*, Kristin, that a woman take advantage of them."

"Don't fret about me, Momma. I remember *everything* you taught me."

Mrs. Shepard spoke slowly, resonantly, sounding an echo of importance, conveying a message that went beyond the word alone. "Then, wherever I am, I'll be relaxed knowing you could never do anything which might harm your sister. I'm worried about Sue Ellen, you see. Keep an eye on her and keep me informed."

"I feel exactly the same way, Momma. I don't think Sue Ellen is doing too well with J.R."

Mrs. Shepard glanced sidelong at her youngest daughter. There was so much of herself in Kristin, and so much more that she neither understood nor was particularly fond of. Kristin had always been older than her years, wiser than her experience, more willing to take subterranean and secret risks than her mother or her sister.

"Sue Ellen may be a little depressed, remember. That often happens after giving birth. But if it turns out she's not entirely happy with the kind of life J.R. has to offer . . ."

Kristin broke in. "Above all, we do want Sue Ellen to be happy."

"We can give her love and support. But if that is the case—well, she'll need to make a new life elsewhere. I would certainly miss having a son-in-law like J.R. I never met a man who enjoys the chase as much as he does . . . almost more than winning."

Kristin examined the chocolate liquid in her cup. "Mother, you let me take care of J.R. Ewing."

"Yes, I will do that. Whatever you do, I know it will be right for all of us, Kristin." Mrs. Shepard laughed, as much in relief as in good humor. "There, don't look so serious, can't have my little girl developing frown lines."

Kristin wore a solemn expression. But her eyes gleamed with the joy of anticipation, the look of the hunter closing in on his prey. "Trust me, mother. I'll never let you down."

Of that, Mrs. Shepard had no doubts.

With the drapes closing out the morning light, the conference room in the offices of Ewing Oil took on a more intimate aspect, the paneled walls less distant, the expensive modern furnishings less forbidding. At one end of the sleek coffin-shaped conference table an automatic slide projector had been set up, sending its conical beam of light the length of the room to splash vividly against a portable screen. A beach scene, tranquil, colorful, the waters smooth, the sands white and sloping gradually toward a line of palm trees. Only a couple of bathers could be seen.

J.R., standing behind the projector, gave a running commentary as slide after slide clicked into place. "As you can see, boys, the beaches are wide enough for our on-shore base. Plenty of room to set up—repair shops, supply dumps, emergency medical rooms, the works. Here's another view. I want to stress to you that there are no off-shore winds in this location and the seas are mild and shallow almost all year round."

A click and a new image slid into view. A lantern-jawed

man in a military uniform. "This is the ultimate leader of the country, boys. The man to do business with, a man you *can* do business with. He is determined, powerful and ambitious. He is someone we can deal with and depend on."

Another click and the light beam faded away, the room lights came up, and the other men around the conference table shifted around to face J.R.

"I tell you, men," he said, "That's a place to be drilling. Better'n anything we have going for us in Texas."

Jordan Lee shook his head. "I don't know, J.R. Southeast Asia's a long way away."

"Going to be bigger than Mexico," J.R. said. "I am doing you boys a favor by letting you in."

Wade Luce smiled mirthlessly—a lean, hard man who looked as if he could do a solid day's labor even today. "Easy to understand you'd want to spread the risk. I'd do the same, J.R."

J.R. kept his manner affable. "There's no risk, Wade, I want you boys to read the geologic reports on this. Study all the information I've gathered. You know me, I'm thorough, I'm slow, and my instincts are never wrong."

Luce shook her head. "Let's lay it on the line: the rest of us are doing just fine right here in our own backyard."

Andy Bradley agreed. "We don't have any problems with the Office of Land Management, J.R. 'Ceptin' when we get too cozy with Ewing Oil. That's when the shit hits the fan, J.R."

The three men broke up into table-pounding laughter, their humor not shared by J.R. He waited for them to quiet down. "Boys, the profits are going to be fantastic."

"If there are profits," Jordan Lee said.

"There's no sky on this one," J.R. said.

Luce nodded. Let's put it this way, we're actually doing you a favor by not going in. Ewing Oil gets to keep it all."

"If," Bradley added, "you can lay hands on that kind of financing."

Jordan Lee leaned forward. "Besides, unlike Ewing Oil, we are all getting top dollar for our product. There's such a thing as having too much oil, as the A-rabs are finding out. Wouldn't want to kill off the golden goose, now, would we?"

Again that raucous laughter, edged with satisfaction

that the joke was on someone else. J.R.'s mind leapfrogged ahead to alternative plans and plots; he hadn't come into this meeting with only one ace up his sleeve. Without warning the laughter expired and attention shifted. J.R. looked around. Kristin had appeared—according to his earlier orders—with a tray of drinks, an ice bucket, and a bottle of Jack Daniels.

"Guess the little celebration I'd planned will turn into a condolence party instead. You boys are getting mighty cautious in your old age. Don't any longer sniff out a bonanza even when it's right under your noses. Well, it's your loss."

If anyone was listening, he gave no sign. All attention was riveted on Kristin as she placed the tray on the conference table, her low-cut peasant blouse falling forward.

"Drinks, gentlemen?" she offered. "Mr. Bradley . . . ?"

Bradley raised a finger as if to identify himself. "Guilty as charged, sugar."

Kristin passed him a glass.

"Mr. Lee?"

Jordan's fingers lingered against hers as he reached for the glass. She smiled warmly at him.

"Just the way I like it," he mumbled.

"Mr. Luce . . . ?"

"Loosey-goosey," he crowed.

Her smile widened. "You said it, I didn't."

"Fast and bright," Luce said. "What's your name, darlin'?"

"Kristin." She bestowed a last smile on each of them, and withdrew without urgency.

"Christ," Jordan Lee breathed. "J.R. you sure must know something about more than just drilling for oil. That is the real goods, I kid you not."

"Keeping that on a string, J.R.?" Luce said. "I give you credit, man."

"Boys," J.R. said cheerfully. "I don't know where your minds are, but that is my wife's sister."

"I know where my mind is," Jordan said into his drink.

"That sweet young thing can park her shoes under my bed any time she likes," Luce said.

"Amen," Andy Bradley echoed.

They were laughing again, enjoying themselves immensely. None of them noticed that J.R. was staring at the door through which Kristin had departed, thinking furiously ahead.

Fort Worth sits at the western end of the swollen urban parallelogram that Texas people call Metroplex. Eleven counties, three million people and uncounted numbers of beef steers, plus the Dallas Cowboys and a major league baseball team.

Fort Worth is smaller than Dallas, not nearly as aggressive, not so brash, built mainly by cattlemen whose elegant Victorian mansions still dominate the city. It is a city of industry and memories and culture, with a quartet of major museums. Fort Worth is a city that grew up with the railroads, and locomotive whistles still punctuate the air day and night, a shrill ode to a fading American past.

None of that was on J.R.'s mind as he entered the Kimbal Art Museum. For that matter, his interest in great art was minimal, too, and he ignored the splendor of El Greco and Tintoretto, Matisse and Rembrandt and more that lined the walls of the galleries. As usual, business occupied J.R.'s thoughts. He was standing in front of a magnificent Goya, his back turned, when he spotted the man he was waiting for.

"Afternoon, J.R.," Loyal Hansen said. He was a small, neat man carefully tailored so as to remain unobtrusive and unforbidding. Hansen went through life offering assurances, guarantees, promises that could be kept. He offended no one, disappointed no one, and therefore was immensely valuable to a variety of persons around the world interested in profit before all else.

"Walk with me, Loyal."

They moved slowly along, paying no mind to the superb and invaluable works of art that marked man's glory through the ages. "Wanted to pick a place no one could overhear," J.R. said. "No possibility of eavesdropping or bugs."

"I appreciate your caution."

"As I told you over the phone, Loyal. I am definitely interested in the situation."

"Yes, I understand. However, there's something I must say—these people I represent, they are of another culture. When they see a group like yours come apart, they wonder why. They grow uneasy."

"Sure they do. So you just get on the horn and tell them Ewing Oil's so high on their country and its prospects that Ewing Oil has decided to go it alone."

"Alone! Does that mean you're not putting together a new syndicate?"

"You ain't hard of hearing, are you, Loyal?"

Hansen's jaw flexed. He glanced over at his companion. "You have any idea how high you're going to bid?"

"As high as I have to."

"You have that kind of financial liquidity available?"

"When it's needed, I'll have it."

"I hope so. Is there anything else, J.R.? I have appointments in Houston this evening."

"Hell, yes, there is. Ewing Oil expects to beat all competition in this matter, Loyal. Expects to put in the highest bid."

"Good luck to you, J.R."

"Exactly how high would you estimate that will have to be?"

"For Heaven's sake, J.R., those bids are sealed. I wouldn't know. . . ."

"I'd certainly appreciate having that kind of information. . . ."

"Look here, J.R.," Hansen said with surprising force. "I am a businessman not a—"

"Now, simmer down, Loyal. No need to get your water hot. Ain't asking you to break the law. Ain't asking you to betray your principles. But you are an expert in these matters. What would you give as your best estimate . . . ?"

"It could only be a guess."

"But an informed guess. The guess of a man who knows how things are done, how they get done. Listen here, Loyal, if Ewing Oil should win these leases we're going to need consultants. Do you know what we pay consultants? By the barrel, man, and that adds up. That's more'n you'll wrangle from anyone else."

Hansen struggled with his conscience and his financial ambitions; it was not much of a battle. "I'm not saying I know anything I shouldn't know . . ."

"Just a guess . . ."

Hansen brought out a memo pad and scratched a number on it, handed the sheet to J.R. "This is an opinion, a consultant's opinion."

J.R. sucked in his breath. The figure was much higher than he'd anticipated.

"The bidding has been fierce, J.R. That number could be low by as much as twenty percent. You want my advice, you'll top that by a wide margin." He snatched the scrap of paper from J.R.'s hand and tucked it into his pocket. "I'll be leavin' now."

J.R. let him go without another word. He'd gotten what he came for.

Two hours later J.R. was ushered into the office of the president of the Cattleman's Bank. Vaughn Leland, a contemporary of J.R.'s, but with the soft pale look of a man who spent almost all his time indoors, came out from behind his desk to shake hands. He invited J.R. to make himself comfortable and did the same. He arranged his face in a pleasant mode, allowing very little to show.

"I'm glad you called, J.R. Always a pleasure to hear from you."

"This is no friendly visit, Vaughn. I told you over the phone what I'm after."

Leland placed a hand on a thick folder on top of his desk. "I've been going through this. As you know, the Cattleman's has financed most all the Ewing ventures since you took over executive responsibilities, J.R. We have always been most proud of that association and believe it's been profitable to us both. In the long run—"

"Jesus H. Christ, Vaughn!" J.R. burst out. "You delivering a commencement address or turning me down? Which?"

Leland was uncomfortable with the role he had been thrust into and it showed. "Southeast Asia's not our field of expertise, J.R. The bank won't take the risk. Even if I personally approved . . ."

"What the hell do you mean—*even!* Vaughn, you are talking to J.R. Ewing."

"J.R.," Leland was pleading for understanding, "even if I did approve, the Loan Committee would certainly turn down the request. You know how bankers are."

J.R. shook his head like an angry predator brushing aside a swarm of offending insects, hardly dangerous but definitely annoying. "It's kind of late in the day for you to talk to me like I was some kind of new customer begging for a auto loan or some such as that. I am Ewing Oil,

Vaughn. And practically speaking, *you* are the Loan Committee."

Leland's mouth drew down and his eyes shifted, tacit admission that J.R.'s words had hit the mark. When he spoke, it was in his most remote banker's voice, flat, lifeless, the echo of hard cash in every dry syllable. "You told me Seth and Jordan and the others would come in with you. Without them, without their backing in real value and in cash, this will take all Ewing owns and then some."

"Doubt, Vaughn? Never thought I'd live long enough to hear doubt about Ewing from the lips of a man who we have befriended and assisted and supported like one of our very own. Yes, sir, it truly pains me. Coming from a man who we fostered all the way up from teller . . ."

"I'm sorry, J.R. I'm giving you an honest professional evaluation."

"I didn't come here for a Sunday school lesson," J.R. bit off. He leaned back, eyes closed, hands meeting prayerfully. "I am remembering, Vaughn. Of the many diverse and private ways in which your career has been advanced . . ."

"Now, J.R. . . ."

"The good men ruined . . ."

"That's not fair, J.R."

"The manner in which you have built a personal fortune of not inconsequential size. Do you recall Charley Donaldson?"

"He was weak, insignificant and I didn't . . ."

"Oh, yes, you did. And there are written records, somewhere or other. And what about Luke Yellowhand? He was one fine fella, best Indian I ever knew. Smart, strong, but too trusting of certain smooth-talking city types. Certain transfers of deeds that took place . . ."

"All right, J.R.! Dammit, our dealings in the past have always been based on mutual trust, and confidentiality."

"Always have been."

"I'll do what I can for you, J.R. But I can't promise . . ."

J.R. smiled that thin, frightening smile of his, his eyes still and without life. "Just get into the pit, buddy-boy, and suck up your gut. Do what needs doing."

"I've always done my best."

"Bust your butt, pal. Nothing less will do."

"J.R., why risk this? Maybe business isn't so great right this very minute, but why take the chance? Ewing Oil can survive bad times. Ewing Oil can survive the O.L.M."

"Survive!" J.R. seemed genuinely surprised. "What ever gave you the idea I was concerned about surviving? I intend to prevail, old friend. I am going to be the biggest and most powerful independent oil operator in Texas." The smile came fading into view, a disembodied shifting of his facial muscles without feeling or warmth. A chilling display. "You better remember that," he said. "Hear . . ."

Pam and Cliff strolled without purpose around Marsalis Park Zoo, stopping occasionally to look at the animals. They lunched on hot dogs, potato chips and Coke—to the casual onlooker two young, attractive people enjoying some time in the sun.

But Cliff was tense and disturbed and finally let it out. "I don't want to hear any more about it, Pam."

"Are you so angry you can't even discuss it?"

"Angry! Hell, yes, I'm angry. And disappointed, depressed and frightened, You're my sister."

"I thought you'd forgotten."

"If I'd forgotten, I wouldn't be so upset. You ask me to meet you and then you lay that kind of shocker on me."

"Cliff, I need my big brother at a time like this. There's no one else I can talk to about this."

"*Abortion,*" he snarled. "I even hate the sound of the word."

"Do you think I like the idea? What else can I do?"

"Have the baby."

She paused to watch two six-year olds chasing each other. I don't think I'm strong enough to do that. I've gone around and around with the idea until I'm dizzy. I can't think straight anymore. I don't believe I can deal with it if I give birth to a baby and it dies after only six months."

"You and I survived."

"But our little brother and sister did not."

"Have you told Bobby yet?"

"No."

"You mean he doesn't know you're pregnant?"

"Not yet."

"Does he know that you have a genetic disease that might kill any child you bear?"

"I tried to tell him. Either the timing was wrong or my courage failed. He wants a baby so much."

"I suggest you tell him, and soon, Pam."

"Why this sudden interest in Bobby's welfare? The Ewings are not your favorite family, to hear you tell it."

"Don't get defensive. We're not discussing politics or oil or money. We're talking about you and your baby. Bobby is the father and your husband."

"Oh, Cliff, I don't know what to do. Sometimes I want the baby so much I can weep. Then I'm willing to take the risk. Other times . . . What a mess it is."

"I wish I could help. This is something you and Bobby have to decide. Together."

"Yes, you're right. I must tell him. I must. It would be so much easier if everyone wasn't under so much pressure —pressure from you, Cliff."

"That's not going to stop until I break J.R. That's the only way I can get my own child back. If I'm lucky my son will live long enough to know who his real father is."

They went on among the families, the rambunctious children playing, each drifting back into private thoughts. Neither able to help the other.

As if some secret sensibility told him she was there, J.R. returned early to the ranch that afternoon. He found Kristin doing laps in the pool. A tall drink in hand he sat and watched until she climbed out of the water, sleek and wet, the black tank suit plastered to her flesh, concealing nothing. She preened in the still hot sunlight, angling her body to catch the westering light and at the same time displaying every facet of herself to J.R.

"I love Southfork," she said.

"We all do," he murmured.

"Everything's so beautiful here."

He examined her frankly. "Everything."

"This place has strength, like the Ewings."

"That appeals to you, Kristin? Strength, I mean."

She stared straight at him. "I appreciate strength in all human activities. Strength is a prerequisite to satisfactory living."

"Is that what you learned at college?"

Her smile was easy, confident, a trifle smug. "Among other things."

He stood up and went over to her. "Are you strong?"

"Better believe it, J.R."

"Strong enough to deal with me, Kristin?" He traced the still damp line of her jaw back to her throat and down.

"Strong as I have to be, J.R." She lifted his finger away as it reached for the swell of her breasts.

"There's something I want, Kristin . . ."

"Oh." There was the wide-eyed look of a little girl on her beautiful face.

"And something you want."

"Oh, there's a great deal I want, J.R."

"Maybe we can make a deal." He reached for her, pulled her close.

"Deals can be terminated, deals can fall through, deals can profit one person and ruin the other. I prefer an arrangement that leaves me secure in my person, able to move into the future with confidence and pleasantly rewarded in this lifetime."

"Sort of a lifetime annuity?"

"In a way."

He stroked her lithe, fleshless side and bent to kiss her. As his lips brushed against hers, she pulled away, disengaged.

"Kristin, you're acting like a schoolgirl."

She laughed over her shoulder. "I *am* a schoolgirl, remember!" She dived smoothly into the pool, sending a wall of water behind to leave him drenched and full of desire. . . .

Dark was beginning to descend over Southfork when Bobby came driving up. As he climbed out of his car, weary but glad to be home, Pam appeared on the patio. One look and she went running forward, clinging to him with unaccustomed force.

He embraced her and felt a slight tremor in her body. The clean scent of her filled his nostrils and wiped away the weariness. His love for this woman was total, powerful and never-ending, he was sure.

If anyone had asked, Bobby could not have defined that love. Nor accounted for it with a catalogue of exceptional qualities. Why this woman and no other? Why was he so strongly and completely committed to making his life with her, whether here at Southfork in luxury and wealth and power, or elsewhere without material well-being, scratching desperately for a living? He understood that as long as he and Pam were together his life would be full and rewarding in ways no words could describe.

"What is it, honey?"

A last shudder and she released him. "I missed you."

The explanation was sufficient. "I missed you, too."

"How was Austin?"

"Hectic, but I'm making progress. I think we're finally going to start seeing results against the O.L.M. I'm sorry, Pam. Your brother has chosen this path, making us enemies."

"He sees it differently."

"I'm sure he does." It was not a subject to be pursued without negative results and so he dropped it fast. "By the way, Dr. Krane's office phoned this morning before I left. Anything wrong?"

"No . . ."

"Your gynecologist. Does that mean something's right?"

She hesitated for a long beat. "I suppose so."

He studied her, and his face broke into a joyous smile. "You're pregnant!"

"I think so."

"Oh, my God!" He let out a cowboy yell and swept her off the ground, whirled her around. "That's fantastic!"

"Easy, mothers-to-be can't fly."

He placed her back down gently. "Why didn't you tell me before?"

"I wanted to be sure."

"That is wonderful, terrific, the best news I've ever heard. Let's celebrate. Get in that car, we are going out on the town, Pam."

"Bobby, there's so much to talk about. Dinner's almost ready and . . ."

"Forget dinner. The family'll never know we're gone. You're right, there's lots to talk about, and talk and talk and talk . . ." He planted a kiss on her mouth. "Let's go!"

"Bobby . . ." She resisted slightly.

"In the car, I said. In, before I'm reduced to using force on a pregnant lady. I've got to tell you, Pam, you've made me the happiest man in the world!"

She was of two minds. Longing to be alone and private

with her husband, to explain the situation and all its terrible ramifications to him; and to surrender to his mood, permit him to remain happy for just a little while longer. To experience his joy herself.

"All right, Bobby. You win."

But once in the car, she sat so he could not see the unsure, troubled expression in her eyes. None of this, she was afraid, could possibly come out well.

The next moning the family gathered on the patio for a buffet breakfast. Sue Ellen, displaying no interest in food, fingered a cup of half-drunk cold coffee. Miss Ellie watched with concern.

"Sue Ellen, can I heat that up for you?"

"No, thank you, Miss Ellie."

"Wouldn't you like some buttered toast, dear?"

"I'm just fine, Miss Ellie."

"Last night, at dinner, you hardly touched your food. Are you feeling poorly?"

"Just trying to lose a pair of unwanted pounds."

Lucy, trying to be helpful, said, "Maybe you need some exercise, Sue Ellen, How about a game of tennis?"

Sue Ellen's manner turned to ice. "If I need your advice, Lucy, I'll come knocking."

"Now wait a minute . . ." Lucy shot back.

"It's all right, Lucy," Kristin said. "You've got to understand that my dear sister's been through so much lately. She has to be allowed to hurt other people as retribution."

"Terrific," Lucy said, her good humor returning. "Now I've got both of you to put up with."

Jock, made gloomy by all this womanly squabbling, moved his scrambled eggs around with the tip of his fork. "Let's put a lid on it, ladies. A man's entitled to some peace and quiet over morning coffee."

"Jock's right," Miss Ellie said.

J.R., who found a certain amount of entertainment value in the caustic exchanges, was the first one to notice Bobby approaching.

"Ah, there you are, little brother. Figured you planned on sleeping the day away."

"Didn't think you cared, J.R."

"Can't do all the work around here by myself, now can I?"

Bobby ignored the comment. "I've got great news, folks."

Coming up behind him, Pam frowned, "Bobby . . ."

Bobby looped an arm around her, pulling her close. "I want everybody to know, especially my family. Pam's pregnant, everybody. There's going to be another baby on Southfork."

The family clustered around Pam, a babble of excited voices interspersed with kisses and hugs.

"I'm so happy," Miss Ellie said. "For both of you."

"Congratulations, son," Jock said.

"Thanks, Daddy."

Lucy put her arms around Pam. "You must be so excited."

"Yes, I suppose I am."

Lucy stepped back, eyes narrowed warily. Pam hardly acted like the happy mother-to-be.

"Well," Jock exulted. "Looks like Little John's going to have a playmate, J.R. Ain't that great news?"

J.R. found it difficult to generate much enthusiasm. "Yes, Daddy."

Sue Ellen worked her way to her husband's side. "A great day for the family, J.R., wouldn't you say? They're finally going to get what they've always wanted. A *legitimate* Ewing heir . . ."

J.R. glared at his wife, determined not to give her the satisfaction of a response. Somehow, he thought, somehow he was going to even the score with her. No matter who got hurt along the way.

Oakside Condominiums were a cluster of expensive townhouses and apartments set amongst rolling lawns and stands of tall trees, each one carefully placed for ultimate privacy and security. The complex included a complete gymnasium, a sauna, a whirlpool and two swimming pools at the center of it all. It was here that Ewing Oil kept an apartment for visiting business contacts, mainly oilmen coming from overseas. It was here that J.R. had arranged for Kristin to live during her stay in Dallas.

He ushered her inside and watched her sweep from room to room with girlish excitement.

"Oh, J.R. it is simply enchanting!"

"I'm glad you like it, Kristin."

"Like it! It is lovely. How long may I stay, J.R.?"

"As long as you want." He made a broad gesture. "You've got your own terrace for sunbathing, with or without clothes on, Kristin."

"Are you suggesting something to me, J.R.?" She giggled.

"I certainly am. Invite me anytime at all."

"Oh, you are naughty."

"I sure as hell do try."

She decided to change the subject. "When may I move in?"

"I'll have one of the ranchhands bring your things over in the morning. Meanwhile, I believe you'll find whatever you need for overnight. What with executives flying in and out, we keep the place pretty well stocked."

"I checked the kitchen, the fridge is packed with goodies."

"And so is the bar, darlin'."

"It is cozy."

"I thought you'd like it. Let me show you the rest." He led her into the bedroom. Furry white rugs, a chaise near the curtained doors leading to the terrace, silk sheets and a comforter on the king-sized bed, lots of polished mirrors. "Well—?"

"It is exotic," she cooed. She opened the nearest closet. "Oh, my, what have we here? Evening dresses, nightgowns, and in a variety of sizes. For business clients, J.R.?"

"In the oil business it pays to be in a position to return a favor now and then."

She came up on her toes and kissed him lightly on the lips. He enveloped her, mouth mashing down on hers, and she arched her belly against him. He responded at once, his groin grinding against her, pulling her tighter to him.

"You mustn't do this," she gasped.

"It's what I've been cravin' for a long time, darlin'. . . ." His hand rode roughly over one breast and then the other, fumbling with the buttons of her blouse. For an extended moment she allowed it and his fingers closed on bare flesh. She moaned and twisted away, backing off, adjusting her clothes.

"No, J.R. No!"

"Why not? Neither of us is a child. You feel the same way . . ."

"I am not after a one-night stand, J.R."

"Of course you aren't . . ." He hesitated. "Neither am I."

"That's what this would be, a one-night stand. With my sister's husband."

"Are you counting on me making promises?"

"I wouldn't do that, J.R. Not ever. It's just that—well, a girl needs a little time to make up her mind, to reflect, to let it all come to a boil. . . ."

That evoked a wide grin. "Well, all right. Just one thing. Don't take too long to reach your decision."

"It won't be forever, J.R."

"And when you do decide, darlin' . . ."

"Yes, J.R.?"

"Make sure it's the right choice."

He left without another word. Kristin shut the door behind him. Soon she dropped down on the great bed, kicking off her shoes, waving her arms and legs in the air, emitting cries of joy. This time everything was going her way. All of it.

J.R. pulled the Mercedes to the curb and strode across the plaza separating the sidewalk from the Ewing Building, almost unaware that it was dark, that the streets of downtown Dallas were, as usual, deserted. Inside the building, the check-in desk was empty, the security man off on rounds or stealing a quick smoke. Not that it mattered. Still, J.R. liked to get what he paid for and made a mental note to tighten security regulations. He rode the elevator up to his office.

The corridor was dark and empty, only the blood-red emergency lights glowing at the far ends. In the reception room, Vaughn Leland sprawled out in one of the sleek leather and polished steel Barcelona chairs, sucking on an unlit cigar.

"You're late, J.R." He looked haggard and worn, a man aging rapidly, displaying the strains of his job. Unlike J.R., Leland was always braced for defeat and failure. Unlike J.R., he never truly believed he belonged in his high station. Unlike J.R., he reveled in his past and feared the future.

"Let's go inside," J.R. commanded, leading the way.

Once in J.R.'s private office, Leland dropped onto the couch, a man whose strength had run out. It occurred to J.R. that Leland had energy and vigor enough for only a certain number of hours each day; after that, he was a dull and beaten fellow.

"You look terrible, Vaughn. Help yourself to a drink."

The banker shook his head, too weary to avail himself of the invitation. "Been a hard day, but I've got good news. The bank can swing it for you on that Asian offshore drilling deal of yours."

J.R. was pleased and he showed it. "That puts you a good two-three days ahead of the pace, as far as I'm concerned, Vaughn."

"There are still some loose ends, but what I did was put together a package—Cattleman's plus three other banks. Each one gets to handle a fourth of the pie."

A fragment of concern alerted J.R. to potential trouble. "I thought I'd be dealing with you, Vaughn."

"Basically you will be. But Cattleman's can't get it up by itself."

"Okay." J.R. conceded that he had run out of options. He needed that money, needed it now. "How high will they go for, in good American dollars?"

Leland filled his lungs with air. "One hundred million, flat out."

J.R. felt like hollering out his joy. He had expected the banks might squeeze him, give him seventy-eighty percent of his needs. Kill the deal with miserliness. Instead he was getting it all, five to ten million more than he might actually use. "That's not bad, Vaughn," he said without expression.

Leland grunted, scratched his ample belly, "The way I see it, J.R., you are going to need it all, looking down the long road, that is. Once the banks are into this, once they are on your hook, if you need a few extra points now and again I'm sure you can work them for it."

"This is a source of great satisfaction to me, Vaughn. Once again, you've justified my faith in you."

"Well, thank you for saying so, J.R. I appreciate that." He blinked and straightened up and some of the tiredness washed out of his face. "There is one other thing . . ."

J.R. felt his stomach muscles clench and his hands go cold. He recognized trouble when he heard it. "Oh," he said mildly, "what thing is that, Vaughn?"

"Just a formality, actually, business procedures . . ."

"Tell me about it."

"Under these circumstances of *special* risk . . ."

"Get to it, Vaughn."

"J.R., there is no need for alarm. I told you, a formality."

"Say it, Vaughn."

"Dammit, man, what if those wells don't come in? What if something goes wrong? You could lose everything and that means the banks would lose, too."

"I won't lose! Now what's the formality?"

"All right. The banks will put up the one hundred million but you are going to have to pledge two hundred thousand acres of prime real estate. . . ."

J.R. sucked in air. He hadn't anticipated *this*. His brain tilted and yawed, finally righted itself, began to function crisply. "You know the only such property I have—the Ewings have . . ."

"I know." Leland appeared to be in spiritual agony. "I can't help it, J.R. That's the deal. The others forced it on me. You are going to have to put up Southfork as security for the loan."

"Southfork! That's ridiculous! No way I can mortgage Southfork."

"Yes, you can. It's part of Ewing Enterprises and you are the president of the company. You have every legal right, every legal power . . ."

"And if I say no?"

Leland shrugged, the pudding face stiffening. "Say no and there will be no loan."

"Do you realize what you're asking? Southfork is my home. My family's home. I was born on that land. It's not a topic for discussion."

"I told you, they forced it on me. The other banks. This time my hands are tied."

"Find another way."

Leland stood up with a surprising finality to the pitch of his massive body. "There is no other way, J.R. Either mortgage Southfork or the deal is null and void."

J.R. stared for a long time at the banker. "All right," he said in a low voice edged with rage and spite. "Consider it done."

Leland went to the door. "I'll have the papers ready in the morning, J.R."

"Do that, Vaughn. And I want you to know, I am never

going to forget the way you handled this matter for me Vaughn. Never ..."

J.R. sat there in the semi-darkness for an hour after Leland left and never moved. His roiled emotions went from simmering hatred to a killing rage and back again, from self-pity and a wide-based suspicion of everyone he dealt with to flickering memories of his boyhood, returning again and again to one particular event of his past.

Jock had taken them bird hunting up in the hill country around Fredericksburg, both J.R. and Bobby, not yet adolescents. They had had a long satisfying day secreted in the blind at the edge of a wide, wild lake, each of them having bagged his limit in mallards. They were tired but happy as they sprawled around a campfire after a supper of bacon and beans and coffee and great chunks of Miss Ellie's homemade bread.

Jock was smoking, spinning tales of his young manhood spent driving the herds to the railhead. Or hunting for gold in the mountains up in Colorado. Or dropping holes in Texas earth in search of oil. There were stories of friends made and enemies conquered, of men who lived short, violent lives, of the insistent compulsion to keep looking for the Pot of Gold.

"Most men never found it," Jock had told them that night. "Most men never found whatever it was they were lookin' for. Most found more trouble than the lookin' was worth and lots of 'em died before they should've."

"Why'd they do it for, Daddy?" Bobby had asked. J.R. had no need to ask; he knew, he understood. Already in him was full-sized lust for riches and power, seeing them as confirmation of a man's reason for being, recognizing that with them came the greatest reward of all—the homage and respect of other men.

Jock had considered Bobby's question in the quiet of that hunter's night before answering. "A man needs a purpose in life, boys, a reason to leave his bedroll in the morning. Something worthwhile to do with hisself. Once upon a time a man went out into the jungle and tracked down his meat for the day, brought food home to his family. There's something of that early man in each of us, I reckon."

"Going after oil ain't just killing a day's meat," Bobby had answered.

Jock granted him that with a wry smile and a self-mocking grunt. "The bug gets to every man. You put away a little more'n you need and a little more after that. Pretty soon it gets to be a habit, accumulating things; more wells, more land, companies, money. Remember this, boys, money only buys the things money can buy."

"People respect you when you're rich," J.R. said.

"No. I reckon not. They shuffle their feet and let you believe they believe you're special and better. But you're not and they know better and so do you, if you're smart. They suck around and kiss your bottom trying to get some of your'n for theirselves. But respect—some of the poorest men I've known were some of those I respected most."

J.R. refused to accept that. But he said nothing.

"There's two things in life that matter most," Jock went on thoughtfully, as somewhere in the night a coyote yipped and another replied. "The family and a man's home, his land. A man has to be ready to fight to protect both of them, to keep them both safe and sound. After your family, boys, value the land above everything else, hear."

The land above everything else; J.R. had never forgotten that; no Ewing could.

J.R. parked the Mercedes in the parking lot outside the Handy Andy the next morning and watched the young housewives as they wheeled shopping carts full of groceries back to their cars. More byGodgood-looking women in Texas than anywhere in the entire world, he told himself. Hot damn, a man could spend all of his time sidling up to 'em, bringing 'em to heel, putting 'em down on their backs. Next to money, next to power, J.R. could think of nothing he enjoyed more than a sexy, ever-loving female.

The door on the passenger side opened and Alan Beam slid into place. He placed an attaché case across his knees and greeted J.R. briskly.

"You're late, Alan."

"I had a few things to clean up at the office."

"You'd best put your priorities in order, Alan. Ewing business first, remember that."

"Yes, sir."

"Now what have you got for me."

"Well, I'm putting together committees all over the district—Cliff Barnes for Congress committees. The Nelsons, the Funts, the Andersons, the Luellyns . . ."

"Spare me the roster of your successes. Just so long as you're getting the job done."

"Oh, I am doing that, J.R. What I'm doing is pulling a group of disparate people together, not too political, no individual with too much real clout, you understand. Grass-roots stuff. The little people."

"Fine, fine. What else?"

Alan brought some sketches out of the attaché case; designs for posters, bumper stickers, advertisements—

DRAFT BARNES

BARNES FOR CONGRESS

WIN WITH BARNES

"Yes, that's good. You're doing good work, Alan."

The younger man was puzzled. J.R. seemed preoccupied, without enthusiasm. Was he losing interest in the campaign? If so, it meant he'd be losing interest in Alan Beam and the lawyer had no intention of alllowing that to happen.

"Just wanted to let you know how your money was being spent . . ."

"Good, very good. Keep up the good work," J.R. said in dismissal.

It occurred to Alan on his way back downtown that he would have to be increasingly careful in his dealings with J.R. He was afloat in a flimsy vessel in a very dangerous sea full of potential deadly dangers.

The Columns was one of those restaurants that seemed to have been transplanted from a New England suburb to Dallas, losing nothing in the move. The walls were red brick, archways lending a sense of space to the various dining rooms. Old Tiffany lamps sent soft yellow light down to the black iron and marble tables and everywhere greenery was growing, plants by the hundreds. Along the walls, at the windows, on the floor and in tall stands, hanging from the beamed ceiling. Waiters—all young men, all handsome, all blonde and bright-eyed—in tight black trousers and equally tight white shirts, open at the neck. Pam was having lunch with her father, Digger Barnes.

They put aside their menus and she smiled at him. "You're looking good, Daddy."

"Feeling good." The grizzled visage displayed no good humor, the eyes alert, never still, as if expecting trouble. "Still on the wagon, if that's what you're thinking. And aim to stay there." He emptied his water glass and made a face. "Damned stuff'll rust a man's plumbling."

"It quenches the thirst."

"It's liquid, is all I can say for it."

"The fisherman's plate is very good here, Daddy."

"Maybe just a bowl of soup. Living with your brother, Cliff, all's I seem to do is lay around and eat. I gotta get back to work."

"The doctors told you to take it easy."

"Doctors! When they don't know what else to tell you they say take it easy. A man my age, working all of his life, there'll be plenty of time to take it easy when I'm dead and buried."

"That's still a long time off."

He made a skeptical sound back in his throat. "Can't say I like the way you're looking, daughter. Seems like you've got the weight of the world on your shoulders. What's the matter?"

She hesitated. With a forced smile, she said, "Daddy, I'm going to have a baby."

The feral glint went out of his eyes and that lined and pouched face broke into a wide and pleased grin. "Pammy! That is terrific news!"

"Is it?"

For a beat he failed to understand. Then it came to him: neurofibromatosis, the genetic disease he carried and was responsible for. She was afraid for her unborn child.

"Hell yes, girl it's good news. Pam, you don't want to get down on yourself. That damned doctor with his diagnosis of neuro-whatever it is . . ."

"Neurofibromatosis."

"Yeah. Look, honey, you let it get to you and you'll ruin everything. Look at it this way. I survived. Cliff survived. And so did you. Think positive, it's the only way."

"I'll tell you what I am thinking."

"What's that?"

"I am thinking about getting an abortion."

The word sliced right through all his defenses to some vital part of his being. All the years of hard work, the years of struggle and conflict, of fighting just to stay alive, were washed away. He felt empty suddenly, and helpless. Unnecessary. "Is that Bobby's idea? Damned Ewings got no respect for human life."

"No, Daddy. I haven't told Bobby about the disease."

"Well, maybe it's best you don't. It's all going to work out in time, you'll see."

"Daddy, my little brother and sister, it didn't work out for them."

Digger felt pangs of guilt as if he had been at fault, had deliberately murdered his own flesh and blood. "Don't dwell on that. It was a long time ago. Things are different now. Doctors know more. New drugs, new treatments . . ."

She took his hand. "I thought you were the one who didn't trust doctors."

"Sometimes," he said without much conviction, "a man has to put his trust in something else. Someone else. When life just gets to be a bit too much for him."

They sat for a long time, not speaking, each dealing with the specter of future terrors in the stillness of mind and conscience, each ultimately alone.

Vaughn Leland had sandwiches and coffee sent in for lunch and while they ate he and J.R. went over the notes and memos and legal documents that authorized the bank loans to Ewing Oil. J.R. read every word on every scrap of paper. Finally he pushed them aside and sat back.

"Looks okay to me, Vaughn. The arrangements are satisfactory. You pull all this together and run it over to Wiggen, of Wiggen and Leitner over in Forth Worth. . . ."

That provoked Leland's interest. "New lawyers. J.R.?"

"That's right. I'm not about to worry Daddy over this deal and you never know when Harv Smithfield might say the wrong thing at the wrong time."

A knock at the door drew Leland's attention and his secretary appeared. "Yes, Janet?"

"Phone call for Mr. Ewing. Line two, sir."

"Thank you, Janet." She withdrew and the banker extended the instrument to J.R. "It's all yours."

"Hello," J.R. said.

"It's Kristin, J.R."

"I thought I told you I wasn't to be interrupted here." The girl would have to learn, the apartment and any relationship they might have was one thing; work was an entirely different and separate matter. He would, given the time, straighten her out. "All right, what's so important?"

"Mr. Loyal Hansen called. Several times. He sounded anxious, said he had something important to tell you."

"Did he leave any kind of message?"

"Well, yes. Just that everything's okay. He said you'd understand. Is there anything I can do, J.R.?"

"Just concentrate on the filing I gave you. And by the way, Kristin, thank you." He hung up.

"Bad news, J.R.?"

"Good news, Vaughn. The leases are mine. The top bid. The loan can go through."

"Then, J.R., you better say a special prayer . . ."

"For a rich strike, you mean?"

"For Southfork . . ."

Kristin hung up the phone and sat at her desk thinking. The other secretary, Connie, was still out to lunch and the office was quiet, no one to bother her. She had dealt carefully with J.R., working him the way a skilled angler worked a trout on his line. But if J.R. was a fish it was of a strong, ruthless and cunning species. King of the sea. His instincts for trouble and danger were sharply honed and he allowed no one inside his head.

Kristin was fascinated by him in a hundred different ways, viewed him as the device by which she might make a rich and productive life for herself. But caution was in order. Caution and information. Information would provide her with strength, eventually with power. She could never expect to control J.R. but it might be possible to manipulate him into stances that favored her. For the time being she was in an advantageous position; J.R. still hungered to possess her sexually, still wasn't sure how she was going to react. Let him keep panting after her, sniffing around. There was no reason to let him believe she was easy, or that she wanted him even more than he wanted her. In the meantime, she might be able to assemble a dossier of facts and innuendos about J.R. Ewing that would one day prove profitable.

She gathered up a handful of letters that needed J.R.'s signature and went into his office. She began flipping through the papers on his desktop, opening drawers, looking for something that might be of eventual value. A single typewritten sheet caught her eye. It read:

ASIAN OIL DEAL

1. Leland—$100,000,000—

2. Hansen—payoff for bid approval

3. Southfork—???

She returned the paper to its place, certain she had acquired some vital information, if she could only decipher it. What, she wondered, did Southfork have to do with oil wells in Asia? She expected that in time she'd find out, she'd find out a great many things. And why not? She certainly held the right cards for the game she was in.

That night J.R. went to the Oakside Condominium. Kristin, wearing a thin negligee, admitted him, drinks already mixed for them both. She led him to the couch and raised her glass in silent toast. They drank and she leaned back.

He looked her over with considerable pleasure. She had never looked lovelier, he had never wanted her more. "You're a very provocative girl, Kristin. Seeing you in that little bit of pink lace gives a man ideas. . . ."

She smiled across her drink. "J.R., you can come well supplied with all sorts of ideas, without my help. That was a mighty long meeting you had today."

"You keeping a stopwatch on me?"

"Just missing your stimulating presence in the office is all."

"Did you give some thought to our last meeting?"

She ignored the question. "I have been thinking. Architectural school isn't all that much, at least not compared to the oil business."

J.R. grew restless. "I'm gratified to hear you say that, Kristin."

"Working with you, J.R., we have so much to share. That's what I find so exciting . . . secrets."

"Secrets! What secrets do we have, Kristin?"

"Not to worry, I won't tell."

"I believe you have a common trait with your sister, my esteemed wife, and that is an extremely vivid imagination."

"I said I wouldn't tell . . ."

He eyed her gravely, that terrible frightening smile twisting around his mouth. "What do you think you know that anyone would be interested in listening to, Kristin?"

"Oh," she said, elaborately casual, "There's the meetings with Mr. Leland, and with Mr. Hansen."

"I meet with lots of different people."

She knew she had to take a chance. "Not to mention the Southeast Asia deal. The hundred million dollars and—" She waited but he made no move to speak. "And Southfork . . ."

There was an indecipherable look on his face and a grudging admiration in his head. She was a sneaky shifty bitch, but much smarter than he'd given her credit for. She knew more than he wanted her to know and now was attempting to use that information against him. Or, if not against him, then for her own benefit. He marked up one minor victory for her side.

"You don't know anything," he said, apparently unruffled.

She gave him that. "You're right, I'm not sure what it's all about. It sounds so glamorous, so exciting, and so involved with lots and lots of money. I'm sure Bobby or Jock could figure it all out, if they knew about it."

"You fascinate me, Kristin. So beautiful and so tricky. Not many men would dare confront me this way. You're bright and courageous and tenacious, and slightly foolhardy. I appreciate the combination, it whets my appetite. Oh, yes, you are a devious bitch."

She laughed a brief brittle laugh. "Why, J.R., I thought you liked deviousness."

"What are you going to do with your new found knowledge?"

"Nothing."

"You're not going to tell Bobby, or my Daddy?"

"Of course not. Your Daddy might just remove you from Ewing Oil and where would that leave me?"

"Very clever girl . . ." He shifted closer to her and they kissed. His hands roamed over her body and she began to moan softly. "Here," he husked out, "hold me here . . ."

"Oh, J.R., what a man you are!"

"Let's go into the bedroom."

"I can't."

"The hell you say!"

"Soon, J.R., soon. When I'm ready I'll come to you, I promise. You won't have to ask. Not for anything. You'll see what I can do for you, what I can be for you. When I'm ready."

He straightened up, barely able to contain his anger. "And what am I supposed to do until then?"

"Oh, J.R., I have a great deal of faith in you," she murmured, stroking his cheek. "You'll think of something . . ."

PART V

The Ewings

TODAY

12

J.R. had given a great deal of thought to this move. His puppets had been allowed freedom enough to bring them to the point where each of them had begun to believe he was master of his fate. The time had come to yank hard on the operating strings, make them dance to his tune, to relearn the limits of their independence. What silly fools they all were, scratching and scuffling in vain attempts to make their own destinies when all the while J.R. was making the decisions that truly counted.

How easy it had all been. *Their* swollen dreams and lust for glory, *their* greed, their pitiful lunges toward power. Small people attempting to play with giants, unable to comprehend the true nature of the game, or what it took to win.

First Lucy. It was time that arrogant little twat was slapped back into line, put on warning for the years ahead. On, yes, Lucy was a Ewing by birth, by every moral and legal right. But she offended J.R. in so many ways and would eventually in her arrogance offer up a threat. Better to deal with her now, make her recognize how inadequate she was to her lofty ambitions, weaken her resolve and undercut her courage. By the time she was old enough, smart enough, experienced enough to cause him any real damage, J.R. expected to have her under tight control.

First Lucy. And then the others, falling like dominoes in a line. Not aware of how vulnerable each was, how inextricably attached to each other, how feeble their efforts to remain private and secret in their moves against *him*. He waited for the best opportunity and it came a few nights later when the family began gathering in the den just before dinner.

Lucy entered the room looking bright and cheerful and vulnerable. Intuitively J.R. moved to the attack. "Nice to have you home for dinner for a change, Lucy." He arranged a pleasantly bland expression on his face.

No less intuitive than J.R., Lucy recognized the hint of danger in his manner. She faced him, brow knitting, wondering what he intended. She didn't have long to wait.

"I've turned over a new leaf," she said, trying to be conciliatory. "I've dedicated myself to family life."

"That a fact!" he challenged.

"Oh, let the girl alone," Sue Ellen protested.

"Haven't raised my hand or voice against her," J.R. said reasonably, eyes fixed on the younger Ewing. "I am glad we are all together here because I have what I consider to be some very disquieting news. . . ."

"Can't it keep till after supper?" Miss Ellie said.

J.R. brought an envelope out of his pocket. When he had everyone's attention, he tapped the envelope with his thumbnail. "What's in here affects us all, the entire Ewing family, I do believe."

"Who do you mean to give pain to, J.R.?" his wife said.

"Stay out of this, Sue Ellen."

"It's me," Lucy heard herself saying. "It's me you're after. What a hateful human being you are, J.R."

"Now, Lucy," Jock rumbled uncomfortably. He was extremely fond of his young granddaughter but was aware of the gap that kept them apart. More than age, there was an entirely different outlook on life. He didn't understand Lucy, and for that matter he found all young people a conundrum, difficult and vaguely unsettling. Perhaps he was getting old, product of a long lost time and place, no longer relevant, as they said. "J.R. don't mean you no harm."

"I have only the good of the family in mind," J.R. said. He withdrew half a dozen photographs from the envelope. "Know what these are, Lucy?"

She shivered with apprehension, said nothing.

J.R. glanced at each photograph in turn, drawing it out. He shook his head.

"What's all this about, son?" Jock said.

J.R. handed the pictures over. Jock looked at them. Bobby moved in to see them. Lucy stood frozen in place.

Jock scowled. "I don't approve of this kind of thing, J.R." His voice was deep in his chest, heavy with simmering anger. "These had best be destroyed."

"You know who those people are, Daddy?"

"Can't say's I do. Without my reading glasses— Don't care to see any more."

"I do believe supper's about ready," Miss Ellie said, trying to move them into the dining room. The effort failed.

"The girl," J.R. said, "is our own Lucy. Without any clothes on . . ."

"J.R.!" Miss Ellie exclaimed.

Sue Ellen muttered an oath.

Bobby took one hard, quick look at the pictures. "I do believe you've committed a breach of good taste here, J.R. Nobody else is to see what you have here."

"When I need your help, little brother, I'll come asking. There you have it—sweet, innocent little Lucy in a compromising position with a man . . ."

"You filthy bastard . . ." Lucy said.

"Watch your language, young lady," Jock said. "Who is the man?"

"Alan Beam," J.R. said.

"You're sure?" Jock said.

"No doubt about it. You intend to deny it, Lucy?"

"How did you get those pictures?" Lucy said, voice unsteady.

"First, what have you got to say for yourself?"

"There doesn't seem to be anything I can say. I didn't know about the pictures. I would never—"

"There they are," J.R. said harshly. "Undeniable in what they present. You and Beam in a disgusting display. You've been seeing him on the sly—"

"On the sly! No, it's been open and above-board."

"Who did you tell about it? Who did Beam tell? No member of this family knew about this relationship—if that's what you want to call it."

"Why are you doing this, J.R.?"

"I am a Ewing. The family must be protected."

"By destroying Lucy?" Sue Ellen said.

"Shut up, Sue Ellen, You play no part in this." He brought his attention back to Lucy. "All these nights you claimed to be studying at your friend's house—Muriel, I believe her name is—you were with Beam, in his apartment. Doing ... *this* ..." He cast the photos onto the coffee table as if they had scorched his fingers. "You make me ashamed, Lucy. You have shamed us all."

"Is that right, Lucy?" Miss Ellie said quietly. "When you were supposed to be studying, is this where you were, with this man?"

"Most of the time, Miss Ellie."

"So we add lying to your other traits," J.R. said.

"What made you feel you had to sneak around?" Jock said. "Don't you trust us? After all, some of us were young once, too. We might have been sympathetic, supportive, even. If you gave us a chance."

"Oh, no," J.R. broke in. "She couldn't be open about it, and with good reason. This Alan Beam, a worthless, gold-digging opportunist. Yes, indeed, our Lucy had to sneak, had to lie."

"I knew how you'd feel, J.R. I didn't want to make trouble. I wanted to avoid it. You hate Alan because he works for Cliff Barnes, because he's instrumental in Cliff's campaign for Congress. Is that why you're doing this, to get at Barnes through Alan? And through me?"

"That's too easy, Lucy," J.R. said. "I despise Beam because I know about him. I've made it a point to know about him, and his activities. He is penniless, ruthless, a social climber, willing to exploit his relationship with you for his eventual profit. He is no good—rotten."

Lucy's eyes stuttered around, seeking a friendly face. She fixed on Bobby. "Bobby, surely you don't go along with J.R. You have to understand ..."

"I've met Beam, Lucy, I would not have handled things the way J.R. did, but I can't approve of Alan Beam. Personally, I believe you could have done a lot better."

Encouraged by this surprising show of support, J.R. leaped ahead three or four laps in his strategy. It was time to drive the last spike all the way home. "Lucy, I forbid you to ever see Alan Beam again!"

Lucy couldn't believe the evidence of her senses. Her

eyes went round and her mouth opened and closed. "What!" she finally uttered.

"You heard me."

"No, I couldn't have heard right. You weren't trying to tell me who to date, who to see."

"That's exactly what I'm doing."

"Go to hell, J.R."

"Please, Lucy," Miss Ellie said. "J.R., this must stop."

"I am telling you what you are going to do," J.R. burst out.

"Wrong."

"You are never going to see Alan Beam again."

"Pull back, J.R.," Bobby said.

"I'd think you'd actively support me in this, little brother. This is your family, too."

"J.R.," Lucy said in a thin, nasty voice. "Understand me good. Not only will I go out with Alan Beam, not only will I continue to be his mistress, but he's asked me to marry him."

"Marry!" J.R. laughed. "*Own* you, is what he means. You're self-destructive, Lucy, but not so much that you'd marry Alan Beam."

Lucy straightened up. "I'd like to take this opportunity to invite you all to the wedding," she said, and marched proudly out of the room.

"She's joking," Jock said. "She must be."

"I hope so," Bobby said.

Miss Ellie shook her head. "I can't believe she means it. Oh, I know Lucy is headstrong and a trifle wild at times. But to marry this Beam fellow, why she hasn't even mentioned his name."

"Of course not," J.R. said, summoning up all the trappings of anger, but privately pleased at the way things were going. "She knew how we'd all react. How we'd feel. Once and for all, I am going to straighten that little girl out."

Miss Ellie's voice hardened. "Let her be, J.R. You've said enough for one evening."

"Let her be!"

"She's a grown woman. She has to make up her own mind about things. Pay the price for whatever she chooses to do. I believe no matter what she'll come out all right. After all, Lucy is a Ewing. . . ."

"I'm just trying to save her from disaster, Momma."

"And nothing else?" Bobby put in.

"You trying to say something to me, little brother?"

"Just asking."

"I don't like that kind of question."

Bobby shrugged and said no more.

"She's not a fool," Jock said, "If this Beam feller turns out to be wrong for her, she's got smarts enough to save herself."

"I'm only thinking of Lucy, Daddy."

"Good enough, Junior. From now on stay out of it, hear."

"Whatever you say, Daddy. I'm minding my own business from here on out."

They watched J.R. go over to the bar and pour a drink. When he turned, he lifted his glass in a silent toast, the wide gleaming smile of victory lighting up his face.

Lucy drove into Dallas and directly to Alan Beam's apartment. He was getting ready to leave when she arrived and her unexpected appearance unnerved him. She mistook his guilt and apprehension for tension in her presence, for fear that he would succumb to her sexual overtures in contradiction of his professed desire to marry her. She was flattered and pleased and her mind was made up.

She embraced him tightly and Alan, geared up for his date with Kristin at the condo, wondered how quickly he could rid himself of her restricting presence.

"Oh, Alan," she said against his chest. "It feels so good to be in your arms. Never, never let me go."

He stroked her hair without feeling. "What's wrong, Lucy?"

She considered telling him what had happened, thought better of it. He might become so angry, she thought, that he'd attack J.R. physically. That would create only larger problems, more trouble for all of them.

"Nothing is wrong. I missed you is all. I missed you and realized how much I love you." Even as she spoke the words, doubts came alive in her mind. Did she in fact love Alan? Had she ever in her eighteen years loved a man? If so, she was unable to name him. Oh, there were so many men she had been drawn to, sexually attracted to and stimulated by. Handsome men, muscular men, men whose raw sexuality had turned her on, made her dizzy and faint with desire. But love? Not so she could remember. Why then was she compelled to say those charged words to Alan?

"Did you mean it?" she went on compulsively. "About wanting to marry me?"

"Of course," he said automatically, his throat thick with desire for Kristin. "But I understand your feelings, your need to remain independent, free. Whatever you want, Lucy, is okay with me. As long as you're happy."

"I will marry you, Alan."

He stepped back. "What?"

"I want to marry you, Alan."

"That's crazy!"

"Why? Why is it any crazier than you wanting to marry me? You do love me, don't you, Alan?"

"Oh, yes. I love you."

"Then it's settled. How soon can we do it?"

"Soon . . ."

"Get married?"

"Well, I don't know. There are arrangements. I'll have to discuss it with your family, with J.R."

"No!"

"What do you mean?"

"This is for you and me, Alan. Leave the Ewings out of it. Especially J.R."

His suspicions were aroused. What had gone wrong to bring her here this way? Certainly some spark had catapulted her into his arms overflowing with love and an overweening hunger for marriage. Instinctively he sensed trouble, some difficulty with J.R. That was something he intended to avoid; J.R. was vital to his future, directly or otherwise, and Beam could do nothing to undercut the relationship unless he was holding all the high cards. His hand was hardly that strong. Not yet anyway.

"I can't do that, Lucy," he said with disarming reasonableness. "One day—no matter what you feel today—you'll want your family close around you. And so will I. We can't do anthing to create a rift, to cause bad feelings."

"You don't know them."

"That isn't the point. The Ewings are your flesh and blood."

"You can't imagine what they're like. J.R. is the worst of them: spiteful, hurtful, always working his deals at the expense of someone else. Maybe I am a Ewing by blood but I've always felt like a stranger in that house. Oh, let's get married right away, Alan. I'll stay here tonight and tomorrow morning we can drive down to Nuevo Laredo. You can get married right away in Mexico and..."

"I don't think that would be wise, Lucy."

"You've changed your mind!" Relief and rage were in sharp conflict, her emotions in turmoil, her thoughts confused.

"I just think we ought to wait, consider, to it the right way."

"You're afraid of them, of J.R."

"Don't be silly."

"And you don't want me anymore. I'm not pretty enough for you, smart enough or sexy enough. Have you got another girl, Alan? Have you had other girls all this time, while we were together? When you made love to me, Alan, were you imagining doing it to somebody else? I loved you, I wanted to marry you, and you're turning away from me. J.R. will be very happy. Was this his doing, Alan? Did J.R. get to you, buy you off, threaten you? Is that why you no longer want to marry me?..."

"Give me a little time. I'll work it all out."

"Never mind, Alan. I know when I'm not wanted. And I know exactly what to do about it...."

She fled, tears streaking her pale young cheeks.

She woke to find herself naked and alone in the bed. A slowly revolving light cast out red and green and blue flashes. The scent of burned grass hung on the air, made acrid by the stench of alcohol. She sat up and tried to remember: where was she, whose bedroom was this? A familiar taste lined her mouth, caused her to struggle harder to penetrate her memory. The taste of sperm accepted and swallowed. She fell back on the pillow, eyes shut tightly, willing this to be Alan Beam's apartment, and knowing, *knowing*, that she had never been here before. That the taste in her mouth was the taste of a stranger and she loathed herself more for what she knew she had done. For what she was turning herself into.

She stood up. A wet trickle brought her attention to her inner thigh. More sperm. A despairing moan escaped her and she searched for her clothes. She discovered her panties under the bed and was about to put them on when he appeared. He was stocky and muscular, barely taller than she was, and equally naked. Behind him, two other men.

"There she is, boys."

"Nice."

"Prime stock."

"Who are you?" Lucy said.

"Never did get around to making introductions," the stocky one said. "Don't seem like names are required at this point. You boys satisfied?"

"You ain't never done better by us, pal."

He held out his hand. "Cash up front."

Each of them placed some bills in his palm. He left them alone with Lucy, closing the door behind himself. The two newcomers began to get undressed.

"I'm going," she said.

They laughed at her. "The hell you say!"

"Whatever he told you, I'm not like that."

"We paid our money, lady. Now it's time to get full value for our dough. Lookee here, sweet pussy, what I have got for you."

The second one circled to one side. "Okay, friend, your choice. First time around, you name it—front or back door?"

"Front."

"You got it. From now on it's every man for hisself. Bet you ten bucks I get to heaven before you."

"You're on!"

They lunged at her and her struggles were futile as they pulled and spread and pressed themselves into her. She screamed and screamed again and that seemed only to excite their passions even more. Giving pain was at least as vital to them as gaining pleasure.

When it was over, they left her bruised and bloodied on the floor. Eventually she was able to dress herself and leave. The stocky man was watching television in the living room but he made no attempt to stop her.

Outside she stumbled along, trying to remember where she'd parked her car. A fugitive thought rippled through her disordered brain. It fled and drifted back, gradually taking form. J.R., she said to herself. J.R. did this to her as surely as if he had been there, conspired in her rape and degradation. J.R. must be made to pay. J.R. had to be punished. Finally dealt with. Made to suffer. To be afraid. His flesh torn apart so that he could never again deal with another human being so cruelly. J.R. must die. . . .

13

$\mathcal{T}$he following morning Bobby and J.R. were in conference in J.R.'s office when his intercom went off. "Yes," he said into the machine.

"J.R.," came his secretary's voice, a modicum of surprise in the ordinarily emotionless voice, "Mr. Cliff Barnes is out here and would like to see you."

J.R. was unable to conceal his own surprise. "What the hell's he want?" he said, not expecting an answer, to Bobby.

Bobby grinned. "A man skilled in the ways of duplicity, big brother. Not to be taken for granted. Not to be anticipated."

"Shall I see him?"

"Unless you do, you'll never know what he's about. I think we both should speak with him."

For one of the few times that he could remember. J.R. was grateful to have Bobby around. He expected nothing good to come of a meeting with Cliff Barnes, but you never could tell. "Send Mr. Barnes in," he said to the intercom.

A moment later the door swung open and Cliff walked into the office. His glance went from J.R. to Bobby and back again, steady and unafraid. He seated himself without being asked in a chair across from J.R. and dropped a brown manila envelope on the desk.

"What are you doing here, Barnes?" J.R. said toughly.

"Good morning, Cliff," Bobby said.

Barnes indicated the envelope. "Open it."

J.R. stared at it as if it were a venomous serpent, coiled to strike. "What's in it?"

"Open it and find out."

Bobby began to laugh. "Oh, for crying out loud! You two are acting like a couple of kids. Cliff, you here to do some business or just kick up some dirt? Whichever, get on it to, man. Some of us got work that needs tending to."

Cliff's expression never changed. "Bobby, of all the Ewings you come closest to being a decent human being. But a Ewing you are and that puts you beyond the pale as far as I'm concerned. J.R., we do it now or we do it in a court of law."

"What the hell are you talking about, Cliff Barnes?"

"The envelope . . ."

J.R. hesitated, then snatched it up, tore it open. He took out a xerox copy of a handwritten document, "Okay, what is this?"

"Read it."

"Don't give me orders in my own office, Barnes."

"Read it out loud so's Bobby here will know what is going down. This has got to do with all the Ewings. . . ."

J.R. looked at him with disgust and loathing. His eyes went down to the xerox and read it quickly. He looked up, cheeks flushed, his eyes narrowed. His voice, when he spoke, was serrated. "You expect me to take this at face value?"

Without a word, Cliff dropped two additional documents on the desk. "These are sworn and attested to, notarized, J.R. Very legal papers. I've had that examined by experts. You don't think I came in here half-assed for you to rip me up, do you? I came armed and ready."

"Will you two tomcats please let me in on the secret," Bobby said. "What is going on?"

"Read it," Barnes said again. "Read it, J.R., so's Bobby can hear for himself."

"All right," J.R. said coldly. He read: " 'It is hereby agreed that all revenues and profits in the oilfield now known as Ewing 23 will be shared equally by John Ewing and Willard Barnes and their heirs in perpetuity.'

"I leave anything out?" J.R. ended bitterly.

Bobby got out of his chair and took the document and read it to himself. He turned to Cliff Barnes. "I just opened those wells, Barnes. You certainly didn't waste any time announcing your interest. . . ."

"Timing counts."

Bobby glanced at the paper in his hand. "You expect to make a claim based on this paper? Our own legal experts will want to study it."

"Help yourself. It won't change things. Half of everything Ewing 23 pumps belongs to me. Half the oil, half the profits."

"Well, Bobby," J.R. said, "you opened those wells and it looks like you've made your brother-in-law a very rich man."

"Are you implying—?"

"Just pointing out the realities of the situation is all."

"It won't break us," Bobby said.

"That's a nice size field," J.R. said.

"Exactly my sentiments," Cliff said.

"Lots of money for whomsoever owns a piece."

"That's me, pardner," Cliff drawled cheerfully.

J.R. went over to the bar. "Looks like a little celebration is in order. What we have here is an interesting turn of events. Enemies become partners. Ain't that a fine kettle of fish, fellers?"

"Save it," Bobby said, eyeballing Cliff Barnes icily. "I'm choosy who I drink with."

"No need to be a sore loser," J.R. intoned.

At the door, Bobby turned back. "Congratulations, Cliff. You finally got what you wanted—revenge on the Ewings and a substantial piece of the action. Guess you're proud of yourself. I don't believe Pamela will be." He left Cliff sitting there with a middling smile on his mouth, feeling less good about things than he figured he would be about now.

"Don't pay him no never-mind," J.R. said, pressing a drink into Barnes' hand. "Bobby tends to be a mite protective where family matters come in. Maybe overly so. Here's to your health, pardner."

Cliff shoved himself erect, put the glass on the desk. "I'll meet with your accountants next week. I want a full breakdown of barrels pumped daily, refinery costs, selling price, profit margins, taxes, and so on and so on. My people will check everything, all the books, all the records."

"My, you sure are a testy litle feller, Cliff. And more than a little bit distrustful of your fellow man. Come on, now, drink up." He picked up the telephone. "Just got to make one itty-bitty call, if you don't mind." He dialed. "Harry Owens, please," he said into the phone. And then to Barnes: "You know ole Harry, foreman out at Ewing 23. Good man, experienced, does what he's told without asking dumb questions, Harry does."

"I have got to admit you are taking it very well, J.R. I expected you to carry on, make a lot of noise. Not that there's anything you can do. This agreement is all legal and binding and what was my daddy's is mine. I'm glad to see you're accepting the inevitable. That you're not going to put up a useless and expensive futile fight."

"Got to roll with the punches, ain't that a fact, Cliff? That's what I always say. What do you always say, Cliff?" Then into the phone: "That you Harry? How yew doin', boy? Well, that is great, Harry, just great." He put his hand over the mouthpiece. "Harry says Ewing 23 is spewing up oil at a record pace. All those gooey black barrels. Man, I sure do hope those OPEC A-rabs get around to upping their asking price again pretty soon." Then, to Harry Owens again: "How many barrels would you say? One thousand a month and going higher. Beautiful." He spoke to Barnes again. "I make your share out to come to maybe half a million dollars the very first year alone and bound to get even better. Man, that is a nice annuity for a man to have."

"I can use the money."

"Sure you can, Cliff. I bet you really can." Back to the telephone: "Harry, you still there. Good boy. Tell you what I want you to do, Harry, so you listen good. Close down Ewing 23. That's right, close it down, the entire field. Every lastgotohellwell. That's right, shut it down. As of this very minute." He hung up the phone. "How's that grab you, Mr. Cliff Barnes, smartass operator? There goes your half a million bucks a year. Still deep down under Texas. Every one of them wells corked shut like a tight asshole and never again to be opened up long as you can walk and talk and breathe."

Cliff Barnes, pale, sucking air, body angled as if about to attack, struggled for words. "You will never get away with this, J.R. This time you've gone too far. If I have to, I'll stop you with my bare hands. Or a bullet in your cold heart . . ."

He heard J.R.'s mocking laughter long after he left.

14

$\mathcal{P}$am returned to Southfork only minutes before the evening meal was to be served. But she had no interest in food, going directly to her room, unpacking her bag, pouring out to Bobby every detail of her time in Corpus, her meeting with the woman who had once known her mother, her experience in the Hall of Records. "I am convinced," she said, looking up finally, "that my mother is alive somewhere, waiting for me to find her."

Bobby withheld the brusque comment that came to his tongue. "I have something to tell you, Pam."

"Oh." She went back to her suitcase, putting her clothes away.

"This could be very important to you, and to Cliff."

"Is it about our mother?"

"No."

"Then I don't really care."

Bobby ignored her response. "It's about Ewing 23, the oilfield . . ."

"I'm not interested in any of your oilfields, Bobby."

"You should be interested in this one, you own part of it."

"I don't know what you mean."

"I mean that your brother Cliff came up with a document proving that your daddy and mine were partners in Ewing 23, down to their heirs in perpetuity. What I'm trying to tell you is that you and Cliff are partners with us Ewings in Ewing 23."

"I don't care about Ewing 23 and some old document Cliff found. I'm not interested in owning an oilfield, or anything else. Not now."

He clenched his jaw. "I love you very much, Pam, but there are times when you are impossible to deal with."

"I'm your wife, not a businessman. Don't make deals with me."

"If you don't want the money, consider Cliff. It could make him financially independent for the rest of his life."

"That's Cliff's business. Let me explain about mine, Bobby. Not only did the Hall of Records in Corpus have no record of my mother's death, neither did the hospital in the area. No one of that name was ever admitted, you see. And that old woman who knew her—what a prize that was, meeting her! Imagine what I'll find out when I really get going." She put the empty suitcase into her closet and began changing clothes for dinner.

He watched her for a minute, admiring her superb young body, wanting very much to embrace her, make love to her. Yet knowing that to do so when she was in this mood would be a mistake, would only establish an even greater distance between them. "Pam, you must listen to me. I understand how important it is to you to find out the truth about your mother. But why now?"

"Don't try to talk me out of it, Bobby. I have to follow through on this. I'm going to give notice at the Store."

"Damn!" he exploded.

"Spare me your disapproval. You were never all that enthusiastic about my working anyway."

"If you wanted to quit for some good and solid reason, I could understand *that. . . .*"

"I see. Finding out about my mother is neither a good nor a solid reason to you. Very well . . ."

"Pam, please. Dr. Danvers said you need a period of mourning. Time to deal with your grief over Digger's death. Time to find yourself again. Decisions you make impulsively may be regretted later on and—"

"I know what I'm doing, Bobby."

"Maybe you need some help. Counseling. Won't you take it slow and . . ."

She stared at him and his warmth and sincerity washed

over her. The resentment drained away and she went over to him, held him close, his head against her bare breasts. "Please, honey, please understand."

"I'm trying."

"And give me time."

"Time is what we both need—with each other. Time to grow closer, to love each other, to be with each other."

"I must do this."

He pulled away. "It isn't right. Not for you, not for me. Not for any of us. When it is right, I'll be right there with you, supporting you in every way. Fighting for you."

"In that case," she said, backing away, "I guess I'll just have to go on without your help. This is something I want to do, must do, something I shall do. Nothing, nobody, is going to stop me. Nobody . . ."

There was, Bobby decided, nothing more for him to say.

Alan Beam didn't want to see Lucy; she was only trouble. But she was the centerpiece of his agreement with J.R. and there was no avoiding her. Her call had been unexpected, unwelcome, an inconvenience; Alan had made a date to visit Kristin in her apartment. Sitting at his desk, going over some business papers, he made a silent comparison of the two women. Though they were not that far apart in years, Kristin was a sophisticated and cunning woman; Lucy, a mere girl, was in many ways formless and without purpose. She had so much to learn about life.

The doorbell drew his attention. He admitted Lucy and turned away from her at once, putting himself in a straight-backed chair in his living room. She trailed after him like a chastened pup.

"Are you still angry with me, Alan?"

"I've never been angry with you. But I'm human. I have feelings, too. I don't enjoy being rejected."

"Oh, no, I never rejected you, Alan." She took up a position in front of him and her nearness reminded him of what she looked like naked—that strong young body, so pliable and anxious to please. Almost too anxious. She had a body most women would envy, he reminded himself, strong and resilient, a body capable of acrobatic gyrations in the passionate pursuit of pleasure. Once, in the middle of their love-making, she had raised up with such swift-

ness and authority that Alan had been rocked loose, sent
spinning off her, off the bed, onto the floor. Now she knelt
in front of him, one hand on each knee. "Did you mean
what you said, Alan?"

"About what?" His throat grew thick, closing up; less in
desire than in the realization of how near he was to
everything he had ever wanted out of life.

"About marrying me? Do you still want to marry me?"

"More than anything in the world," he answered soberly. Her hands slid along his thighs and her cheek came to
rest on one leg. His muscles tensed and he became aware
of his body responding. And so did she. She said his name
softly and reached for him.

Anguish and desire mingled in his gut, a low-swinging
passion charged by resentment and a simmering rage. All
that she was, all that she offered, all that she gave was
nothing when compared with what J.R. promised. Oh,
God, how he wanted! Wanted it all. But without strings.
Without this clinging female whose sexuality was draped
in a scatter of neuroses, all gathered under the heading:
Love.

He pushed her hand away.

"Don't you want me anymore, Alan?"

"I told you—no more like a couple of scared kids
groping each other in the back seat of a car. No more
stolen kisses, no more illicit feels, no more dirty sex."

"I want you so much, Alan."

"And I want you, Lucy. Really want you."

The words rushed up into her mouth, struggling for
release. And all she could think of was J.R. and the hatred
she felt for him. How much joy she could find in his pain,
his eventual destruction. She would do anything to hurt
him, cause him real damage, subvert his power over her.

"I will marry you, Alan."

"You really want it?"

"I never meant anything more."

"A proper wedding, everything right?"

"Whatever you want, Alan." She reached for him again.
"Oh," she said with exaggerated concern. "Where has
dear, dear Peter gone?"

"Maybe we ought to wait until after we are married . . ."

"That's not fair."

"You really want it?"

"Never wanted anything more."

"Convince me."

She began to undo his trousers. "Whatever you want . . ."

"Whatever?"

"Just tell me."

"Beg."

"What?"

"Beg, I want to hear you beg."

"You bastard," she muttered, pushing her face between his moist thighs.

"It's what you want."

"Yes."

He took hold of her blond hair and yanked her head up. "Beg, I want to hear you beg."

"Please, Alan. Please, let me have what I want, what I need. Please let me do to you. With my hands. With my face. With my insides."

"I'm going to use you."

"Yes, yes. Use me. Just for you, for your pleasure."

"You can service me."

"Ah, yes. I want to service you. I want to make you happy."

"Just another body. Another face. Another pair of hands."

"Whatever you want it to be, only let me kiss you, love you, take you into my mouth."

"Go on, do it. The way you've done it so many times to so many different men."

She obeyed, head swimming, eyes clamped shut, the thick smell of his sweat drifting into the cavities of her skull. She imagined she was stripped bare and bright lights flooded every inch of her skin and hundreds of people watched avidly as she performed and cries of excitement went up as they saw the pleasure she provided him with, cries urging her on to greater, more varied activities, telling her how skilled she was, how much better than other women, the best. The best head in all of Texas . . .

Until the image disintegrated and came together again. This time she was inside a great silent cathedral, all in white, moving gracefully down the center aisle toward Alan who waited with the preacher. And she came closer, closer to becoming a married lady, a wife. And Alan's hand reached out for her, guiding her onto her knees in front of the preacher until she saw that he was naked from the waist down. And Alan pushed her head forward against the preacher and told her what to do, and she did so.

And the cheering rose up all around her and her eyes rolled and she saw the preacher smiling down at her that terrible dangerous smile that she knew so well. The preacher was J.R. She bit down hard as she could.

"Jesus!" Alan said. "Watch what you're doing. That hurt."

"Sorry," she mumbled.

"If you can't do it right, don't do it."

"Oh, please, Alan, let me. I'll be good, I'll be good."

And she was.

McSween looked like a cop. Or more precisely, he resembled Hollywood's version of a hard-nosed, dumb cop, the sort who populated all those private eye movies back in the thirties and forties.

In fact, McSween was a cop. He had a mashed in face, a nose broken a dozen times, a long ugly scar twisting from under his left eye along his heavy jaw under his ear. McSween was patient, a trait he had developed from a thousand futile stakeouts over the years. Patient and cunning, acting always in his own self-interest. He was a man without scruples or morals, functioning on a purely pragmatic level, exploiting every situation for possible profit and pleasure, squeezing the guilty and the helpless for every drop of satisfaction he could extract. His patience, however, was beginning to wear thin. He checked his watch; Beam should've been home by now. Probably out humping some fancy cooze while McSween sat in his car sipping flat Dr. Pepper and chomping on stale Doritos.

A car pulled into the parking area and swung into the space next to McSween. He swallowed the last of the Dr. Pepper and got out, went around to where Beam was climbing out of his car. McSween felt he owed the young lawyer one; without warning, he punched him hard in the kidneys. A scream rose out of Alan's throat, cut off by McSween's big hand clamped down over his mouth.

"Not a sound, boy," McSween said harshly. "Else I am going to kick your ass from here to hell and gone. You follow me?"

Alan Beam managed a nod. McSween removed his hand. "We'll go in my car."

"Who are you?"

McSween shoved him along.

"What do you want?"

"Get in, shut up. I'm in a pisspoor mood so don't press your luck."

They drove out of the parking area. "Where are you taking me?"

McSween dealt a backhand that caught Alan in the solar plexus. He gasped and wheezed.

"You puke all over my car," McSween said, matter-of-factly, "and I am goin' to git belly-crawlin', grass-grabbin', dirt-diggin' mad at you, boy. Better jes sit there and be good till we git where we are goin' . . . ."

J.R. was at his desk in his office. He sat with his fingers laced under his chin, staring into the night sky of Dallas. Without shifting his eyes very much he marked the lighted sign of the Southland Life Building, the clock above the Central Stock Manager's Tower, the soft coppery glow of the tinted glass facade of Texas Banking and Loan—all reflected in one of the nearby lakes. J.R. enjoyed being part of Dallas, enjoyed the sleek modern beauty of the city, the energy and excitement that rippled through the town day and night. A sound brought him swiveling around to see Alan Beam approaching, McSween behind him. When the lawyer hesitated, McSween shoved him forward.

"What the hell is this?" Beam said.

J.R. appreciated the young man's technique: attack, attack, attack. But in Alan's case it was much ado about nothing; he functioned out of weakness and ignorance, was doomed to defeat.

"He give you any trouble, McSween?"

"Him? No way he could trouble me, Mr. Ewing."

"Call your gorilla off, J.R. You want to see me all you had to do is ask."

"Now, Alan, don't you go insulting the sergeant. You'll hurt his feelings."

"Why the rough stuff?"

"To let you know the limits of your freedom, Alan. You're right, I could have invited you and you would have been glad to accommodate me. I chose this method in order to impress on you the extent of my authority, my influence, my power. Sergeant McSween here is a police officer who, from time to time, does small jobs on my behalf. If I give him the word, he'll run you out of town. Or arrest you. Or put a bullet in your brain." J.R. arranged an ingenuous expression on his open face.

Alan shuddered. "I don't understand any of this."

J.R. pushed himself to his feet, came around to the front of his desk. He measured Alan carefully. "You ready to talk to me, boy?"

"Sure, J.R. What would you like to know?"

"Don't get flip with me, son. It ain't fit." He jabbed a stiff forefinger against Alan's chest. "Now. You tell me this. What do you and Kristin think you are doing?"

The blood rushed out of Alan's face. His palms turned moist and cold. His knees went soft.

"I don't know what you're talking about."

J.R. leaned and the nearness of the other man increased Alan's unease. He averted his eyes, took a single step away.

"Stand still," J.R. commanded. "Look at me. You must never lie to me, Alan. It distresses me, makes me angry, puts unsettling ideas into my head. Shall we get back to you—and Kristin?"

"I don't know anything . . ."

J.R. nodded once and McSween drove his fist into Alan's back, sending him down to the floor. J.R. leaned against his desk, waiting patiently until Alan was again standing. "Talk to me, Alan . . ."

"Whatever Kristin told you," Alan managed to gasp out, "it isn't true. I don't know anything . . ."

"You and Kristin," J.R. said, almost in wonder that such a coupling was possible. "Two insignificant characters in search of a future. Whatever possessed you, man? I showed you the way to a secure and reasonably good life. You and Lucy . . ."

Alan grasped at his last hope. "Lucy," he said, voice hoarse. "Lucy agreed to marry me. . . ."

"Of course she did. I manipulated her so that she would. But that wasn't sufficient for you—Lucy, your own law office in Chicago. Oh, no, you and Kristin had to conspire against me. I do believe you intended to cause me some harm, Alan, and I cannot in all frankness permit that to happen. So it's off, Alan, your marriage to Lucy."

"You can't do that to me!"

"Our deal is terminated. No law office for you this time."

Alan summoned up a last rush of strength and courage. "I won't let you do this to me."

"You have no choice in the matter. You're finished here—get out of Dallas. By noon tomorrow, Alan."

"Who do you think you are! You can't treat me this way. You can't do a damned thing to me, not a damned thing."

J.R. made no effort to conceal his amusement. "How do you intend to earn a living from now on? You got some private income I don't know about?"

"I'm a lawyer, a good one. I'll get a job. I shall continue to practice law."

"I don't think so," J.R. said thinly. "Sergeant McSween, what is the penalty for rape?"

McSween stared sullenly at Beam; no words were required. Beam felt a stab of panic set in. "I haven't raped anybody."

"I imagine McSween can come up with someone to testify otherwise."

"You'd frame me!"

"Can you find such a woman, Harry?" J.R. said to the detective.

"Blonde, brunette or redhead?"

J.R. smiled in Alan's direction. "See what I mean, Alan?"

"Why are you dong this to me?" Alan whined.

"You had a clear choice, Alan. Work *for* me or *against* me. You and Kristin chose the latter. When you make a mistake in this world, you must pay for it. Now get out of my sight. You're weak and stupid and you leave a bad taste in my mouth."

At the door, Alan swung around, his narrow eyes going from McSween to J.R. When he spoke, his voice was cold and steady, edged with hatred.

"You won't get away with this, J.R. You just leaned too hard on the wrong guy. I'll find a way to make you pay, to take it out of your hide. One night someone will say your name, J.R., and when you turn around it'll be me and you'll be sorry. . . ."

McSween made a lunge at the lawyer but Alan slipped

out the door first. "Let him go," J.R. said. "He's not the first one to make threats, he won't be the last."

"You want me to take care of him?"

"Not worth the effort, Harry. He's harmless, they all are. Talkers, every one of them. Not the kind you worry about."

"I hope you're right, Mr. Ewing."

J.R. was startled by the detective's sober reaction. He wondered if this time he had made a mistake.

15

"*I'*m sorry, Kristin."

Vaughn Leland kept repeating the words as if saying them over and over would somehow wipe away the disgrace. The shame. The flaw in his manhood.

"There's nothing to be sorry about, honey," she anered automatically. Her mind drifted from peak to peak, seeking answers, creating plans and plots that fell apart under close examination, crying out silently for justice. Revenge. Victory.

"This never happened to me before."

"It could happen to anybody."

"I guess you think I'm not much of a man."

She touched his naked thigh reassuringly, having already dismissed him as a source of pleasure or profit. J.R. had done a good job on Vaughn Leland, the ultimate job. As if reading her thoughts, he moaned and rolled her way. saying: "The bastard deballed me just as sure as if I was one of those Southfork bulls, cut off my manhood as easy as slicing down a crop of winter wheat."

"Don't make too much of it, Vaughn."

He put his hands on her, feeling her without passion, seeking in that young firm flesh the answers to his problems. She shifted position, enough to break the contact. His touch offended Kristin, the clammy touch of a stranger, or worse—an enemy. If the banker was to be no help to her then he might very well be an albatross she chose not to carry around. If not Leland, she wondered, who?

There were so many wealthy, successful men in Dallas. Men of power. Men who would enjoy having a beautiful young girl available to them during the week. A sensual afternoon, a passionate, fulfilling evening. With no emotional strings attached. No danger to existing relationships. To other lovers. To wives. To marriages. And all she asked in return was a fraction of that wealth and power, the promise of greater things to come. To hell with J.R. Ewing. To hell with his threats. She would confront the problem later.

He pushed himself against her, mouth closing on one breast. The intimacy reminded of her how much time she had wasted on this useless person; she pushed him away and stood up, padded into the bathroom.

"Get dressed, Vaughn," she tossed over her shoulder. "It's getting late."

Minutes later she returned to discover him still curled up in bed in the fetal position, weeping pitifully. "What am I going to do?" he wailed.

"You could kill yourself," she said casually. "The way Seth Stone did."

"You heartless bitch."

She slipped on a summer robe that concealed nothing, made her even more enticing. "Well, crying won't do anybody any good. Give it some thought, Vaughn. You've got friends, contacts, you've still got your job. There must be some positive action you can take." A reptilian smile played at the corners of her voluptuous mouth, but her eyes were flat and lifeless. "If you can't kill yourself, why not kill J.R. then? That would make you a hero in this town."

He sat up. "Don't think I wouldn't like to."

"But you won't."

"I might surprise you."

"I don't think you've got the belly for it, Vaughn. Now get your clothes on. The sight of your pale little body makes me kind've queasy, if you get my meaning."

He raised his hand as if to strike her. She stared him down, laughing softly when he lowered his fist. She made a gesture of dismissal just as the phone rang. She picked up the instrument, never taking her eyes off Leland.

"Yes?" she said.

"It's Alan, Kristin. I have to see you right away."

"Sorry. I'm not in the mood, dear boy. One disappointment a day is my quota."

"I don't know what that means and I don't care. This is important, Kristin. It's about J.R."

She watched approvingly as Leland began to dress himself. "Everything is. All right, if you must talk to me do it now."

"Not over the phone. I'll be there in twenty minutes."

"Make it an hour," she said firmly.

"An hour," he agreed and hung up.

"Who was that?" Leland said with some bitterness. "The next shift?"

"Someone younger and prettier, Vaughn. Someone whose career is on the rise, someone who can still get it up like a man. Does that answer your question, lover?"

He found it impossible to respond.

"I'm going to take a shower, Vaughn. And when I'm finished, I want you to be out of here. Is that understood?"

He nodded without meeting her eyes, still unable to comprehend how his life had disintegrated this way. Everything he had ever been, or ever wanted to be, was destroyed. Career, personal life, pride; all gone. He yearned to make the single dramatic gesture that would redeem him in his own eyes, transform him into a real man again.

But how?

Exactly sixty-one minutes later, Alan Beam presented himself to Kristin. She hadn't decided yet whether permitting him to make this visit was a wise move on her part. She admired Alan's raw ambition, his hustle, his high-powered lust for position and power. Yet something was missing, some essential element that she couldn't isolate and give a name to; Alan managed, despite everything, to be less than he should have been.

Still, Alan had been tight with J.R. and that was worth a great deal. She believed she could use that relationship to her benefit, until Alan opened his mouth and shot her down without any warning.

He heaved himself into a deep chair, legs outstetched, ankles crossed, the lean, feral face taut and jittery. "J.R. just gave me the gate, Kristin."

The words exploded deep into her brain, one after another. Bright painful bursts. She staggered as if struck; her life was unraveling right in front of her eyes and there seemed to be nothing she could do about it. Her allies had turned into paper tigers, useless, futile, all their bravado of no use to her now.

"What happened?"

"Lucy came to me, said she was ready to get married."

"That's what you wanted, what J.R. wanted." She saw no hope in the news, aware that Alan intended to dole out the bad news piecemeal.

"J.R. sent for me. One of his legal goons . . ."

"McSween?"

"You know him?"

"He's dangerous. Whenever there's dirty work—"

"J.R. told me the wedding was off. The Chicago law office was finished. I am to get out of Dallas."

"J.R. is intent on eliminating all of us undesirables. Go on."

"He found out about us."

"Damn! You told him. You shot your mouth off. Couldn't you keep quiet? Couldn't . . ."

Alan interrupted. "I told him nothing. The guy's got eyes and ears all over this town. I get the feeling he knows every private thing I've ever done, or wanted to do."

"That means you're finished here."

"Maybe not."

She rocked back and forth as if in lament over lost opportunities. Vaughn Leland, Jordan Lee, Alan Beam; all had failed her. All would continue to fail her.

"Take my advice, if J.R. said get out of Dallas—get!"

"He's not so smart, Kristin. Not so tough. I'm going to strike back."

She looked at him now and he seemed to be shrinking before her eyes. Growing less and less significant, a dwarfed reminder of the man he'd once been. There was, she knew, nothing more to say. Alan Beam had outlived his usefulness as far as she was concerned.

"Thank you for coming, Alan." she said formally, and rose, ushering him to the door.

"Listen," he said, reaching for her. "You and me, we're terrific together. There's no reason to give it up. We can still work as a team, in bed and out. We're young, smart, and full of energy. We'll outthink J.R., outfight him, out-smart him."

She opened the door. "J.R. Ewing goes at two speeds, Alan—wide-assed open and asleep. Mostly he's wide-assed open. And I'm not at all sure he ever does sleep. You've overstayed your welcome, Alan. I've got some very heavy thinking to do and frankly, honey, you are in the way."

She guided him into the hallway and shut the door firmly, irrevocably behind him.

Bobby entered the apartment and looked around as if seeing it for the first time. "You've put your mark on the place, Kristin," he said, in greeting.

"I'm pleased that you approve, Bobby. Can I get you a drink?"

"Maybe a beer, if you've got it."

"I know what you like. Be right back." She returned with two Lone Stars on a tray. "Shall I pour?"

"I'll take mine out of the bottle, thanks." He took a long pull and made himself comfortable. "I've got to tell you, Kristin, your call came as a surprise."

"Not to me, Bobby." She sat next to him on the couch. Close but not too close. She had prepared carefully for this meeting, making herself attractive without being obvious. She wore a floor-length hostess gown from Lord & Taylor that set her figure off spectacularly yet managed to conceal her charms quite effectively. Let him wonder, was her idea. Let him grow curious. Let him want to see more. "I've been thinking a great deal about you lately."

He decided to let that pass and drank some more beer.

"I've never forgotten how it was with us," she said.

"How was it, Kristin?"

She smiled ruefully. "Perhaps it was only for me, I can't be sure now. But at the time I thought—well, I always figured there was a great deal of feeling on both sides."

He shifted around to face her. "Why do I get the nasty idea that you are after something, Kristin?"

There was no point trying to be cute or subtle or devious with brother Bobby. He was no J.R. to be played with. J.R. enjoyed the game as much as the result; Bobby was direct, honest, forthright.

"I want you, Bobby," she said softly.

He examined the Lone Star label as if seeing it for the first time. "That presents at least two severe problems, as I see it."

She touched his cheek, traced the jawline from ear to chin, caressed his mouth delicately. "You are a very beautiful man, Bobby Ewing, and no amount of problems are going to stand between us."

"One," he ticked off. "You and J.R."

She made a face. "That's over."

"Oh?"

"Absolutely, positively, completely over."

"When did that happen?"

She pursed her lips. "I can't remember that there ever was anything between J.R. and me."

"Two," he said. "I am a married man."

She moved closer. "Bobby," she husked. "No way I am going to pretend to be some naive little virgin just in off the farm. I have been around. Been around enough to know what is good and what is bad. To know what I want and what I need. You are what I want, you are what I need."

"You flatter me, Kristin. But that nasty idea is still with me. What are you after, Kristin?"

"A girl could get piqued at a man like you, Bobby Ewing. Here I am practically throwing myself at you shamelessly and you keep dwelling on that same old subject—what am I after? I told you, it is you. Only you."

"What put an end to you and J.R.? I know him, I think I know a little bit about you. Neither one of you lets go of a good deal willingly. What made it stop being a good deal?"

She leaned against him, her breast soft and heavy against his shoulder, her lips drifting across his cheek. "Why don't we end all this gabbing and begin kissing and hugging, do a little fooling around, huh?"

"You tempt me, Kristin. You surely do tempt me."

"Give in, honey." She brought his hand onto her breast and moaned at the touch. She stroked his chest, letting her fingers hook into his belt briefly, then go lower. "Ah, baby, see! I knew you felt the same way."

He stood up. "You're a beautiful woman, Kristin, and I'm a normal man. But don't be faked out by reflexive reactions. We went through this once before, you coming on strong, as if I was the beginning and the end of time for you. I didn't believe it then, I don't believe it now."

She swallowed her rage. She couldn't afford to turn him against her, too. An ally within the Ewing family was vital to her future. If sex couldn't win Bobby over to her side, maybe the truth would.

"All right," she said. "There is something on my mind. But that doesn't change my feelings, Bobby. Anytime you want me all you have to do is reach out and take hold, hear. You turn me on, you truly do."

"Okay. Now what's on your mind?"

She straightened up. "J.R.'s ordered me to leave Dallas."

"Why, he can't do that!"

"That's what I told him but he insisted."

Bobby laughed humorlessly. "Big brother must think Dallas is still a little ole cowtown and he's the marshall up against the bad guys."

"I hope I'm not one of the bad guys, Bobby."

"The longer I live the less sure I am who the bad guys are. Maybe we all are. Maybe it's only a myth about good guys winning in the end. Maybe it's just a question of who has the most muscle and who writes the history books. What's this all about, Kristin?"

"Oh, J.R. has it in his head that I'm trying to do him out of something, do him in. Which just isn't the way it is at all. I have always been loyal to him, to all the Ewings, to Ewing Oil. After all, I am practically one of the family."

"So you came after me."

"I need a friend at court, Bobby."

"At Southfork, you mean."

"Exactly. J.R. is railroading me out of town, out of the family, out of my own future. I want to stay around here, do good things for myself."

"I see. How can I help?"

"If you stood up for me—against J.R. . . ."

"I don't know if I can do that, Kristin."

"Why not? You don't like him anymore than I do. J.R. is low-down mean and rotten, Bobby. Everybody knows that. You know it."

"Maybe so. But there's one thing you've overlooked . . ."
Her heart missed a beat. "What's that?"

"That I'm a Ewing, too. J.R. and me, we're family and always will be. . . ."

16

$\mathcal{B}$obby returned to Southfork early the next evening. He switched off the ignition of his car and sat staring at some unseen point in middle space as if transfixed by visions of private demons. Images snapped onto the screen of his mind without order or intellectual coherence, reminders of events long past and nearly forgotten, words still vivid and biting as he relived their being spoken. Too much too fast. Life unreeling in quick-time, speeded up beyond the ability of his frontal lobes to accept and comprehend and categorize it satisfactorily.

He reached for the newspaper on the seat next to him. The headlines leaped out at him, black symbols of a life gone wrong. Of lives lived without morality or spiritual concerns. Freedom under God and law transmuted by some warped philosophical sleight of hand into license to damage and do in your friends and neighbors in the eternal quest for profit and more power. He was on an ethical treadmill, forced to go faster and faster simply to stay in place.

He got out of the car, then paused. What if J.R. was right? Right to put ends before means in every matter. Right to disregard the old ways as outmoded and useless: loyalty, friendship, personal decency. Had all these once treasured human values fallen into disrepute—useless, ancient baggage now too cumbersome to carry around anymore?

An enticing image of Kristin came to mind. And a

weakness seeped up into his groin, the heavy shift of desire. Most men would have leaped at the opportunity to make love to her. To experience her in all those thick, secret ways that a woman like Kristin evoked and promised. Kristin Shepard was not created for love so much as for love-*making*, for hot wet moments in semi-darkness, with hints of the forbidden always present in the shadows. To roll with that lush nakedness would give free rein to that portion of himself—that portion no man was without, he was convinced—that brought out no pride, no honor, no hope; only despair wrought of transient sensations and dark longings.

J.R. entertained no such thoughts, he knew. No doubts. No questions. What J.R. wanted he went after. He bought his way. He bullied, threatend, cajoled. Bargained. The laws of the marketplace governed his behavior and when those proved too restrictive, J.R. made up his own laws. No price was too high for J.R. to pay if he wanted something, certain that in the end he always received an extraordinarily high return on his investment. J.R. knew how the game was played. J.R. knew how to win.

He went inside the house. In the den, his father and J.R. were having a before-dinner drink. Bobby tossed the paper to his father and lifted the glass out of J.R.'s hand. He drank and gestured.

"You see the evening paper, Daddy?"

Jock, those cool plainsman's eyes missing nothing, measured Bobby at length before glancing at the front page. "What's this?" he said automatically.

Bobby read off the headline: "Banker In Loan Fraud Scandal—Vaughn Leland Flees—Investigation Under Way."

"What's this all about?" Jock said. He had long ago taught himself to create time cushions for himself, to allow himself time to figure out what was going on. Time to think about and digest unexpected information. Time to plot the proper response.

"Vaughn's on the run is what," Bobby said. He finished the drink and went after another.

"Easy does it, little brother," J.R. said. He glanced at the newspaper. "Vaughn has never been a strong person."

Bobby spun around. "That's it, J.R.! Are those your final

words on the subject? Vaughn Leland was not strong.
Seth Stone was a craven coward. This one is too stupid to
play and that one not stupid enough."

"What in hell are you babbling about, Bobby?" J.R.
said.

A hot lump of rage lodged in Bobby's throat and he
struggled to contain it, to force it back into the dark
corner from which it had sprung.

"Don't you see what's happening? J.R.? Daddy? Seth
and Leland, these men were our friends. Business partners. They've been ruined, unable to face their friends,
their families. One dead, one on the run. Is that what you
intended, J.R.?"

"Bobby . . ." Jock said in warning.

"That's all right, Daddy. Bobby's just drinking a little
too much a little too fast. I'm used to that kind of
behavior . . . ." His lips were thinned out and mocking
when he finished speaking.

Bobby took one long threatening step his way.

"Bobby!" Jock said, coming to his feet.

J.R. moved off to one side, watching his brother warily.
"Let me tell you, Bobby. Folks shouldn't play if they can't
afford to lose."

"J.R.," Bobby said, issuing each syllable separately.
"You are all heart."

"I'm a businessman."

"You're a pirate."

Jock interrupted. "Look here, you two. This is my home
and we are family here."

J.R. gathered force. "Are you defending Vaughn Leland, Bobby? Let me remind you, he would have happily
turned us out of our home. He didn't think twice about
foreclosing on Southfork, you forgotten that?"

"I haven't forgotten that it was you who mortgaged this
ranch."

J.R. held his ground, neither embarrassed nor troubled.
"This time the tables are turned. Leland is a vulture and
whatever his troubles are it couldn't happen to a more
deserving bird."

Bobby struck without thinking. "J.R., have you mentioned to Daddy that we have a new partner?"

If looks could kill, J.R. directed a lethal stare his
brother's way. "What's that supposed to mean?" His eyes
skittered from Bobby to Jock and back again.

"What are you talking about?" Jock said.

"The document, J.R." Bobby held himself in check, not happy with the path he had chosen to travel, yet determined to see it through.

Jock shook his head like an angry lion shaking away a swarm of offending flies. "What document is that, son?"

"The paper that you and Digger signed, Daddy."

Jock growled. "Dammit, Bobby, spit it out in words a man can understand. Documents, papers. What's Digger got to do with all this?"

So much and so little, Bobby thought. That pathetic roustabout had lived a hard life, died a hard death, all without it being necessary. What he had labored for so long and so hard was his by moral and legal reason, but he had never known that. Everything he had ever wanted, and was entitled to, had been taken away, the rewards of a lifetime deprived to the old man. Now J.R. intended to ramrod a similar injustice against his children.

"Let's have it, Bobby!" Jock said, voice rising, his weathered face flushed.

"Don't get excited, Daddy," J.R. cautioned with genuine concern. "Seems like Cliff brought in some old document—doesn't mean a cotton-picking thing."

Bobby confronted his father straight on. "You remember signing a paper sharing Ewing 23 with Digger Barnes?"

Jock frowned, thought about it. "Dammit, Bobby. That Digger and me, we signed more papers than we dug wells. Maybe my memory's not so good anymore. Sometimes I feel like my head's as empty as a sucked out straw. Fill me in, boy."

"This particular document made Digger a partner in Ewing 23 in perpetuity. Which means his heirs are partners in the field."

"Pamela?"

"Yes, and Cliff Barnes, too."

"Cliff! A partner of mine! I'd rather go to hell in a basket than—"

J.R. took a step toward his father. "No need to get all worked up over this, Daddy. Just like always, I took care of Cliff Barnes."

"Took care of him?" Bobby said uneasily. "that's a legal paper, J.R. Cliff is a partner."

J.R. was beginning to enjoy himself. "Well, I guess he

is, little brother. Only he is a partner in a nonproducing field."

"Nonproducing?" Jock said.

"What in hell are you talking about?" Bobby said. "I opened that field myself."

"And I," J.R. retorted deliberately, "shut it down. Not a well pumping crude in Ewing 23."

The rage rose in Bobby again. His hands folded into white-knuckled fists, lips drawing back over his clenched teeth. "Who told you to do that?"

"Didn't need any telling, brother. J.R. made the decision by himself, gave the order by himself. It's done, a fact of life."

Bobby addressed his father. "You gave me the authority to open that field, start pumping oil. No one closes it down unless I say so."

"Would you have closed them?" J.R. said in a small taunting voice.

"You know damned well I wouldn't. If Cliff has a legal right to half the profits, then by God, we are going to have to live with it."

"Is that right, Daddy?" J.R. said.

Jock inspected the toes of his black lizard Tony Lama boots. Nothing was easy anymore, nothing was simple. Maybe time had passed him by. Maybe he would do better by divying up all the Ewing holdings, let Bobby run his part and J.R. the rest. Maybe. But not quite yet.

"J.R. did right," he said."

"You approve of what he did?"

"I do not want Cliff Barnes as my partner, no way."

"But it's wrong . . ."

A tough unyielding note came into Jock's voice. "I would have done the same thing myself."

Bobby retreated as if unable to remain in close contact with his father and his brother. "I was afraid you'd say that, Daddy. J.R., you are no damned good and somebody's going to make you pay for your crimes. Some poor soul's going to take it out of your hide in pain and blood one day."

"Not you, little brother."

Bobby paused in the doorway. "Don't push your luck, J.R. I'm a Ewing, remember that. I've got my share of Ewing meanness and orneriness. Bet on what I'm likely to

do, J.R., and you may lose everything you hold dear."
Then he was gone.

J.R. spread his hands in resignation. "Daddy, I do
believe Bobby's gone weak on us. Lost his nerve. What we
just heard, Daddy, that didn't sound like a true Ewing to
me anymore. . . ."

Unable to answer, Jock turned away. J.R. took his
silence for consent and treated himself to another drink in
celebration.

Pam was getting dressed for dinner when Bobby burst
into the room. His eyes were narrow and his mouth
twisted out of shape.

"What's wrong?" she said, rising to greet him.

"Five minutes in the same room with J.R. and I feel like
I've been wallowing in a pigsty."

She tried to embrace him, but he moved away. "What
happened, Bobby?"

"I still can't believe it."

"Believe what? I have no idea what you're talking
about."

"I finally found out where my daddy stands. . . ."

"Jock . . . ?"

"Squarely behind J.R., no matter how dirty his tricks
are. Dammit, this family is coming apart at the seams."

"What set this off!"

"Those wells I opened? Ewing 23."

"What about them?"

"Seems *my* brother closed down those wells when he
found out you and your brother are entitled to fifty percent of the profits. On his own. And this is the binder—
Daddy approves. I hate to think this, let alone say it out
loud—but Daddy's no better than J.R."

"You don't truly believe that, Bobby."

"The hell I don't! I've had a bellyful, Pam. If I stay
around Southfork there's no telling what I'm liable to do."

"What do you want to do?"

He looked deep into her eyes, trying to discover what
her feelings were, what she was thinking. He drew a
blank; nowhere was there any help. The decision was his
alone to make; he made it.

"Tomorrow morning, Pam. First thing, we are getting
out of here. Leaving Southfork once and for all."

She shook her head. "You don't mean that."

"I thought you'd be pleased."

"How I feel doesn't mater. Bobby. Not in something as important as this. After all, you're a Ewing. This is your family."

"No. No more . . . it isn't. I've got to get out now. While I still recognize the difference between right and wrong."

She wrapped her arms around his waist, holding tight. "Take the advice you give me so often. Wait. Cool off. Give yourself time to think."

"No. I've put up with all the wheeling and dealing and shabby tricks I can tolerate. It's over for me. I'm leaving in the morning. I hope you are coming with me."

She didn't know what to say. From the look on his face, she knew there was no way to change his mind. And the next decision was hers to make. By herself.

PART VI

The Ewings

YESTERDAY

*M*nths earlier, on a crisp morning under a high blue Texas sky, Valene Ewing returned to Dallas. She arrived in a dusty sedan of uncertain vintage bearing Kansas plates, rolling down the interstate and into the maze of ramps and cloverleaves that would soon be jammed with the day's first traffic. But now the driving was easy.

Yet she felt tension in every line of her body. Her hands held tightly to the wheel despite her efforts to relax. Her fingers flexed and she blinked against the morning glare. Coming home this way unloosed a barrage of alien sentiments in Valene. And fear. The fear gave birth to more fears that plucked at her for more attention than she cared to provide.

How strange that she should think of Dallas as home. In fact, nothing could be farther from the truth. A home was what she lacked. A place secure and comforting, a place alive with warmth and affection, with a sense of belonging. Dallas was simply a way station on a journey to— where? The only answers that came frightened her even more, and she was tempted to turn around, retrace her path. Or head to some distant, new part of the country. Start all over. By herself.

But that, she understood, was impossible.

At almost the same time, Pam Ewing, wearing jeans and a faded Levi's shirt, made her way from the main house on Southfork to the stables. Behind a white-painted split rail fence, a dozen horses were at pasture. Snorts and whinnies greeted the new sun spreading its warmth over the prairie, and the small herd swept away as one from the rail to race around the perimeter of the corral, manes' and tails blowing.

Pam watched. That is, her eyes followed the running steeds, but her mind was back in the nursery in the main house. Back with John Ewing III, son of Sue Ellen and

J.R. Except that Pam knew, as J.R. knew, that he was not the father. That honor went to Pam's brother Cliff; which meant that Little John, like Cliff, like Pam, was cursed by neurofibromatosis, that awful genetic burden passed on from one Barnes to another.

Shedding her profound concern for Little John, Pam wondered about herself, and Bobby, and any child that they might produce. Would he too be cursed? Would his life be inevitably brief? Or if he should survive to manhood, would he pass on the disease to his offspring? Where would it end? Would it ever end? A shudder racked her body and tears welled up behind her eyes. She never heard Ray Krebs come up behind her.

"Want me to saddle one up for you?"

He spoke in a soft Texas drawl, a lean bony man with remarkable personal appeal. With the authentic presence and appearance no Marlboro man ever projected, a cowboy in every line and angle of his long, strong frame. Here was a man who belonged on a ranch, around horses and cattle, the smell of leather, in sun or rain, the genuine article. Rare even for Texas, Pam had come to understand.

"Oh. Good morning, Ray."

"Sorry, didn't mean to give you a start."

"Just lost in my daydreams."

"Ain't nothin' wrong with that. You sit a horse eyeballin' a grazing herd of cows long enough, your head goes off on trips by itself, day or night."

"I guess cowboying is a lonely life."

"You're by yourself a lot, but not always lonely."

"My," she said. "You are deep, Ray."

He blushed. "Only thing I'm tryin' to say is mornin' is the right time of day for thinkin'."

"I agree . . ."

"About that horse?"

"Oh, no. No, thanks. Some other time."

"You name it." She started back to the house. "How's Little John coming along?"

Now what did he mean by *that?* But his weathered face was without guile. Hardly a man to dissemble, Ray Krebs would surely ask if he wanted to know something. "The baby . . ." she said, trying to collect her thoughts. "He's fine, just fine. You ought to come up to the house and visit."

"Well, I might just do that one of these days. I just might."

"See you, Ray." She walked away.

He tripped his battered Stetson in her direction. "Have a nice day, ma'am . . ."

On the patio of the main house, two servants were setting up a buffet breakfast on a long table made of black iron and Mexican tile. Fifty feet away, Bobby plunged headlong into the pool and swam laps with strong sure strokes. As he went, he spied Pam returning from the stables; he kept swimming. When he was finished, he climbed out onto the stone apron of the pool. Pam approached, tossed him a towel from six feet away. He began to dry himself.

"Morning," he said.

"Morning." More than physical space separated them this morning and Pam suspected that he was as aware of it as she was. "Did you sleep well?"

He threw her a quick sidelong glance. "I was surprised you were already up and gone before I got out of bed this morning."

"I had a bad night . . ."

"I know. I woke up around three o'clock and you weren't there."

She looked off to the horizon. It seemed so far away, remote, unreachable. Everything in Texas suggested distance and separation, as if intimacy was a fault frowned upon out of some long tradition. "I heard Little John crying . . ."

"And you went to him?"

"I went to him."

"I know," he said aggressively. "I saw you in the nursery."

"Why didn't you come in?"

"I didn't want to disturb you. It was such a pretty picture, you holding the baby."

"I was only trying to get him back to sleep."

He considered his words with care. "Little John has a nurse, Pam. He also has a mother."

"You know how Sue Ellen is—"

"Yes, I know. But there's something you don't seem to know."

"And that is?"

"Little John is not your baby."

"That's not fair."

"Fair? Fair is you trying to get *our* baby to sleep, not your sister-in-law's."

"We decided to wait. You know that."

"*We?* Uhuh. We decided to have a baby. *You* decided to wait. And the worst of it is I don't know why. I see you with Little John. I can see that you care for him, love him. There has to be a reason why you don't want our baby."

"It's not like that. It's not that I don't want our children."

"Tell me. Tell me how it is, then?"

Before she could answer, Jock and Miss Ellie appeared on the patio. Jock called down to them. "Mornin', Bobby . . . Pam!"

"Morning," Bobby said.

"Morning," Pam said.

"I think we ought to join them for breakfast."

"All right. But please don't be angry with me. Try to understand."

"I am trying. But I don't understand and I guess I won't be able to until you explain it to me."

"Can we discuss it another time?"

"I imagine, under the circumstances, we'll have to."

By the time they reached the patio, Jock and Miss Ellie were at work on their morning meal. Jock ate swiftly, with gusto, as if stoking up for a long day's work.

"Slow down," his wife said. "You're just gulping your food."

"No time to dawdle, woman. We have got places to be."

"The stores don't open till ten."

"I know that. But the rate you're nibblin' your victuals we won't be in Dallas before noontime."

"I don't think it matters. There can't be anything left to buy the baby."

"Nothin' left! Why I've just begun."

"You're going to spoil him rotten."

"Did the same thing with Bobby and he turned out all right, ain't that a fact, Pamela?"

"Just terrific," she said automatically, watching Bobby pour some coffee for himself. "Well," she said, "I'm due at the Store."

Bobby muttered a farewell, not looking at her, and she left. Neither of his parents seemed to notice anything was wrong.

"That all you going to eat, son?" Jock said.

"I'm not very hungry, Daddy. Anyway, I'm heading over to Little Creek with Ray."

"Problems?"

"Just loading some stock. See you all later."

On his way he passed J.R. arriving for breakfast. He nodded and moved on. J.R. went directly to the buffet, began heaping food on his plate.

His mother watched him for a moment. "Something wrong, J.R.?"

"Wrong, Momma? Why should anything be wrong?"

"The more things bother you, the more you eat."

He placed himself in an empty chair and examined his plate. A rueful smile lifted the corners of his mouth. "Didn't realize I was make such a hog of myself. Funny thing is I am not particularly hungry."

Jock lifted his eyes. "Is there something we should know about. Things all right at he office?"

"Same as usual, Daddy. Still trying to figure out how to get Cliff Barnes off my back."

"Anything I can do to help?"

"I can handle it," he said quickly. He didn't want Jock at the office, looking over his shoulder, undercutting his authority. "Matter of fact," he said casually, "I'm getting together with some lawyers today to work on it."

"Tell you what," Jock said. "We were going into town to do a little shopping, but this might be more important. Maybe I'll just come into the office for that meeting."

"No need for that, Daddy."

Miss Ellie turned a sharp look his way. "Your father ran Ewing Oil for a good many years, J.R. Don't discount his help."

"Yes, ma'am. Just that lawyer talk does tend to be mighty dull."

"That is a true fact," Jock agreed.

J.R. hoped that put an end to it and when Lucy came bouncing out onto the patio he was glad of the interruption.

"Morning, everybody," she enthused.

"Well, you certainly are in an up mood this morning, Lucy," J.R. said.

She skipped over to where Jock was sitting, planted a noisy kiss on his cheek.

"Morning, sweetheart," he said.

"You seem in very good spirits this morning," Miss Ellie said.

"I am. The finals for the cheerleading squad are this afternoon. I am sure I am going to make it."

"How about that!" Jock said.

"I didn't even know you tried out," Miss Ellie said.

Lucy grinned happily. "I didn't want to say anything till I saw how I did."

"Well," J.R. drawled, "isn't that nice. Maybe you ought to stop by the university this afternoon, Daddy, give our Lucy some encouragement."

"Oh, no," she shot back. "I'd be too nervous if Granddaddy was there."

Miss Ellie kept her eyes on J.R. "Besides, your Daddy's coming into the office this afternoon. Give me a chance to take care of some chores of my own."

"That's right," J.R. said with forced brightness. "So he is."

Lucy drank some juice and headed for her car. "Wish me luck!"

They all did. Jock watched her drive off. "Well, good thing we've got Little John around here now. Looks like our little Lucy is just about all grown up and going out on her own. . . ."

Miss Ellie, sketchbook in hand, decided to do some drawing back of the main house, near the stables. Out onto the patio, she paused to greet Sue Ellen on her way inside.

"Good morning, dear."

"Good morning, Miss Ellie."

"How are you feeling?"

"Reasonably well, I'd guess. I was just going inside to do some reading."

"It's such a beautiful day. Why don't you come out with me? Bring your book. You read, I'll sketch. I'd love the company."

"I don't believe I'm up to that quite yet, Miss Ellie. Actually, I was planning to read until I felt drowsy."

"Sue Ellen, I don't want to push you. I do understand

what a trying experience you've had, but you don't want to coop yourself up in this house all day."

Sue Ellen allowed nothing to show on her finely etched face. "Excuse me, Miss Ellie. I think I heard the baby."

Miss Ellie watched her go. If Sue Ellen had heard the baby, it was only in her mind. Presently, Miss Ellie turned away and made her way toward the stables. She arranged herself comfortably near one of the barns and began sketching the landscape when Bobby came riding in. He swung down from his horse and greeted his mother with a kiss on the cheek.

"Daddy around?"

"No. Why?"

"Just wanted to go over some figures on the herd with him. I think he'll be pleased."

"Well, good. He went into town. He and J.R. are having a meeting."

"Bet J.R.'s tickled to death about that."

Miss Ellie gave him a knowing grin. She and Bobby had a common understanding of J.R.

"Fact is," she said with conscious understatement, "J.R. didn't seem overjoyed at the prospect. Seems J.R. is still having problems with the Office of Land Management. Your Daddy's just trying to lend a helping hand."

"Cliff Barnes again. My wonderful brother-in-law. I'm crazy about Pamela but I sure could have done better when it comes to picking a family to marry into."

"I'm sure Pam must have similar ideas about us Ewings from time to time."

"I'm not sure I know what she thinks anymore," he replied softly, his good humor fading swiftly. Miss Ellie put aside her charcoal stick and looked up at her middle son. Bobby went on: "I don't know, maybe it's because she was a Barnes. Maybe it's just because she's a woman."

"Hey, son, is that a touch of male chauvinism I hear creeping in? I may be living out here in the country, but I keep up with what's going down, as they say." She grinned.

He grinned back. "Call it a touch of male confusion. What I want to know is how the heck you and Daddy have done it all these years? You don't seem to fight, or even disagree about most things."

She raised her brows and cocked her head. "About most

things we don't. But if you think we don't fight, it's because you haven't happened to be around for some of our whing-dingers. Let me remind you, son, you Ewings are not the easiest men in the world to live with."

"We Ewings! After all this time, don't you think of yourself as a Ewing?"

"Mostly. But there's still a part of me that's Ellie Southworth. Always will be, I reckon. Just like there's a part of Pamela that will always be a Barnes."

"Well, that's true enough. Doesn't make it easier, though."

His mother hesitated. "Bobby, if there is something you want to say about you and Pamela, say it. If not, stop hinting around."

Bobby, grinning again, said, "Momma, you are about the most direct person I know. But I don't really have anything to say. I just think I was unfair to her this morning."

"And she's a bit fired up at you?"

"You might say so."

"Then apologize."

"I don't think I was *that* unfair. There's a big part of our life we can't agree on. I wish I knew why."

Miss Ellie opened her mouth to speak, thought better of it and waited for her son to go on.

"It's not your problem, Momma. It's mine, and Pam's. We'll work it out, at least I hope we will. Guess I just wanted to run off at the mouth a little. Ever since I was a little kid, you've been the one I could talk to."

She squeezed his hand. "You're still a little boy to me. And as hard as you may find to believe it, so is J.R., warts and all. Now you scoot out of here, I've got some serious drawing to do...."

She watched him wheel away, heading back up to the house. Sometimes, she told herself, being a mother wasn't all that bad. Sometimes...

The parking lot at Southern Methodist University was filling up rapidly with students hurrying to their classes. Lucy, intent on finding a spot, didn't notice the dusty sedan with the Kansas plates rolling behind her. When Lucy parked, the car with the Kansas plates did likewise.

Carrying some books, Lucy headed toward her first class of the day. The driver of the dusty sedan hurried to catch up. Valene Ewing was taller than Lucy, but with the same sun-bleached hair, long and finely-spun. She was a pretty woman; but a concerned expression caused her mouth to be twisted up to one side. When she was no more than twenty feet away from Lucy, Valene called out.

"Lucy!"

Lucy froze in place. For a microsecond, all bodily functions ceased. There was no mistaking that voice, no forgetting the musical rise and fall of it, the soft way it caressed all within range. Lucy kept herself from turning.

"Lucy, it's me."

Now Lucy did come around. Without urgency. In firm control of her limbs. With grace and apparent confidence. Her chin came up and her eyes glazed over.

Valene slowed her pace. No affectionate invitation beckoned her on. No welcoming smile creased that lovely girlish mouth. She paused, allowing students to rush past, eyes fixed on Lucy. Another stride brought her within touching distance of Lucy, but her hands remained at her side.

"Hello, baby," she cooed.

A shudder convulsed Lucy's body. When she spoke, her manner was icy and mean. "Hello, Momma."

"You're looking good, baby. Very good."

"Spare me the smooth talk, Momma. What I want to know is what you are doing back here in Texas?"

Pain rippled through Valene's breast, stabbing swiftly downward. A cry of protest and anguish lodged in her throat, a tide of tears was dammed up before it reached her eyes.

"I am not totally unprepared for such a reaction on your part, baby."

"What do you want?"

"But I had hoped for something better from you."

"You give me too much credit, Momma."

"You were always a sweet and loving child. Those qualities have surely not disappeared. I don't believe you feel as antagonistic toward me as you seem."

"Believe whatever you wish. Now, if you'll excuse me, I have a class and I'm already late."

"I came to see you, Lucy."

"Oh. That's why you're here."

"Sarcasm does not become you, Lucy."

Lucy braced herself. "You should have come by the

ranch first. Made an appointment. Perhaps I could have fit you into my day, Momma. And maybe J.R. would have given you some more money and you could have left again. Without seeing me at all . . ."

Then she was running along the path until she disappeared into a building. To Valene, Lucy seemed very young and defenseless, frightened and vulnerable. She breathed out, struggling to control her emotions as she returned to her car. Things were much worse than she thought they could be.

Pam Ewing sat on the table in the examining room draped in a soft green examining gown. Her legs dangled over the side, arms rested lifelessly in her lap, her shoulders slumped. Doctors, hospitals, examinations; none of it had ever troubled or frightened her before. But now waves of apprehension alternately chilled and made her flushed with heat, waves of guilt more than fear. For whatever she learned here today would affect not only her own life but the future of her husband, all the Ewings, and the lives of her still unborn children.

Behind her the door opened and Dr. Paul Holliston entered, carrying a clipboard in one hand. "Mrs. Ewing," he intoned in the ponderous voice of authority all doctors seem to slip into so easily.

She turned his way and shrugged, as if to shed the pessimism she wore along with that examining gown. "Doctor?"

Holliston tapped the test results on the clipboard with one long finger. "The lab hasn't completed all the tests yet. What I have here are just preliminary results. . . ."

"Do I have it?"

His lips pursed. "There are no symptoms of neurofibromatosis, if that's what you mean."

"Then I don't have it?"

"Mrs. Ewing." The voice was tutorial, strict, larded with warning. "All I can tell you is that there are no symptoms. In cases such as this, that is not at all unusual. Look at how late in life your father's symptoms surfaced. But even if they should show up later on, at your age they are probably not fatal."

Pam was listening with a highly selective ear. "Then I don't see how, if I don't have any symptoms, I can possibly transmit the disease to my children."

"I understood you to say that you didn't have any children, Mrs. Ewing."

"I don't. But I intend to have children. My husband and I want a family very much. We both love children. . . ."

Holliston placed the clipboard on a counter nearby. He squared it up, a man very exacting in his work and life. "Mrs. Ewing, neurofibromatosis is a genetic disese. Each generation passes it on to the next. Even in infants, however, it is not always fatal."

"Not always, but often."

"Often enough," he said drily. "As in your brother's case, you both survived, but you both do carry the strain. Of that there can be no doubt, no doubt at all. I thought I made that quite clear when I examined your father."

"You did. But somehow I thought . . . I thought that if somehow . . . if I wasn't displaying symptoms . . . I might not be carrying it . . . if I had a child. . . ."

He tried to be gentle.

"Mrs. Ewing, I wish I could give you some hope that your children could be born safely. Perhaps they will be, perhaps not. The disease is random in whom it strikes and when and with what ferocity. You might have children and all would pass through life unscathed. . . ."

Her eyes fluttered shut and she squeezed out the words. "But a child of mine might die before he or she was a year old."

"Yes," he said. "I am sorry. I want to help you, but at the moment there is no way. Still, don't despair. Other diseases have been cured. One day we'll cure this one."

"Tomorrow?" she said ruefully.

"Not likely."

"Nor next week. Or even next year." From the helpless expression on his face, she knew the answers. "Don't say it, doctor—you're sorry. I'm even sorrier. But it's not your fault, is it?"

"It's no one's fault, Mrs. Ewing. You must remember that. Tay-Sachs, various forms of leukemia, Sickle Cell Anemia, a predisposition for cancer, heart disease; nature plays many cruel tricks on human beings. No, no one's to blame. Neurofibromatosis is simply something the Barnes family carries." He took a backward step. "I'll leave you to get dressed now." He left the room, closing the door quietly behind him.

Pam remained in place on the examining table. Her

spirit crushed, all color drained out of her face. The future promised no hope for her. No hope at all.

"Something the Barnes family carries," she murmured aloud. "Who else is to blame, then?"

That afternoon, in J.R.'s office, they gathered: J.R., Jock, Alan Beam and Harve Smithfield. They were settled around J.R.'s desk, studying charts and graphs, making reference to balance sheets, trying to make sense of what was going on.

"I don't quite understand what Cliff Barnes is after," Smithfield, a senior member of the law firm that bore his name, said.

"He's after *us*," J.R. said. "Trying to ruin Ewing Oil, put us out of business. That man has put a restraining order on the test drilling on the new sections in Midlands Odessa. They're investigating our refinery operations. . . ."

"How's that?" Jock said.

"Making sure that if old oil goes in, old oil comes out."

"Smarmy little sucker," Jock said. "His father was a real man. You could admire Digger, respect him no matter the differences . . ."

"Worst thing is," J.R. said, "he's keeping us down close to the break-even point."

Jock growled his displeasure. "Seems to me, every other oil man in this state is drillin' anywhere it even smells like a gusher. We can't get a drill a foot underground before that damned O.L.M. gets down on us."

"You're not the only ones, Jock," Smithfield said. "He's stopped other drilling too."

J.R. nodded. "But only in and around where Ewing has oil rights. He's after us, all right."

Alan Beam spoke up, full of deference for his elders and betters, yet plainly aggressive. "You'll pardon me for saying so, but Barnes is no fool. He can't be too obvious about putting the screws exclusively to Ewing Oil. If he stops other drilling, it's just to make himself look good."

Jock raised one oversized fist in the air. "Harve, you've been my lawyer since near day one. You mean to tell me there is nothing we can do to stop Barnes? Can't get an injunction or restraining order?"

"We've tried, Jock. But Barnes has got every ecological

group in this state behind him. Making himself out to be a regular hero, he is. People say he's doing a great job. Aside from which, so far the courts have agreed he's stayed within his authority."

"So we get back to the same old bone—how to get rid of Cliff Barnes?"

Alan spoke softly, the words unmistakable. "Can he be bribed?"

Harve gave him a hard, disapproving look. "That's hardly a question I'd expect to hear from a member of my legal firm."

Jock said, "Hold on there. Harve! Ain't such a bad question as you make out."

"The answer is no," J.R. said. "I know. Point is there's not enough money in the State of Texas to get Barnes off our backs."

Alan spoke again. "There must be something Barnes wants. Everybody wants something . . ."

"He wants to see us Ewings down and out. Like that drunk daddy of his. There's nothing could drag him away from the O.L.M."

Alan addressed himself to Jock. "But, sir, before O.L.M. he did run for public office."

"And had to quit before the election. Man couldn't raise two bits worth of support in the whole state."

J.R. eased his chair forward, all senses honed. An idea had begun to form back in his brain, taking size and shape, gradually moving to where he could see it clearly, name it, make it work for him.

"Cliff surely did want to be elected. He just yearned for public office, for the power and the glory, you might say. The people's choice, that's his style. A big government office, influence, folks sucking around all the time. And dreams of moving up in the world; the Senate, Governor of Texas, maybe even President of the entire U.S. of A."

"Barnes for President," Alan said, grinning. "I bet he'd quit O.L.M. fast enough for that."

"I believe he would," J.R. said.

Jock snorted in annoyance. "All this chatter ain't helping us even a little bit. No matter how good it sounds, there's not a man in Texas fool enough to back Cliff Barnes for office. Not a one."

J.R. let his eyes drift to Alan, who sat without moving,

taking it all in. Then back to Jock. "I reckon you are one hundred percent correct, Daddy. Who'd even dream of trying to put Barnes up for election? Nobody crazy enough to do that. Least not anybody we know . . ." But a hint of a smile played around the corners of his otherwise flat, stiff mouth.

It was midday on the university campus and students came pouring out of the buildings, heading for the dining halls or setting up picnic lunches on the grass. Lucy, accompanied by two other girls, was on her way to the stadium and the tryouts for the cheerleaders.

The girl called Sherril said, "Can't you just see it! The team's in the Cotton Bowl and there we are, leading cheers on TV!"

Wanda, a pert redhead, giggled. "I just hope we get better outfits than they had last year. They were so old-fashioned."

"I'd like something real deep cut," Sherril said, "something that ties in front, but not too much."

"And short, short shorts," Wanda added.

"I just hope I make the finals," Lucy said.

"Are you kidding!" Wanda said. "You have nothing to worry about, sugar."

Lucy clapped a hand to her brow. "I left my shoes in the car. See you all over at the field . . ."

She hurried over to the parking lot and located her car, retrieved her Nikes from the trunk. She wasn't aware of Valene until her mother spoke to her.

"Lucy . . ."

She came around. "You still here, Momma? I thought by now you'd have latched onto your money and split."

"Honey, I wrote you and explained I didn't take any money from J.R."

"Why should I have believed that?"

"Because it's true. Because I'm your mother. I see I've got a lot more explaining to do to you."

"Don't bother. None of it matters to me, nothing you can say."

Val took a step closer and Lucy retreated, one hand coming up as if to ward off a blow.

"Honey, I know how you must feel."

"No, you don't, Momma. If you did you would never

have gone off and left me behind. You don't know anything about me." She spun away, going past Val toward the stadium and the tryouts. Val's words stopped her dead in her tracks.

"I know this—I gave birth to you. I love you. I always have."

"You love me like you love my daddy? You ran off and left him, too."

"I never did. We never had a chance."

"Oh, we had a chance, all right. We were all together at the ranch. We could have made it together. But it got too rough for you, for the two of you, so you just took off, the two of you. In a way that's funny, it was too rough for you. But it was perfectly okay for you to leave me there. By myself."

"It was your home. It's where you were brought up. They love you at Southfork."

Lucy snarled out a reply. "The way you make it sound, everybody loves me. That is just grand, grand. Only I don't feel loved. Not by anybody. You want to know how I do feel? I'll tell you, Momma. I feel as if I don't belong to anybody at all."

"You belong to me, and to your daddy. And we belong to you."

"Is that a fact! If I belonged to you, where were you when I was growing up? When grandma had to take me out shopping for clothes. And when boys called me for dates and I needed somebody to talk to about it, where were you? And when I was graduated from high school, all the Ewings were there, but not you. Not Daddy. And—oh, what's the use. The pain's all there, but you and Daddy weren't." Tears streaked her cheeks.

"Baby . . ." Val was crying, too. She reached out for her daughter but clutched only empty space.

"I'll tell you something, Momma. I hurt sometimes, but I can handle it. I learned how. What I haven't learned to handle is you showing up this way and making me think I really do have a momma when I know damned well it isn't true."

"I'm here, I love you, I—"

"And one day you'll be gone again. Without warning. So don't bother me, lady. I'm on to your ways. Don't try to get your hooks into me again. It just isn't going to work.

Not ever again . . ." She ran off across the campus, the Nikes dangling from one hand.

Val watched her go. "Baby," she said aloud. "Oh, my poor sweet baby . . ."

John Ewing III slept fitfully in his nursery, unaware of his surroundings, of his family importance, of his destiny. A shadow fell across the crib and Little John remained unaware that Sue Ellen, his mother, was gazing down at him.

To her the baby was a source of pain and a trigger for the powerful pangs of guilt that rendered her helpless and weak. This child, a daily reminder of how badly she had been used by all the men in her life. And yet, she had conceived him, had carried him to term, birthed him.

The baby moved and began to cry. Sue Ellen's hand went out as if to comfort him, then drew back. "Mrs. Reeves!" She backed away from the crib.

From an adjoining room, Mrs. Reeves appeared and started soothing the baby. "There, there, little fella. We'll just get you comfortable in a minute. Don't you fret . . ."

"What's wrong with him?" Sue Ellen said.

"Just doesn't like lying there in his own wet, is all. Would you like to change him, Mrs. Ewing?"

Sue Ellen stared at the woman. "That's what I'm paying you for."

She started to leave and faltered at the sight of Miss Ellie standing in the doorway. Behind her the baby began to wail louder. Without a second glance, Sue Ellen marched past her mother-in law and out of the nursery.

"God in heaven," Miss Ellen said to herself, "what has gone wrong . . . ?"

Bobby was in his office when his secretary appeared. "There's a call for you, a woman. Won't say her name or what it's in reference to, just that it's about Lucy and is important. You want to take it?"

Bobby nodded and reached for the phone and the secretary withdrew. "Bobby Ewing," he said into the instrument.

"Bobby, it's Val, Valene Ewing."

"Val! Val, how are you? Where are you?"

"In Dallas. Sorry about giving your girl such a hard time but I was afraid to give my name in case J.R. was hanging around."

"Can't say that I blame you. Have you heard from Gary? When can I see you?"

"Bobby, I don't want to go into too much over the phone, but I do want to see you. I need to see you. But not at your office, not at Southfork."

"Name it. Anytime, any place."

"Is tomorrow all right? I'm working from four to midnight in a little cafe. I don't want to be late my first night."

"Tomorrow's fine. Where and when?"

"How about Bachman Bridge—is that okay?"

"Just fine."

"About ten tomorrow morning?"

"See you then . . ."

"Thank you, Bobby."

At almost the precise moment that Bobby was talking to Valene, his wife was herself making a phone call.

"Dr. Holliston," she began, "this is Pamela Ewing."

"Thank you for returning my call, Mrs. Ewing. I said it was *Mr.* Holliston calling when I spoke to your mother-in-law. I didn't know if you'd talked to anyone about your visit to my office and I didn't want to chance opening an unwanted discussion."

"I appreciate that. I take it you have the final test results." Her heart was pounding and her eyes burned.

"Not all of them, but soon. However, enough information is available to me now to indicate that there may be a problem."

Pam filled her lungs with air. "With the disease?"

"In a way," he replied soberly. "Your blood and urinalysis samples show one thing for sure. You are definitely pregnant, Mrs. Ewing . . ."

Pam could think of nothing else. She was going to have a baby. Joy and despair mingled in her like conflicting tides, muddying her emotions, her thoughts; leaving her without purpose or hope.

Night descended over Southfork and Pam, still clad as

she had been during the day, lay motionless on her bed as darkness filled in the room. Through the morass that clogged her mind came the awareness that her husband would soon appear. What would she say to him? Could she inform him that she was pregnant, knowing that more than anything in the world he craved a son and an heir, that more than any man she had ever known he yearned to be a father, to have a true and growing family.

Bobby, his roots deep in the soil of Southfork, was so much a natural man, linked in his blood to the seasons, to the rise and fall of the sun, to the forces of nature and the inevitable turn of the earth. How to make him understand the fears that ran through her? How to tell him that with the fetus in her belly less than a month along she could not keep from considering an abortion?

Do it without Bobby ever knowing, she commanded herself, and the soft flow of tears filled up the spaces behind her eyes. Was she strong enough to make that awful move? And what if Bobby should somehow discover what she had done? Would he understand? Would he forgive? Would he love her still?

And finally the most damning question of them all: Would she be able to forgive herself?

As if to underscore her anguish and uncertainty, a car pulled into the driveway outside. She heard the slam of a door and booted feet striding across the patio and into the house. She knew those footsteps better than she knew her own. Bobby . . .

She lay without moving, unaware of the tension that gripped her limbs. Unaware that she had ceased thinking. Ceased feeling anything but an overwhelming love for her husband. Her breathing was shallow, her heartbeat rapid, her eyes fixed on the darkened ceiling.

A rectangular shaft of soft light abruptly flooded the room as the door opened and Bobby walked in. He moved toward her, looming large and threatening—and ancient childhood guilts rippled across her middle, made her anticipate swift and dire punishment for misdeeds committed and imagined.

"Pam . . ."

She made no answer, unable to speak.

"Are you all right, honey?"

He lowered himself to the edge of the bed, kissed her

gently on the brow, held her hand in his. "You not feeling first-rate, Pam?"

"Just tired." The words sounded false and contrived in her ears and she realized that in all the time of her life with Bobby she had almost never lied, never dissembled, never maneuvered for personal gain.

He accepted the words as spoken. "Hey," he said cheerfully. "Guess who called me today?"

"Who?"

"Valene."

She had to struggle to put a face with the name. "Valene?"

"Lucy's momma. She's back in Dallas."

"That's nice."

He frowned. "I thought you liked Valene."

"Oh. I do, I do."

"I'm meeting her tomorow. Why don't you come with me? I know she'd like to see you."

Valene, Gary, Lucy. The Ewings in all their manifestations, she reminded herself, had problems. And she was in no mood for anyone else's problems.

"I don't think so. I'm going to be tied up all day."

She heaved herself off the bed and went past him to the mirror to stare at her reflection. Mouth drawn down, eyes hooded, the lines in her face suddenly more pronounced. What kind of woman was she turning into?

Bobby watched her. Was she still angry over the dispute they'd had that morning? Well, why not? Hadn't it bothered him on and off through the day? His love for Pam, his respect for her and the life they were building together; none of it came without struggle, effort or pain. The important thing was that they were bonded forever, a sound pair, till death do them part. He moved up behind her.

"I'm sorry about this morning. I shouldn't have jumped on you that way."

"I'm sorry I gave you cause to."

"But you didn't. Not really. I shouldn't press you about having a baby. . . ."

Pain stabbed into her, made her flinch.

". . . It's just that when I see you with Little John, Pam, I guess I wish he was ours."

"Do you think I don't know how much our baby would mean to you?"

"Sometimes," he drawled, "that's exactly what I do think—"

The words slid onto her tongue and she had to set her teeth against uttering them, against saying: I AM PREGNANT!

He went on, smiling gently. "Other times I don't know. But if it came to it, I'd rather never have a baby than have it cause trouble between you and me, Pam."

"Bobby," she said, turning to face him. "Can I tell you one thing and then not talk about it again?"

"Yes."

"In this world, there is nothing that I would want more than for us to have a baby. A little boy that would grow up to be just as strong and beautiful and honest as you are . . ."

He cocked his head. "There's a 'but' in there someplace."

She could not reply, averted her gaze.

"All right," he said. "But whatever's wrong, whatever reasons you have, whatever's bothering you, you're going to have to tell me. And soon."

"Yes," she said, oh, so softly. so distantly, so full of apprehension. "I know . . ."

J.R. woke the next morning in high good humor. A quick shave and a shower and a choice of clothes, all done to a cheerful tune whistled. He stood in front of the mirror knotting his tie when Sue Ellen appeared out of her dressing room to stand at a distance behind him, as if seeing him for the first time.

"My," she said sarcastically, "aren't we in a good mood."

"You should be, sweetheart. After all, your momma's gonna be here soon."

"Is that what's got you all juiced up, J.R.? Momma coming, or Momma bringing my dear little baby sister with her?"

"Now what is that supposed to mean?"

"Just that you have never turned away from a pretty face or a well-turned bottom, J.R., and Kristin is well endowed in face and fanny both."

"You surely do have a dreadful mind, Sue Ellen. Your own sister, shame. I had hoped when you stopped lapping up the whiskey your outlook would improve. Course that was too much to hope for."

Sue Ellen's laugh was bitter, sardonic, meant to declare her hurt and deliver pain to her husband. "There was a time when what you said would have mattered to me. No more. As Mr. Rhett Butler said, 'Frankly my dear, I don't give a damn.'"

"Don't you? Then what keeps you here? Here at South-fork? Here in my bedroom? In my bed?"

She bared her teeth. "What keeps me here is seeing your face when your precious daddy tells you how proud he is of Little John. How much he looks like you, J.R. And all the time you're just never sure that he doesn't look more like Cliff Barnes than J.R Ewing."

"You are a bitch."

"Perhaps so. But no name would rightly describe you, my dear."

He cast a withering glance her way. "Perhaps you should start drinking again, Sue Ellen. At least when you were drunk you didn't talk so much or so vulgarly. As for Cliff Barnes . . . well, I have a strong feeling he is liable to fall off that high horse of his." He started out, but her voice brought him around.

"Knocked off, you mean?"

"Exactly, sweetheart. Knocked off hard. And by yours truly, J.R. Ewing . . ." That sent him out of the room humming a lively little tune, ready to confront the day and enjoy every damned minute of it, too.

Later that morning Cliff Barnes fell into stride with his sister, Pamela, on a busy street in downtown Dallas. "Well, now, sis, what's so goshdarned important you couldn't tell me over the phone or come on up to my office for a little talk?"

She kept walking. "I'm going to have an abortion."

"Abortion! Don't just throw that word around, Pam."

She sniffed. "The doctor told me that if the baby *does* have neurofibromatosis, no signs—none—will show up until at least four to six months after he's born. Am I supposed to sit and wait? And that's after carrying the child for nine months. Never knowing, always fearing the worst. And then all I have to do is sit back and wait for him to die before he's even a year old. And you think I'm looking for easy way out?"

"Isn't that what you're doing?"

"What would you have told Sue Ellen if you knew your son might die in a year?"

Cliff hesitated, trying to be forthright, honest with Pam and himself. "I don't know. But whatever I would have wanted, it had to be better than it is now. He's my son and and he may die. And to make it even worse, I don't know if I will ever get to see him again."

Her face was drawn, grim, determined. "Then wouldn't it have been better for him not to be born at all?"

"I can't believe that!"

"Why? Why can't you accept nonexistence as preferable to birth and a short life that makes everyone who loves the child miserable?"

Cliff tried to wade through the miasma of emotions he experienced. "What if the baby's not sick? What if your baby will be born healthy? Can you take that chance?"

"I don't know," she said helplessly. "Oh, God, I don't know what to do, who to turn to. I thought you might be able to help, to understand. That's asking too much of you or anybody else. I'm sorry. I just need to talk to someone and there's no one else. I had to hear what it sounds like out loud."

"I want to help and if I could I would. But I feel strongly you should tell Bobby."

"And if I do? It's not only my baby. I'd have to tell him about the disease. He knows you're the father of Sue Ellen's baby. He'll understand that Little John might die. Is that fair, Cliff, to burden him with all that? Our tragedy, his and mine and yours and Sue Ellen's, not to forget J.R. I can't do that to Bobby. I just can't do it to him."

Cliff started to reply, thought better of it. He put his arm around her and they walked on in silence, each with a private fount of misery.

At that very moment, Bobby parked his car close to Bachman Bridge. It seemed to him an idyllic setting, the green expanse of grass, the sparkling lake, all the young and carefree people enjoying themselves. He spied Valene standing on the bridge and waved, hurried to join her, delighted to see his second sister-in-law. But she greeted him hesitantly.

"Bobby, it's so good to see you again, Thank you for meeting me this way."

He embraced her and felt her body stiffen and resist. He released her. "You look great, Val. How've you been?" He inspected her face for evidence of damage and perceived a glint of wariness in her so very blue eyes.

"Fine," she said without conviction. "Fine."

"Have you gotten in touch with Lucy yet?"

She nodded. "That's why I wanted to see you."

"Trouble?"

"I followed her to school yesterday, tried to talk to her. She doesn't want to have anything to do with me, Bobby."

He took her arm and they strolled without haste. "She was hurt last time, Val. You've got to expect something like this. The girl is being protective."

"I suppose so. But she was so . . . spiteful. Guess there is no good reason why she should feel different. Like she said, I never was a mother to her. Maybe I was wrong to come back this way."

"Why did you come back?"

"To see Lucy."

"Why now? What's different than it was before?"

"Some things are . . . I've been in touch with Gary. More than once, Bobby."

Bobby's eyes lit up. "Well, that's just great! How is he? Where is he?"

She filled her lungs with air and exhaled slowly, as if using the time to reflect. "He's been pretty good, Bobby." She glanced sidelong at him, seeking his reaction. His expression told her nothing. "Doesn't drink at all."

"That's great," he said flatly.

"Been workin' out on the West Coast. Tells me he's even been puttin' a little money aside. That's what I wanted to tell Lucy. Not that I could promise anything, not that Gary can. But Gary and me been talkin' and, I don't know—maybe we'll try to see each other again soon. I'd like that a lot, see if we can work out something between us."

"Don't you think it's a little early to get Lucy's hopes up?"

"I just wanted to talk to her. I thought—maybe you could help. That's all."

His brows contracted and his eyes darkened. "I'm not sure I should, Val."

"We were always friends."

"Yes. But I'm thinking of Lucy now. You know how she's been hurt. These days, she's got herself back together pretty well. She's happy now. Seeing you, starting to think you can all be one happy family again ... What if it doesn't turn out that way? Who can say what she might do? I don't know if she can take getting her hopes up and then losing you all again."

"I appreciate you sayin' that, Bobby. Whatever went on before, the last thing I wanted was to hurt her."

"I know that. Still—things happen."

"I don't intend to make her no promises. There's only two things in this world I love ... your brother Gary, and my little girl. I don't believe I can stand livin' without us at least bein' friends." She paused and looked up into his face. "Please, Bobby, I need your help ...."

There was no way he could not give it, no way he could not trust Val's love for Lucy, her sincerity. "All right," he said. "We'll go see her after school. Where can I pick you up?"

"Over at the Big Sky Motel, on Lemon over by Love Field."

"See you then."

"And Bobby, please, don't say anything about my bein' here. 'Specially to the family. Last thing I want is for J.R. Ewing to know I'm within five hundred miles of Dallas ..."

The cheerleaders were working out in front of the grandstand on the athletic field. The girls were young, uniformly pretty and possessed of tight, voluptuous bodies. In scanty satin shorts and tight blouses they bounced and danced and jiggled enticingly, all to the approval of a group of spectators, mostly male.

Across the field, Bobby parked as close as possible. He and Valene watched the proceedings briefly.

"There she is," he said. "In the center of the group. The girl's really good. ..."

They both got out of the car, started onto the field.

Valene placed a restraining hand on Bobby's arm. "Do me a favor, Bobby?"

"What's that?"

"Why don't you just sort of amble over there and ask Lucy to come over here and talk to me? She might not be too happy, me just blowin' in there with her friends and all."

"Whatever you say, Val." He strode toward the cheerleaders, arriving just as they finished an intricate yell-and-dance number to the applause of the onlookers and the approval of their coach. The girls split up into small groups, chattering, congratulating each other; bright clusters of youth and happiness against the green carpet of the field.

Bobby spotted Lucy and called her name.

She waved and hurried to join him. "Hi, Bobby!" She kissed him on the cheek. "Well, what did you think? Were we pretty good or were we pretty good?"

"You were pretty good. Now, Lucy—" He gestured back toward the car. "I've got Valene with me . . ."

Lucy pulled back as if struck, her face frozen into a mask of pain and fright.

"She wants to talk to you, Lucy, I think you ought to listen."

Lucy's head began to rock from side to side.

"It might be in your best interests, all of you."

"So she got you to come and ask me. Well, you tell her she could have saved herself and you the trouble, hear. I don't want any part of this."

"At least listen to her."

"You want to hear what she's got to say—you listen. Dammit, Bobby, you listen to her." She dashed back to where her friends were waiting. Bobby turned back to the car as a whistle blew summoning the girls back to practice.

In the car, Val saw Bobby coming alone and she fought to hold back the tears.

"I'm sorry," he said, climbing in next to her. "I'll talk to her again, try again. Later, at home"

She nodded, unable to speak.

He started up the car and drove away.

Behind them, in the stands, concealed in the group of spectators, J.R. watched them go through a pair of high-powered binoculars. He hadn't wanted to come out to watch the cheerleaders, yet had allowed himself to be talked into it. Sort of a public service, good of the community. The kind of thing that got your picture in the pages of the Dallas papers with a complimentary caption underneath. The kind of thing that won people over to your side. He hadn't expected it to prove to be profitable as all this. Valene back in Dallas; well, what do you know! Nothing like a little private information to give a man an edge in his war against Life. Nothing like an edge to make him a winner. And winning was what life was all about for J.R.

Miss Ellie was watering her flower beds alongside the patio that afternoon when Pam joined her.

"How was your day?" Miss Ellie said.

"Not the best. Yours?"

"Slightly boring. I'm used to the men going into town. I used to have Sue Ellen to talk to, but she still stays pretty close to her room."

"She'll be feeling better soon."

"Let's hope so. If I didn't have Little John to play with . . . I don't know what I'd do."

"It's easy to get attached to him, isn't it?"

"Too attached, Pam. It's been a long time since there's been a baby at Southfork."

"Did you miss having babies around before Little John was born?"

"Not as much as Jock did. I raised three of my own. That's enough to keep any woman for a while."

Pam laughed shortly. "Have you ever thought what it would have been like if you'd never had children?"

Miss Ellie gave a pensive little smile. "There were times when it might have been looked on as a blessing."

"Would your marriage, your life with Jock have been so much different without children?"

"Different, yes. I'm not saying better or worse. But definitely different."

Pam nodded, looked away.

Miss Ellie went on. "I didn't marry Jock just to have children. The children were sort of a by-product of our love for each other. We'd have missed a great deal of joy without our boys. And a great deal of sorrow as well. But through it all we've always loved each other. Always been honest with each other. With or without children, I think we'd have had a good life together." She broke off with a little laugh. "Listen to me, you ask a simple question and I tell you the story of my life."

"I wanted to know. It's very important that I know."

Miss Ellie understood that something troubling was eating at her daughter-in-law. The younger woman had come seeking something—but what?

"Why is it so important, Pam?" she asked gently.

"Because children are so important to Bobby. If we don't have a family—I don't think our marriage can survive that!"

She fled into the house sobbing. Miss Ellie watched her go, not knowing what she could say or do to help.

That evening, in the living room of the ranchhouse, J.R. and Jock were waiting for the rest of the family to join them before dinner. Drinks in hand, they were talking. Or rather, J.R. was talking, making a strong sales pitch.

"Tell you the truth, Daddy, I think it's just fine that Bobby's runnin' Southfork these days. The ranch requires a strong hand, a member of the family."

"I agree."

"But he could be a great help in Austin."

"You're goin' to have to spell that out for me, son."

"Yes, sir, I will. The more heat we can put on Cliff Barnes from that end the more likely he is to jump at something else that looks good to him."

"You still got your mind set on Barnes runnin' for Congress?"

"I am. You'd be surprised how many folks believe he'd make a good congressman. Might not be a bad idea for us to climb on that wagon."

Jock frowned. "Seems to me we'd be worse off with him working his mischief off in Washington than we are now."

J.R. grinned. "Well, sir, there is a heap of difference between runnin' and gettin' elected. I'm just sayin' we might be better off with Bobby in Austin layin' on the pressure while I'm maneuvering Barnes around."

"What's all that?" Bobby said as he entered the living room with Miss Ellie and Pam.

Jock answered. "Bobby, J.R. here thinks you ought to

hustle on down to Austin. Start callin' in some markers for us."

"What markers are those, Daddy?"

"The kind that would get some fire stirred up under the O.L.M. is what I'm talkin' about."

"They've got us over a barrel," J.R. said. "And I am talkin' about a barrel of oil."

Bobby shook his head. "We tried it before, Daddy. It didn't work."

"But it might now," J.R. said quickly. "Barnes has stepped on other toes lately. People up in the State House might be willin' to listen now."

Bobby considered it. He distrusted his older brother in motive and operation, believed J.R. always did what he did for concealed reasons, reasons that stood to profit him at someone else's expense. On the other hand, he had no love for Cliff Barnes. And the O.L.M. was indeed putting a strain on Ewing Oil that had to be relieved before it resulted in a family disaster.

"When do you think I ought to go down there?" he said.

"No reason to wait past tomorrow morning," J.R. said sweetly.

"Got things to do tomorrow."

Jock took a pull on his drink. "Bobby, I have to side with J.R."

"Daddy, if it'll help, I'll do it. But not tomorrow." Carrying his drink, he left the room.

J.R. made a face. "You surely did raise a stubborn son, Daddy."

Jock scowled. "He said he'd help. Let it go at that."

"Yes, sir, I will," J.R. said, pleased with himself. "I have a few things to take care of tomorrow myself."

A rooster crowed as if to welcome the break of the new day over Southfork. In the east, the sky turned pink and light splashed over the prairie in a swift soft tide bringing with it a hint of the heat that was to come. On the patio, Bobby in jeans and sombrero drank black coffee out of a white ceramic mug, his chair tilted back against the wall, boots hooked in the chair rung, enjoying the quiet, the solitude, the peaceful reminder of what Texas had been like years before. He hardly stirred when the back door opened and Lucy materialized, moving very quietly, very careful to call no attention to herself.

"Mornin'," he said.

She pulled around, startled, dismayed, trying not to show it. "Oh, Bobby, it's you."

"I waited up for you last night. Till about two o'clock."

"I had a date."

"Why do I have the feeling you're trying to avoid me? Especially you leaving this early?"

"We have got practice at school."

"At six in the morning? We are going to have to talk about Valene sometime."

"I've done all the talking I'm going to do."

"You sure are a spiney critter, little Lucy."

She smiled. "I take that as a compliment and say likewise to you."

"The difference between us is I'm willing to listen to reason."

Her face seemed about to melt. "But she *ran*. Without ever saying word one to me. No explanations, no goodbyes."

"Honey, I said everything to Val you can say to me. Whatever she did before, she came back 'cause she loves you."

"Ah, love. The magic word."

"Okay, let's forget about love. You owe her something. She is your momma. You think it was easy for her to come back? She knows what you think of her. She's not gonna hurt you, Lucy. She only wants a few minutes to talk."

The silence lay heavily between them. "All right," she said finally.

Bobby got to his feet. "Let's go."

"Now?"

"No better time."

"No. I have to think. And I do have an early practice. Pick me up this afternoon. I'll go with you. I promise."

"Before four, that's when Val goes to work."

"Three o'clock, at the practice field."

"I'll be there. I'll call Val and let her know we're coming."

At exactly thirty minutes past three that afternoon, Val paced nervously across the width of her motel room. She checked her watch, chewed her lips, straightened her hair. When there was a knock at the door, she hesitated before hurrying to open it. Standing there, big and ominous, was J.R. Ewing, a wide, biting grin on his bland face.

Without a word, he moved past her into the room, looking around as if he really cared. "Not much, this place. Sleazy. And undoubtedly cheap. In keeping with what you are and always have been, Valene." He pivoted around to face her. "Never expected to see you in Dallas again, Valene."

"How'd you find me?"

"Not at all hard. Some of my friends checked around, all the tackiest places. I told them that's where you'll find Valene holed up, in her accustomed style."

"Get the hell out of here."

J.R. circled her like a wary animal, a frightening glint in his eyes. "What does it take to keep you away from us? I warned you what would happen if you came back."

"I want to see my daughter."

"I bet you do. And I bet I know why."

"You'd never understand why, not in a million years."

"I understand you'd like nothing better than you and that drunken brother of mine to be living back at Southfork, gettin' your cut of the pie before it's too late."

"To your way of thinkin', money's the answer to everything. Well, this time you're wrong, J.R."

"I do believe it's the answer to you, Valene. Money can always buy your kind and you're using Lucy to get to some of it."

"I don't care what you think. You're wrong. And I'm not leaving here till I do see Lucy."

"That's where *you* are wrong. You are gonna be on your way before nightfall. . . ."

"Get out of here, J.R. I swear I'll call the police if you don't."

He laughed. "That's your sense of humor at work. I like that. Now you just get your bags packed, 'cause in five minutes you're gonna be leaving' Dallas or—"

"Or what?"

"Or a certain friend of mine on the police force is going to put the heavy hand of the law on you . . ."

"What for?"

"For soliciting with intent to commit prostitution, Valene. Look at you, brassy blonde, tight dress, nice big breasts. Ain't nobody would doubt your callin' for a minute . . ."

"You filthy bastard."

"Pack. You are not gonna see Lucy. You are not gonna see anybody in the family. You are finished in this city for all time."

She braced herself. "I've run from you for the last time J.R. You can't scare me anymore. There's nothing left for you to do, no way to hurt me anymore. I've got nothing left to lose except Lucy, and I do not intend to lose her ever again."

"You already have, you just don't know it."

From the still open doorway, a familiar voice answered. "I don't think so, J.R."

They swung around to see Bobby and Lucy standing there. It was clear they had been listening, had heard everything. Bobby ushered Lucy ahead of him into the motel room.

J.R.'s mind was racing. How to get out of this bind? How to turn it to his advantage? He spoke to Lucy, "Lucy, I'm glad you showed up to hear. I was doin' it for you, darlin'. No way I was going to let her hurt you again."

Lucy turned to Valene. "Thank you, Momma, for standing up to him."

Bobby took a step toward J.R. "Lucy you stay here and talk to your momma. You can take my car home. J.R.'s gonna give me a ride back to Southfork. There are a few things we can talk about on the way. . . ." He took J.R. by the elbow and directed him out of the motel room, ignoring his brother's protests, keeping the bigger man firmly in his grasp.

Lucy and Val stood an arm's length apart, looking at each other as if neither of them knew exactly what to do or say. Then Lucy broke the impasse by taking her mother's hand.

"I'm sorry, Momma, for everything I said."

"Oh, you were right, baby. I never was a good momma to you. But not because I didn't want to be. I always loved you."

"I know that now."

"Our lives are kind of mixed up right now. I can't

promise it's gonna get better, but if we could start by likin' each other, by bein' friends. It's a place to start."

"I want to, Momma. I want to. But what about J.R.?"

Val's face hardened. "If he interferes again, I'll take care of him for good and all."

Lucy flung her arms around her mother. "Oh, Momma, I love you so."

"And I love you, baby."

PART VII

The Ewings

TODAY

17

$\mathcal{I}$t was another morning on Southfork. Breakfast in the dining room as members of the family came, fed themselves, and went. As always, the constant remained Jock and Miss Ellie, lingering over their *huevos Mexicana* and strong black coffee, exchanging a few words with each member of their brood.

Now it was Lucy gulping her food, pecking Jock on the top of his white-maned head, hugging Miss Ellie, cheerful and bright-eyed, anxious to get about the business of living her life.

"I won't be home for dinner, Grandma."

"Where you off to tonight?"

"Studying—" She smiled coquettishly. "With Muriel."

Jock looked suspiciously at his granddaughter. Lucy disarmed him with a girlish laugh. "Really, Grandpa. The truth." On her way out she passed Bobby.

"Bye, Bobby," she said automatically. "See you later."

He spoke so softly she didn't actually hear him. "Goodbye, Lucy." He entered the dining room, poured himself some coffee and took a chair opposite his parents.

The troubled expression on his strong-boned face was not lost to Miss Ellie. "What is it, Bobby, are you all right?"

After a long beat, he answered. "No, Momma, I am not. Momma, Daddy, Pam and I are leaving Southfork."

Jock came to his feet. "What?"

Miss Ellie paled. "Bobby . . . why . . . ?"

"I'm sorry, Momma. I can't live here any longer. I can't live in the same house as J.R."

263

Jock cleared his throat. "Now, listen here to me, Bobby. That's a helluva decision to make without talking it over with us."

"There's nothing to talk about, Daddy. Unless you want to talk about decency and morality. We don't hear about those words much around here. We don't hear about fair play, either."

"Bobby," Miss Ellie said. "Please don't go. Whatever is wrong between you and J.R. can be worked out."

"No, Momma. I have stopped kidding myself. It can't be worked out. Not this time. Not ever."

"Jock, don't let him go."

"You can stand up to J.R., son."

"I can't go into that office downtown every day and punch him out. Daddy. I can't fight him every inch of the way. Fighting all the time, I don't want to live that way."

"You're not going to quit on me, Bobby. I don't like you running out."

"I never ran out on anything in my life. But this is impossible. Daddy. I'm sorry to have to say this, but I can't fight you and J.R. both. You put me back into Ewing Oil to watch J.R., but when it came right down to it, you backed him."

"I thought he was right."

"That's why I can't stay." He took his mother's hand, struggling to ignore her tears. "I'm sorry, Momma, I tried. I tried for a long time. I lost."

"Son," Jock said in that slow heavy drawl of his. "Whatever differences we have, you're still a Ewing. We only have each other. We got to stick together."

"At the expense of everyone else? No, Daddy, I can't live that way."

"Where will you go?" Miss Ellie said.

"I'm not sure. All I know is, I have to get as far away from J.R. as possible."

He shook hands with his father. He kissed his mother and said; "I'm sorry, Momma," before he left.

Only minutes later, J.R. and Sue Ellen entered the dining room. Both were startled to see Miss Ellie weeping and Jock attempting to comfort her.

"Momma, what's wrong?"

"Miss Ellie, are you all right?"

"It's Bobby," Miss Ellie sobbed. "He's left us."

"Left . . . ?"

"That's right, J.R.," Jock said. "Left Southfork. He feels the differences between you are too great and can't be resolved."

A harsh rasping sound broke out of Sue Ellen. "There you have it, J.R., what you always wanted. You drove your brother Gary away. And now Bobby. You tried to bribe Valene and you tried to make it seem that Pam was a hooker. You treat me badly and you cheat your friends and business associates. There is nothing you won't do to get what you want. And at last you've got it—you are now the Ewings' only son. Congratulations."

"Momma," J.R. cried. "Daddy! You know I don't want Bobby to leave. You have to know that."

Miss Ellie raised her chin, her expression set, her eyes steady. "All I know, J.R., is that two of my boys have left home. Somebody has got to be responsible. . . ." She marched out of the room with Jock close behind her.

Alone with Sue Ellen, J.R. lashed out. "Pleased with yourself, aren't you? Making me look bad to my momma and my daddy. Well, let me tell you something, darlin', you have had your last say in this house. Nobody talks to me like that in front of Momma and Daddy. Nobody. *Nobody.*

"You are a drunk and an adultress, an unfit wife and an unfit mother. You are losing your reason, all control is gone. The sooner you are back in that sanitarium the better. And this time I mean for you to stay there for good!"

She stared at his retreating back.

"No!" she screamed inside her head. "No, I won't let you do that to me. I'll kill you first. I'll kill you. . . ."

In Kristin's condo, she and Alan Beam were having their morning coffee. He was fully dressed, ready to go, but Kristin wore only a flimsy dressing gown that did little to conceal her strong young body.

Despite a long, active night that had left him weak with satisfaction, he still found himself responding to her charms, never content with what had passed between them. She was, he acknowledged, like no other woman he had ever been with. He restrained the urge to touch her, to feel those firm breasts again, to press his nakedness against her, to plunge himself deep into her and hear her moans, feel her clawed fingers raking his back. He had always believed that sex alone would not be enough to keep him coming back to any woman; Kristin was clearly an exception.

He indicated his attaché case on the coffee table between them. "I'd like you to keep this for me."

"What's in it?"

"A few things I'd rather not have at my place."

Kristin eyed the attaché case as if it were some dangerous creature likely to spring at her any moment. She had learned in her comparatively young life to compartmentalize the elements of her existence: money, love, sex, ambition. For her, they overlapped only when one might advance the cause of the other; otherwise, nothing clouded her thinking. Kristin always knew what she was after and let nothing stand in her way.

She opened the case. There were several folders. A ledger. Some sealed envelopes. And a .38 revolver.

"Why the gun?" she said coldly.

"Don't worry, I've got its twin brother." He tapped his belt. "You never know when one of those babies will come in handy."

"You planning to shoot somebody, Alan?"

His gray eyes met hers and neither wavered. "There is someone I'd like to shoot."

"Yes," she said lightly. "So would I, in principle. But would either of us actually do it—?"

A loud knock at the door brought her head around. "I'm not expecting anybody," she said.

"Better see who it is."

She went to the door. "Yes?"

"Police," came a harsh voice. "Open up."

Alan and Kristin exchanged a look. He closed and locked the attaché case, then nodded. she opened the door. Sergeant McSween pushed his way inside.

"What is it? What do you want?"

The big policeman looked her over. "Nice." he drawled. "Very nice. But too expensive for a poor policeman on salary."

"Look here, McSween," Alan said.

"Shut up, mister. This is police business."

"I don't understand," Kristin said.

"I've got a warrant for your arrest. . . ."

"Arrest? I've done nothing—"

"This is harassment," Alan said. "J.R. Ewing variety."

"Mister," McSween said. "You are interfering with an officer in the performance of his duty. That can get you locked up. And disbarred, Mr. Attorney."

"What am I charged with?" Kristin said, voice trembling.

"Prostitution."

McSween looked over at Alan. "She must be pretty good, huh?"

"That's impossible," she managed to get out, guilt coloring her words. What else was she but a prostitute, she asked herself, operating at a very lofty level, safe from the dangers her sisters in the street chanced every day.

McSween turned his heavy face her way. "You're a lucky lady, I'd say. You've got friends in high places. I'll hold this warrant for twenty-four hours. Give you a chance to get out of town, a long way out. Permanently." He lumbered to the door, fearsome in his bulk, all muscle and menace. He pointed at Alan. "Same goes for you, attorney. Time is running out on you. Take the first stage out or else you are going to have visitors you won't much like. . . ."

Alone, Kristin swung toward Alan. For a long time neither of them could speak. She staggered over to the couch, collapsed on it unaware of her nakedness, her cheeks blotched, her mouth twitching. "J.R." she muttered wetly. "I'll kill him. I swear it, I am going to kill him."

"Stand in line, lady. There are a few of us ahead of you waiting for the chance. . . ."

─── 18 ───

J.R. sat behind his desk lost in thought. The phone rang and he picked it up. "J.R. Ewing here."

"Listen to me, you scummy motherfucker," came Vaughn Leland's voice, tighter than usual, pitched higher as if it would rise beyond the capacity of man to hear, but definitely Leland's. "I'm going to give you one last chance. Ask you for the very last time. Return that money to me."

"Now, Vaughn, you know I can't do that."

"J.R., I am warning you."

"Hey, Vaughn, where are you anyway? They got half the Dallas police force, the Rangers, and the Federal Bureau of Investigation on your trail. Man, you are kicking up a hell of a lot of dust. Why not turn yourself in and let them call off the posse?"

"I'll tell you where I am, J.R. I'm close enough to get you for what you've done to me."

"Now, Vaughn, you don't mean that."

"The hell I don't. I'll see to it that you've pulled your last crooked deal, I kid you not." He hung up.

J.R. looked at the dead instrument in his hand, then shook his head. Talking wasn't doing and men like Vaughn Leland were no threat to him, that was for damned sure. He went about his business as if it were a normal day.

19

Sue Ellen sat on her bed staring at the .38 revolver that lay heavily in her lap. She hefted it, aware of its ponderous lethal quality, of the terror it endangered in her. She put it aside and stood up, walked over to the window. Looking down she could see the patio where so often the Ewings ate breakfast; but not this morning. This morning was different. Strange. Ominous.

Bobby was gone.

Soon only J.R. would be left on Southfork. Master of it all. Rich and powerful and growing richer and more powerful every day. Dispensing pain and humiliation as if by divine right. She went back to the bed and stared at the .38.

She checked her watch. It was time to go. She took a coat from the closet and her purse from the dresser, returned to the bed. The revolver seemed to cry out to her in its smoky passivity, to provide leadership and purpose. She reached out for it. Cold, sticky to the touch. She dropped it into her purse and briskly left the room. There was so much she had to do first.

20

$\mathcal{A}$t the very moment that Sue Ellen left Southfork that morning, Cliff Barnes arrived at the cemetary. He made his way slowly to Digger's grave which was set deep within the grounds on a low, grassy knoll. He stood for a long time without moving, looking down at the mount that covered his father. His shoulders were slumped, he seemed weary, older than his years.

"I'm sorry, Daddy. They beat me, the Ewings did. Tricked me into running for Congress, faked me out of the O.L.M., the only power I had. J.R. whipped me, just like Jock Ewing did you. There's not a whole lot left for me to do. Except stop J.R. for good. I don't know for sure if that'll make you rest any better or not, Daddy. But it's got to be done. I have got to do it. And I will.

"Goodbye, Daddy."

21

$\mathcal{B}$obby stood on the sidewalk in front of the Ewing Building looking up. How far they had all come from their beginnings as a family. Ewings and Southworths both. Roustabouts and wranglers, diggers and dust-eaters. To become ranchers and oil millionaires, men still wearing the trappings of the Old West while spending almost all their time in sleek air-cooled offices in buildings like this one. How far Dallas had come ...

But it couldn't go on the way it was. Not with a man like J.R. ramrodding his way through everybody's life. Dumping on friends and enemies alike, treating family like dirt, without honesty or scruple. Something had to be done. Someone had to do it. Bobby concluded there was no one but himself. No one at all.

He made up his mind.

EPILOGUE

A cleaning woman, making her rounds of the Ewing Building that night, discovered the door to J.R.'s office ajar, a light on. She knocked. She called J.R. by name. She entered tentatively. She found J.R. on the floor unconscious, bleeding profusely. She let out a piercing scream.

Within ten minutes an ambulance was on the scene. Within forty minutes J.R. was on the operating table at Dallas General. Phone calls were made. To Southfork, and elsewhere. And the members of the family began to assemble at the hospital. By the time they had all arrived, the surgical procedures were almost completed. They gathered in a waiting lounge down the corridor from the O.R., hushed and strained, touching each other occasionally, trying not to talk too much, eyes not meeting.

A doctor appeared in his surgical greens, removing his face mask. His eyes raked the Ewings as they waited for him to speak.

"Will he be all right, doctor?" Jock said.

"I can't tell you that, Mr. Ewing. The wounds are severe, he lost considerable blood and was very weak when he was brought in. We were able to remove one bullet. The other, unfortunately, is lodged in his spine. We haven't been able to remove it. I won't lie to you, Mr. Ewing, it's an extremely critical situation. If I were a praying man, I'd pray to my God."

"Has he said anything?" Sue Ellen said.

"Did he say who shot him?" Bobby asked.

"We allowed a detective from the homicide division a few seconds with J.R., when he came out of the anesthesia. J.R. was reasonably alert. My impression—and the police tend to agree with me on this—my impression is that he may know who did this thing but refuses to name the assailant."

"Who could have done this terrible thing?" Miss Ellie cried.

"Almost anybody," Bobby said flatly. "J.R. has made more mortal enemies than any man in all of Texas. He has caused men to die, destroyed careers and marriages, ruined lives. His enemies are legion, the hate he's incurred is deep and infinite. . . ."

"I can't believe that," Miss Ellie said.

"I'm afraid it's true, Miss Ellie," Sue Ellen said, trying to comfort the older woman.

Miss Ellie looked around as if seeking unspoken answers. "Why?" she said finally. "Why wouldn't J.R. say who shot him?" Her eyes came to rest on the doctor.

He shrugged, excused himself, and disappeared down the long corridor.

"Why?" she said again.

"I can think of one good reason," Jock said tightly. "Revenge."

"Revenge," Pam said in disbelief.

Jock spoke with nostalgic pride. "J.R.'s a Ewing. He'll come through this and track down the bushwhacker who shot him, get even in his own way."

"Oh my God!" Miss Ellie gasped.

"The law of the open range," Bobby said, voice lined with irony. "Can't you understand—those days are ended. Revenge. Gunfights. Killings. Those are the things of the past. This is attempted murder, maybe murder, if J.R. doesn't make it. The police will deal with the killer."

"Besides," Pam said, "there may be a second reason why J.R. won't name the man who shot him."

All eyes shifted her way.

"What's that?" Jock said.

"That he knew who did it and is protecting him . . ."

"Or her," Pam added.

Miss Ellie buried her face in her hands. "Oh, dear God in heaven, how could this have happened?"

There was a long silence. Everyone was lost in their own thoughts and memories.

Suddenly Sue Ellen spoke, "This may be hard for all of you to understand. But in my own way I still love J.R.

Love and hate, opposite ends of the same stick, I suppose. Love is why I married him. Why I've stayed with him in spite of everything. I tried every way I know to make him love *me.* . . ."

Bobby embraced her briefly. "I understand what you're feeling, Sue Ellen. J.R. and me, we've always had our differences, but we're brothers and neither of us ever forgot that. Remember the time we were in that plane crash, Daddy . . . ?"

"Thought we'd lost both you boys that time," Jock said.

"I was out cold for more'n three hours. The pilot, he was hurt too bad to do anything. But J.R., he never hesitated, beat up as he was. Pulled us clear of that plane, built us a shelter, and kept us warm. Sent out rescue signals and kept talking to us, keeping our spirits up. Saying it was all gonna turn out okay, and it did. He took care of us, Daddy, he saved us."

"He remembered all those things I taught him as a boy," Jock said. "How to survive in the wilderness. He did real good that time, J.R. did. Bobby, I know he hasn't treated you all that well all the time—pushing you into the background, trying to run Ewing Oil all by himself. But that's just been J.R.'s way. When the chips were down, he was right there being your blood kin."

"Maybe that's so," Pam said slowly. "We had lunch one day, Bobby. J.R. and me. He tried to warn me about that old college pal of yours, Guzzler, tried to get me to talk you out of doing business with Guzzler."

"He was right about that, though I had a lot of old good feelings for Guzzler."

"And I got to remind you," Jock said. "When I had my heart attack, it was J.R. who saved me, got help, got me to the hospital. Not everybody can act when the bacon falls into the fire. . . ."

Miss Ellie looked up. "When Jock and I got married, my daddy didn't like it at all."

Jock grinned. "He didn't approve of the 'Wild Man of the Plains.'"

"Daddy said our marriage wouldn't stretch out for even five years. He was wrong by nearly forty and we're still going strong. Folks aren't always what they seem. Folks change. They grow. J.R. belongs in business, that's his talent, his gift from God. Bobby, you have a knack for working the ranch, the stock. You're at home with the soil, the naturalness of things."

"And my daddy?" Lucy said in a frightened little girl's voice.

"Gary," said Jock, hawking his throat clear of sentiment. "Gary's the prodigal son, isn't he? He'll turn it around, find himself, make a good life yet. I believe in him, and in the future. After all, he's a Ewing, isn't he?"

"So are we all," Miss Ellie said. "A family named Ewing."

"That's right," Bobby said, looking around. "Whatever our differences, we have to hold on to each other."

"What if J.R. doesn't make it?" Sue Ellen said.

"J.R.'s a fighter," Miss Ellie said. "He'll give it his best shot."

"And meanwhile," Jock said, "we'll hang in and pray and hope and wait, always together. Hells bells, we're Ewings, aren't we? We're family. And in the end that's all that really matters, isn't it?"

They moved in closer to each other, silently waiting, finding courage and strength in each other. Standing as one. Always together.

The Ewings of Dallas.

ABOUT THE AUTHOR

BURT HIRSCHFELD was born in Manhattan and raised in the Bronx. He left school at the age of seventeen and took a series of menial jobs. Immediately after Pearl Harbor he enlisted, and spent three of his four years in service overseas. After the war, he attended a southern college for several years. For the next fifteen years he worked on and off for movie companies and also did some radio and acting work. Burt Hirschfeld did not write his first novel until he was in his early thirties. He worked on it for three years and, when it only earned $1,500, he abandoned writing for several years. At thirty-seven, he decided to find out once and for all whether he had the makings of a successful writer and began to freelance. He wrote everything—from comic books to movie reviews. He also wrote numerous paperback novels under various pseudonyms and eleven nonfiction books for teenagers which were very well received. *Fire Island* was his first major success. His recent novels include *Key West, Aspen, Provincetown* and *Why Not Everything?* Burt Hirschfeld lives in Westport, Connecticut.

COMING IN FEBRUARY

The provocative second novel in the new series
about television's most notorious family

THE WOMEN OF DALLAS

By Burt Hirschfeld,
Author of ASPEN, PROVINCETOWN
and KEY WEST

*This new volume probes the shocking secrets, the
haunting passions and the surprising lives of the
Dallas women, stars of the #1 rated CBS-TV series.*

SUE ELLEN, the ex-beauty queen, an alcoholic who
finds happiness neither in marriage nor motherhood.
Married to one of the richest men in Texas, she finds
love in the arms of a cowboy.

PAM, who gives little J.R. III the love his mother
withholds, but who longs for a child of her own. She
searches desperately to unravel the secret of her past
that will allow her to find happiness in the present.

KRISTIN, Sue Ellen's sister, a determined beauty
who will stop at nothing—even seducing her brother-
in-law—in her drive for power.

LUCY, the virtual orphan who never felt at home at
Southfork. The quest for her own identity leads her
into a shocking life-style.

MISS ELLIE, who tries to keep the family together
and maintain peace between her three very different
sons. She, too, is a woman with a shocking past.

*Meet THE WOMEN OF DALLAS, a Bantam Book
available February 1st, wherever paperbacks are sold.*

THE EWINGS OF DALLAS

The Ewings of Dallas—the most closely watched family of America. Now, you can follow TV's most fascinating family in these three new titles from Bantam. You'll want to complete your own set and order additional copies as gifts for fellow Dallas addicts.

THE DALLAS FAMILY ALBUM (01289-4) $6.95

This large format (8⅜"x10⅞") book contains over 150 photographs (many in color), narrative captions, and star biographies which bring the illustrious Ewing family to life.

THE EWINGS OF DALLAS (14439-1) $2.75
Burt Hirschfeld

Follow the escapades of the Ewings—the oil barons of Texas who love, hate, and wheel and deal their way to fortune.

THE QUOTATIONS OF J.R. EWING (14440-5) $1.50

The pithy sayings of America's favorite villain. "Not since John Milton gave Satan all the good lines in *Paradise Lost* has a villain so appalled—and fascinated—the world."—*People Magazine*

Bantam Book Catalog

Here's your up-to-the-minute listing of over 1,400 titles by your favorite authors.

This illustrated, large format catalog gives a description of each title. For your convenience, it is divided into categories in fiction and non-fiction—gothics, science fiction, westerns, mysteries, cookbooks, mysticism and occult, biographies, history, family living, health, psychology, art.

So don't delay—take advantage of this special opportunity to increase your reading pleasure.

Just send us your name and address and 50¢ (to help defray postage and handling costs).